THE TAIL OF NIGHTSHADE

HELEN WHISTBERRY

Helen Whistberry

The Tail Of Nightshade

WITH 31 ORIGINAL ILLUSTRATIONS BY THE AUTHOR

Other Works by Helen Whistberry

The Melody of Trees: Ten Tales from the Forest

The Jim Malhaven Mysteries series:
The Weird Sisters
The Avenging Angel
The Ghostly Groom

Take My Hand at Midnight: A Gothic Ghost Tale

Short stories in the following collections:
Creating Cinderella
Autumn Nights: 12 Chilling Tales for Midnight
Of Cottages and Cauldrons
Villainous
Duplicitous
Ravens and Roses
Autumn Nights: 10 Sinister Stories
In Somnio
Autumn Nights: Nine Stories to Nibble at Your Nape

This one is for Pru and Ian,
Nightshade's most ardent fans

CONTENTS

CONTENT NOTE FROM THE AUTHOR

T HIS STORY WAS CREATED as a weekly serial over the course of a year. The adventure that unfolded was as much of a surprise to its author as it was to its readers. I have since edited the fifty-two episodes into the novel you hold in your hands and created thirty-one original illustrations to accompany it.

This is a classic quest adventure following the trials and travails of our young mouse friend, Nightshade, and the many weird and wonderful friends they make along the way. Please be warned, especially for younger readers, that there are brief moments of violence, instances of death and other kinds of mayhem you might expect in a fantasy story. But also be reassured that it is a tale full of hope, love, and the beauty of staying true.

Speed

Chapter 1

THE INFERNAL MACHINE

A MOUSE SCRABBLED ALONG under crisp, fallen leaves, whiskers twitching. Death, disguised as an owl, kept watch high above, unblinking eyes orbed bright in the moonlight.

"Home soon, home soon," Nightshade chanted to themself, a spell to ward off danger.

They were an itty-bitty thing. Fur grey as slate. Teeth so sharp, *snap snap*! Ears that twitched and caught the soft crinkle of another leaf tumbling to the ground. Quick as a whip and fierce when cornered. If they were larger, what a formidable creature they would be, but they were only tiny, so they'd learned to hide and wait, ever patient.

Death screeched overhead and Nightshade trembled. Not good to be caught so far from home (just a hollow beneath the twisting roots of an ancient oak, but it was warm and dry and safe and oh, what they would have given to be there now). Driven out into the night by hunger but filled with regret. Should've waited 'til daylight when the golden-eyed hunter sleeps.

But that was neither here nor there. "What's done is done," as their old ma used to say. "Time only passes one way. Forwarder and forwarder."

There was a rumble in the earth. A puttering vibration underfoot grew ever more violent until Nightshade's teeth and bones and claws chattered and shook. What a rackety noise! The owl, startled, took to the air in a flurry of wing and feather, nearly careening into a tall pine in its panic to escape.

To flee or stay? The mouse's curiosity to see this rumbling creature overcame their natural instincts. And what a sight indeed! It was a bear, brown as a chestnut, with googly eyes and a shell over its head, perched on the most complicated metal beast ever seen. The thing sputtered and growled, then choked and died.

"Blast and botheration," the bear muttered, pulling off its helmet and goggles. "Fuming flames!" it cried as it dismounted and stamped its great paws on the earth.

Nightshade couldn't help but giggle at the giant's frustration.

"Eh? Who's there?" The bear's eyesight and sense of smell were keen. It pushed its snout down to the ground, blowing hot air and scattering dried leaves around.

"A wee mouse, is it? Think it funny do 'e?" the bear thundered, unfolding himself to his utmost height, arms outstretched.

"Abject apologies. It's just I never saw nor heard such as you before."

"I'd think not." The bear chuckled, thumping its chest with pride. "As far as I'm aware, I'm t' only bear what rides a motosickle. A useful machine when it works, but nowt but a nuisance when it don't, which is far too often for my liking."

"Wherever did you get such a thing?"

"Now that is a story and not a short 'un neither. Suffice to say I did a man a service once and this is my reward."

"A man? A human man? Whatever did you help a human for? They are the worst of our enemies. None are safe when a human is in the forest."

The bear crouched down on all fours so as to be more comfortable for this unexpected debate. "I suppose 'tis true we've much to fear from a hooman. But not all hoomans are one and the same, same as none o' us are. This man I met was mated to a woman, bold and generous and kind. Her hair was as brown as my fur and her eyes also so. I met her in the woods, all a surprise, not unlike our own meeting. She weren't afeared o' me and that is a wondrous thing when you're used to others running away at sight o' you! We had many a pleasant talk, me and her."

Nightshade was amazed at the idea of speaking to a human. They had been taught from earliest age to fear and avoid all such, for humans were even more dangerous than the owl or the fox or the cunning weasel.

The bear looked pensive. "Then one day, she came no more to the place we met. I went in search o' her. Followed her scent what smelled of bluebells and daffodils and every good spring flower. Found her still and cold on the forest floor. I went to fetch her man, tho' we'd never met. She must've told him o' me, for he was unafraid and followed right willingly. 'Twas an awful thing to see how he keened over her. I helped him dig a hole deep as deep. Bears are fearful diggers, you know."

"How sad," the mouse said, moved at this pitiful tale despite their antipathy to humans. "What did the man do next? Find another mate?"

"You'd think so, wouldn't you? But he was a faithful one and vowed ne'er to leave her side even in death. He bid me go to their cottage and take anything I wanted, for he had need o' it no more. I seen men from time to time on these machines and thought I'd like one for my own. Save some wear and tear on my paws as none of us grow younger, do we?"

"And you taught yourself to use it?"

"Aye. I'm a smarter bear than I might appear."

"You must be the cleverest bear that ever lived," marveled Nightshade.

The bear bellowed with laughter. "Perhaps. Perhaps, young 'un. But we ain't been introduced proper." He extended a paw. "I am Mister Chester Charles Farthington."

The mouse grasped the very tip of one large bear claw in both their tiny hands and shook solemnly. "Pleased to meet you Mister Farthington. I am Nightshade."

"Now would that be Mister or Miss or even Missus?"

"None of those, I don't think. I am just Nightshade."

"You must call me Chester then. We shan't stand on the formalities. And what're you doing out in the woods this time o' night? There are many and many an enemy for one such as yourself, both on the prowl and on the wing."

Nightshade shivered. "Well I know it. I was fearfully hungry, so I ventured out, but I wish I hadn't."

"But then we should not have met and that would be a pity. It ain't so easy to meet a new friend."

"Are we friends?"

"I don't see why we shouldn't be. You're far too small a morsel to fill my belly and I prefer talking to eating you at any rate."

The mouse couldn't help but be grateful for the bear's viewpoint. "I've had no friends since my mother died and my littermates scattered to the four winds."

"That's a shame, ain't it," said Chester. "Say, how'd you like to go on a bit o' an adventure with me?"

Nightshade's ears perked up and their nose wiggled. "An adventure?"

"That's right. I'm on my way back to check on the man what gave me this machine. Like as not he has followed his mate by now and deserves proper burial. Their cottage has good things to eat in it. Plenty for a wee thing such as yourself and even a big fella like me."

Nightshade considered this proposal carefully. They didn't like the sound of being so close to a human but if the man was dead, he could pose no threat. They did like the sound of good things to eat very much. It had been a harsh autumn and winter was just around the corner.

"I suppose," they agreed hesitantly.

"That's the spirit!" Chester scooped up the mouse and set them carefully on one shoulder. "I've discovered if I jiggle this thing here and kick this bit a few times..." The machine roared back to life and the bear climbed aboard. "What did I tell you? Hold on tight as tight there. There may be a fair bit o' wind."

A bit was an understatement. Nightshade burrowed deep into the bear's fur and anchored themselves with their tail. Their heart raced as the forest flew by faster than they could ever have imagined. Their empty stomach began to feel rather peculiar, and they decided it was best to shut their eyes.

As the wind rushed through their ears at an alarming rate, Nightshade regretted more and more their rash choice to take up the bear's invitation for a wild ride on his infernal machine. After the folly of venturing out at night to try and find a morsel of food, this seemed like yet another poor decision. The tiny grey mouse resolved to be more careful and stick close to home if they ever got back to their warm hole in the ground. But home seemed farther and farther away as Chester revved the machine's motor and they rocketed through the towering pines.

The bear hummed a growly tune, well-pleased with himself for mastering a hooman device. No sooner than he had this thought when he saw a large obstacle in his path. No time to swerve or react, he hit the thing with a mighty thump. Events after that, I must report, became a bit confused. There was a certain amount of swirling and twirling, tumbling and bumbling, even a smidgen of bouncing and pouncing.

Nightshade somehow managed to keep their grip on the bear's thick fur. Through sheer good fortune, the bear rolled to a stop in such a way as to avoid crushing his fragile passenger.

"Eh, there, little one," Chester called anxiously, "still among the living, are you?"

Nightshade was too shaken up to reply sensibly but managed a quivering squeak that reassured the bear.

"Glad to hear it. Afraid we've met with an accident. Hit a rock, I think."

"I beg your pardon," a deep, slow voice protested. "I have been called many things in my time, but I am not an inanimate object, good sir."

"An what?" Chester said, peering around to see who was speaking. He was taken aback to spy the largest tortoise he had ever seen, grey and grim and grizzled with an extraordinary pair of pince-nez (which are simply a terribly old-fashioned type of eyeglasses) perched on its nose.

"An inanimate object. An insensible entity. In short, a thing. I am a living, breathing animal and I do believe you owe me an apology for not only insinuating otherwise but attempting to run me down with whatever that is." The tortoise nodded its head toward a twisted pile of metal.

The bear leapt to his feet and bent over the wreckage, laying one paw on the ruins. "My motosickle! 'Tis a goner, I fear."

Nightshade gave a shudder of relief on the bear's shoulder. They'd had quite enough of traveling as humans do and hoped their remaining journey would be much more sedate.

"Good riddance," the stranger said. "What a racket you were making! I heard you coming from miles away. Don't you have sense enough to keep silent in these woods? Calling such unnecessary attention to yourself rarely ends well."

Chester scoffed. "None can hurt me but a hooman with the courage o' one of those noisy, fiery things they carry, but few venture this far into the forest."

"There are other threats than humans here. Have you never heard of the Keeylas?"

A thrill ran down Nightshade's spine; a distant memory of ghost stories exchanged with their siblings at their mother's side before they went their separate ways. Tales of a white cat as large as the mightiest stag and with the antlers of one too. Three swishing tails and six paws instead of four, the better to trap and claw the unwary. The mouse gave out an involuntary squeal of terror at the memory.

"And what have you there?" the tortoise asked, craning its head to peer at the bear's passenger. "You are infested, sir."

Chester chuckled. "Infested? Nay, 'tis a friend o' mine. Nightshade is their name, and I am Mister Chester Charles Farthington, though my friends call me Chester. Now, I'm not sure if we are to be friends or no, but I'd be right glad to learn your name."

"I am Sibyl by name and sibyl by nature."

"And what might that be?"

"Females with exceptional insight and the ability to see into the future."

Chester was much struck by the august dignity of this unique personage. His jaw dropped in awe, but Nightshade was less impressed.

"Nobody can tell the future," they protested, "for no one has ever been there."

"The mouse speaks!" Sibyl cried. "And what would such a one as you know? What have you experienced of the world in your brief life that makes you so sure, compared to one such as I who have been alive hundreds of years?"

"Hunderd of years? Hunderd of years?" The bear sat down heavily on the ground, shaking his head in wonderment. "Is it possible any beast can live so long?"

"I don't know about beasts, but it is certainly possible for a sibyl. I've witnessed such events as you could never imagine. I have seen outside of this world into the farthest reaches of the universe. Such chaos there, it is impossible to describe, and yet it is beautiful too, beyond anything you will ever witness."

Nightshade thought this all nonsense and was more concerned with Sibyl's warning. "Is there really such a thing as a keeylas?"

"Not *a* keeylas. *The* Keeylas. A giant cat, white as frost with a rack of antlers wide as a man is tall and sharp as a scold's tongue. I have seen it many a time and seen what it can do. A formidable foe. There are none mightier within the forest or without. No human or animal can withstand its power. Pray you never meet it. It may be the last sight you ever see!"

"Now, now," Chester objected, feeling Nightshade quivering in fright on his shoulder. "No need to upset my wee friend. I'm no youngster and have traveled near and far in these same woods and ne'er once set eyes on such a thing."

"Then I suppose it can't possibly exist if you've not seen it," Sibyl said mockingly. "Don't come crying to me when you feel its hot breath upon your neck."

"I shan't, for such a thing ain't likely to happen. Have you anything else to tell us before we part ways, Madame Sibyl?"

"Only this. Pay close attention when a raven speaks. It is the wisest of birds and means you no ill will. They do prefer to speak in riddles, however. An unpleasant habit they find hard to break. Make sure you understand the answer well before taking its advice."

With that, the enormous tortoise went on its ponderous way as Chester and Nightshade watched it warily.

The bear sighed. "That was a remarkable meeting and an unfortunate one, no mistake, for my motosickle is dead and we needs must proceed without."

Nightshade thought this no tragedy, but out of respect for their new friend's feelings, said only, "Do you believe her? About the Keeylas and the raven?"

"Barking mad, I should think. If she's lived even half as long as she claimed, plenty o' time to lose her marbles."

"What are marbles?"

"A hooman game. The woman showed me how to play. I'll teach you if you like. There are some in that cottage. It's not too far now. Won't take us long, even by paw. Hang on, my friend."

The bear set off on all fours at a pace that seemed to Nightshade no less than when they rode the machine. Hungry and weary of adventuring, the mouse climbed ever higher on Chester's back until they could burrow deep into the deepest part of his dense brown fur and, against all odds, drift off to sleep.

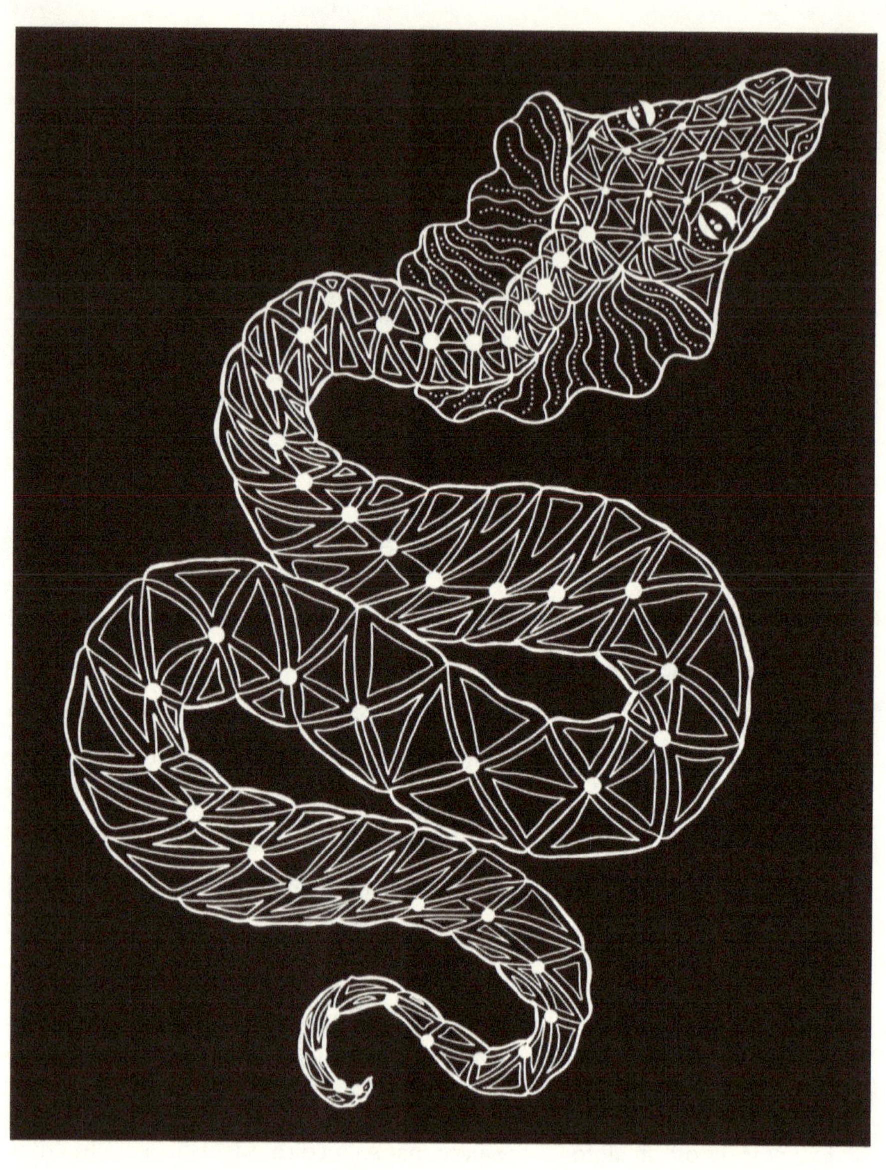

CHAPTER 2

THE CREATURE UNDER THE BED

Nightshade woke to the warming rays of morning sunshine on their belly. Blearily, they opened their eyes and found they were cradled in the outstretched leaf of a sprawling cabbage. Stomach rumbling, they nibbled eagerly on the fresh green leaf.

"My friend, we can find better grub than that!" Chester's enormous face peered down, his fur lit up like a golden halo from the sun rising over his head. He reached out a paw and the tiny mouse jumped on, holding tight as they were whooshed through the air. "I set you there while I took care o' my grave business. The man has gone to join his mate in the cold ground."

"How sad," Nightshade lamented.

"Sadder still to be the one left behind alone, I'd think. Wouldn't know. Never found a mate. Never even seen another bear since I was a wee one myself. They say we are extinct."

"And what is that?"

"Means died out. Departed. Done for."

"You are the last one left in all the world?"

Chester chuckled. "Can't say for certain, can I? Ain't seen the whole world. These woods are vast, 'tis sure, but I heard tell there are vaster still beyond its bounds. I'd like to think there are more like me out there roaming somewhere."

"I'm sure there are none exactly like you," the mouse said sincerely, for they had come to think Chester was entirely unique.

"I'll take that as a compliment and thank 'ee kindly for it. Come inside and see what treats there are in store!"

The bear carried Nightshade through a neglected flower garden to a white-washed stone cottage, small but neat. He pushed open the rough wooden door and stepped in. There was one large room with a huge fireplace for cooking, a rustic table and chairs for eating at, and a straw-stuffed mattress with colorful quilts on a roughly built platform in one corner for sleeping. A humble dwelling by human standards, but to a very tiny mouse, it was as impressive as the grandest castle would be to us.

A large iron kettle was bubbling merrily over a roaring fire that spit warmth out to chase away the cold.

"I started some stew while you slept," said Chester.

"Isn't heating food a human thing?"

"Aye. The woman taught me. She was lonely, poor thing. Her man was often away on the hunt or trading vegetables in town. I'll not turn down fresh meat, but I've learned a taste for a daintily seasoned dish. I found potaters and rutabagers down the cellar, along with some nicely cured venison. I cut the bits and bobs up with my claws, mix it into water. Add some of these powders and potions you see here, let it swirl around a bit and a while, and then look what you have."

Chester ladled out a generous bowl for himself and a small saucer for his guest. Nightshade sniffed suspiciously at the unfamiliar food. Something made them sneeze hard enough to knock them over backwards.

"Dear, dear, too much o' the black stuff perhaps," Chester muttered, but it did not stop him from slurping down the steaming mix.

Nightshade cautiously followed suit. At first, the highly seasoned dish felt as an assault on their senses, but gradually, they grew accustomed to the foreign tastes and even enjoyed it. Hunger adds spice to any meal, and it had been long since they had so much to eat. They liked the warmth that spread from inside out. Along with the cheery fire, it chased away their near permanent chill for the first time in months. They were abashed when a large burp escaped (which was really more like a polite squeak), but Chester laughed and let out a mighty belch of his own that blasted Nightshade's ears back against their head.

A small chirruping sound interrupted their merriment.

"Eh? And what's that?" cried Chester, craning his neck around. "Is somebody there?"

"No, nobody here."

The bear looked at Nightshade. "Strange, in'it? Thought I heard someone, but I am told not."

"But, Chester," the mouse objected, "something must be there to tell you there is nothing there!"

"Sound sense, my friend. What say you, Nobody?"

There was silence, then a soft rustling.

"Coming from under the mattress, I think." Chester bent double from his chair, his great bulk making him awkward as he stood nearly upon his head to gain a better view. Nightshade ran to the edge of the table and likewise peered closely at the dark space under the bed.

"Is only a wyrm," the voice said. "Nothing worth worrying about."

"An earthworm?" asked Nightshade, smacking their lips and thinking of the many deliciously juicy meals they had made of such a one.

An indignant pair of glowing eyes appeared from out of the gloom. "Not a worm, a wyrm with a y!"

"A wyrm with a y," echoed Chester thoughtfully. "And what is that when it's at home, supposing you are at home here and not an interloper."

"Bold talk from one who has invaded this place and stolen what you like!"

"Hold on there. The man what owned all this, and the woman too, were right glad to invite me in and bid me make free use o' it. Can you say the same?"

A harsh, keening sound erupted. "She is gone. She is gone. O, fairest one." A pool of water seeped out from under the bed, a stream of tears for the woman who was no more.

Chester, being a very sympathetic bear, began to weep himself, reminded of his own sorrow.

Nightshade dithered, unused to comforting others after having lived alone so long. "There, there," they said, venturing close to their furry friend and patting one paw gently. "There, there."

"'Tis hard when I remember her beauty and grace," said Chester.

"And her warmth and kind heart," said the wyrm.

"Her long brown hair..."

"And shining eyes..." The eyes beneath the bed blinked and burned. Bit by bit, they were moving closer and closer to the light. Nightshade strained to see what creature might emerge into view.

It was a weird one indeed. Somewhat like an overgrown worm, somewhat like a snake, yet with a triangular head and delicate frills on either side of its neck that quivered with the beast's emotions. Its scales were a swirling mix of amethyst and emerald that sparkled as it oozed out into a sunspot near the window. Most notable though was its oversized mouth, full of sharp, cruel spikes, and a leathery tongue that unfurled and twitched as though it were tasting the very air.

"Eek!" cried Nightshade, clambering quickly to the top of Chester's head. "It is a *monster*!"

The wyrm cried all the harder at the mouse's obvious fear.

"Is it a monster, though?" the bear asked. "An unusual sight to be sure, but best never judge too hasty, I've found. Do you mean to be friend or foe to me and my companion here?"

The wyrm hiccupped. "We've no grudge against one who remembers our lady fair. She was never afraid of us, invited us into her home, made us a cozy den under the bed and fed us tidbits with her own sweet hand. Kept us secret from all but her husband."

"Aye, sounds like the sort o' thing she would do. She had a loving heart and a generous nature. You say you are a wyrm with a y? I never heard o' such nor seen one like you before."

"We are rare these days, I believe, and becoming rarer still, for most humans seek to destroy us on sight. We were fortunate to find safety here, but now we must seek out a new haven. It will be only a matter of time before another human finds this place and takes it for their own. It is their way."

"I'm surprised hoomans would harm you," Chester commented. "You are of no size to threaten them, though I suppose your bite might sting a bit as your teeth are uncommon long."

"It might do more than sting, for we have a deadly venom we can release at will. And as to size, we are but a youth. When we are full-grown, we shall be bigger around than this cottage and longer than your eye can see. We must find somewhere to hide ourself away before that happens, or we will never have peace again."

Nightshade had been slowly creeping down from their high perch on the bear's head as they listened to this conversation. There was no doubt the wyrm was a beautiful creature if one could overlook its too-toothy grin. Its scales flashed and undulated most pleasingly as its body curled and twisted gracefully.

"Perhaps..." the mouse said tentatively, "perhaps we could help you."

Chester beamed and clapped his mighty paws together with a thunderous sound. "A splendid idea! And it could be quite the adventure as well! Chester Charles Farthington, at your service, and my friend here is called Nightshade. And who might you be?"

"Our mother named us Celestyna, for she said we were as bright and shining as the lights in the night sky. We were the only daughter she had out of a clutch of one hundred eggs."

"A hunderd eggs!" cried Chester. "Does that mean you've ninety and nine brothers?" he added, for he was that uncommon bear that had a talent for mathematics.

"Not all broke through their eggs nor survived long if they did. Our kind are tiny when we are hatched and have many enemies."

Being tiny and having many enemies themselves, Nightshade's sympathy was aroused. "Do you know where any of your brothers are now?" they asked.

"We were sent our separate ways by Mother. She thought it more likely we would escape notice and survive if we were not bunched together. She used to speak of a safe, high, far-off place. A place where we might gather out of the sight and reach of humans."

"There you go," said Chester. "We shall escort you. Where is it?"

"That is just the thing," Celestyna cried mournfully. "We've only the vaguest idea. The knowledge of it has forsaken us as our family has and the woman of this place did."

"We shall not abandon you," Nightshade promised. "What can you remember?"

The wyrm cocked her head to one side as though deep in thought. "We know first you must cross a silver river and then fly up into the sky above the clouds."

The bear's eyes grew round in amazement. "Above the clouds! Think o' that! I always thought there was nowt there but the moon and the sun and the stars. What creatures are they that could climb so high? A soaring bird, perhaps."

"I've often watched a hawk so far away it was but a speck in the blue, but still I knew it for what it was," Nightshade offered with a shudder at the memory of that sharp-eyed foe. "But surely there is no bird so large it could—nor so generous it would—take us there."

"You see, it is hopeless." Celestyna sighed.

"Don't believe anything's hopeless," said Chester. "Often, it only takes a bit o' determination I've found. And I may not know how to soar above the clouds, but I do know of a silver river, for I have caught many a slippery fish in one and fallen asleep on its mossy banks. We shall start with that and see how we go as you never can tell unless you try."

"And both of you would undertake such a journey, destination unknown, for us—a stranger?"

"Chester is so courageous and daring," said Nightshade. "He learned to ride a human machine and to make a delicious stew. I don't think there is anything beyond his power."

"And what about you, young mouse?"

"I'm afraid I may not be of much use on the trek, for I am only very small and powerless, but I would like to see the silver river and what lies above the clouds. I promise to at least be of as little trouble as possible if I may accompany you."

Chester picked the mouse up gently and settled them behind one ear. "Course you are a-coming. We shall make a party o' it. A trio of resolute and valiant adventurers. Adventuring is not about the size of your body but the size of your spirit."

So saying, the bear carefully doused the kitchen fire and tidied the cottage. Though the woman and her mate were gone, he knew they would want things left neat for whoever might stumble upon their home hereafter, so others might see the pride they once took in it.

Lastly, he unwound the long scarf from his neck and wound the wyrm round it instead. Celestyna hugged him close but not so tight as to steal his breath. She rested her delicate head on top of his large one so she could keep one eye on their path and one eye on Nightshade to make sure the mouse was safe in their ursine perch.

And so, three companions strode off together into the forest in search of the silver river. A peculiar sight but they cared not a whit, so full of excitement and hope were they.

CHAPTER 3

A WISP OF SMOKE

THE TRIO OF ADVENTURERS had not journeyed far before a commotion up ahead in the forest caught their attention. A wild-eyed brown rabbit jolted into view, dashing in a patchworked, zigzag fashion.

"Flee, flee!" it screamed before disappearing behind them into the tangled underbrush again.

"That were an odd thing, weren't it?" asked Chester, scrubbing one clawed paw against his chin.

"Should we run?" asked Nightshade fearfully from their roost near the bear's right ear, for running and hiding was their natural impulse in nearly any situation.

"Naw. Rabbits are skittish things. Always with the thumping o' the foot and the flashing o' the tail at the slightest ruckus. I'm sure it is nowt."

Celestyna and Nightshade exchanged a glance of concern. The rabbit had seemed truly panicked, but Chester carried on galumphing forward as though he hadn't a care in the world.

A flock of raucous crows flew overhead, cawing, "Danger. Danger. Danger."

"We are becoming concerned," the wyrm commented.

"What was they?" said Chester. "Crows? Right rowdy bunch they are and notable pranksters. I should pay it no mind."

A few more steps, then a growing drone of noise preceded a multitude of moles, a plethora of porcupines, and a superfluity of squirrels scurrying underfoot and through the trees as they muttered their own alarms. There was such a cacophony of voices, it was hard to understand what any of them were saying, but their general air of panic spoke volumes.

"Dear Chester," Nightshade said. "I do believe there may be something amiss up ahead. Shouldn't we turn back?"

"I will admit something seems to have these folks in a bit o' a tizzy, but this is the way to the silver river. Besides, there is not much in the forest that can threaten a bear, you know. You're safe with me."

Next, they encountered a small army of insects.

"Better get hopping," scolded the grasshoppers.

"Better get buzzing," opined the bees.

"Better get to beetling," warned the beetles.

The ants were far too busy and said nothing at all but simply marched by at an impressive pace in neat, soldierly lines.

The wyrm and mouse held their tongues as well, for Chester seemed bound and determined to let nothing sway him from his path. They only kept their eyes peeled for further developments.

Up ahead, more movement. A tiny white thing, filmy and flimsy, dancing and darting. It looked harmless until they got close. Nightshade's powerful sense of smell gave warning.

"It's smoke. There is flame ahead. A fire in the forest!" the mouse squeaked.

Most animals have an instinctual fear of fire even if they have never seen it. Some ancestral memory deep in their bones of this greatest of enemies, implacable, unbeatable, merciless and cruel. Even Chester, that brave bear who had learned to master the mysteries of the human hearth, paused in his tracks as a chill chased up and down his spine.

"Perhaps," he ventured. "Only perhaps, mind ye, it might be an idea to turn back and find a way round. Though it be only the smallest wisp o' a bit o' smoke when you get right down to it."

Even as he spoke though, the puff of smoke was joined in company by others. More and more, larger and larger, spinning through the air until the forest became choked with their madcap waltz. Chester was not usually one to beat a hasty retreat from any foe, but he had his passengers to think of. At least, that is what he told himself as he turned and trundled in a hurried but dignified manner after the other escaping animals.

Had they left it too late? The fumes were thick and it was becoming hard to see. A roaring noise like growling thunder approached on either side. The hearts of the three companions beat faster and faster. No more words were exchanged, no recriminations or reproaches. Only a yearning for fresh air, a cool place away from the growing heat. Blue sky rather than the flickers of orange that teased them to their right and left.

Chester wheezed and Nightshade coughed. Only Celestyna was unaffected as wyrms are closely related to dragons and other creatures of fire and fume, but concern for her newly found friends weighed heavily.

The bear's eyes were burning and watering so, he no longer could see where he was going as he blundered here and there, attempting to find a way through. The crack and screeching death knells of withering trees echoed around him, confusing him still further. He blamed himself for not heeding the rabbit's first warning but had little time to think on it as he struggled to save himself and his companions.

His hope fizzled as another roaring noise was heard directly in front of them.

"I am sorry," he croaked out roughly, as sweat pooled and puddled in his bristling fur. "Sounds like more fire ahead. I think we're done for."

"You did your best," said the wyrm, giving the bear a light squeeze with her coils.

"You're very brave," said Nightshade softly into Chester's ear. "I am proud to have met you."

Tears rose in the bear's eyes to hear such praise. The saltwater cleared his vision for a moment. "Look there. What's that?"

The three strained to see through the billowing smoke. A massive shape loomed, impossible to make out except for an improbably large set of antlers.

Nightshade quivered. "It is the Keeylas!" they cried in terror.

"The what?" asked the wyrm.

"A fearsome creature we were told about by a sibyl," answered the bear.

"By a what?"

"No time to explain," said Chester, "but it is not a thing we particular want to meet up with if the old gal told true."

But they had no choice as there seemed no escape whichever way they looked.

Chester lifted Celestyna from his neck and wrapped her around a branch on a tree that had not yet begun to smolder. He set Nightshade gently beside the wyrm.

He'd never yet met a foe he could not easily overmatch with his size and strength and claws. He rose on his back legs to his fullest height and roared a mighty war cry as he prepared to charge into battle. His challenge ricocheted through the forest. Had any other creatures been left to hear it, they would have cowered at the sound.

Proud he was of his prowess and fearless too. He would never give up until all hope was lost, but whether the fire or the monster would get him first, who could say?

As Chester prepared to charge into battle with the barely visible foe, a gentle yet commanding voice stopped him in his tracks. "Good sir, this way is blocked. You and your friends should come with us."

The bear dropped to all fours in his surprise as the wyrm and mouse kept watch from the tree. A creature stepped forward, but it was no mythical monster such as the Keeylas. It was a magnificent stag, his sleek coat shining red and gold in the firelight. His head supported a set of shining antlers so large it seemed impossible he had the strength to carry them. A formidable sight, but his dark eyes were kind and full of concern.

"Yes, do come with us and hurry!" A doe stepped beside her mate as two small fawns pranced forward, excited and oblivious to their danger in the way only small ones who have not yet experienced the perils of life can be.

"Papa is leading us to the river. It is a game!" they cried, unaware of the jeopardy they were in. "We must stay very close!"

Chester was an impulsive bear at heart, and in truth, there wasn't much of a choice to be made. If this was a friend and not foe, and if there was any chance the stag could lead them to safety, they must take it. He hastily retrieved the wyrm and mouse from their perch and followed.

The stag seemed to have an eerie sense of where the fire was and had been. He threaded his way carefully but confidently through the flames. The fire burned close enough to scorch their skin at times. Even the two little fawns grew serious and frightened before long, but their father never wavered, only turning his head from time to time to encourage and cajole everyone on.

"It's not much farther. An eagle reported to me the fire has not crossed the river. We can swim across to safety on the other side."

Nightshade was quite unnerved and decided to hide inside of Chester's ear. It was devilishly ticklish, but the bear resisted the urge to shake his head. Celestyna was rather enjoying herself, for wyrms are cold-blooded and love warmth of any kind. They can slither directly through fire without a bit of harm, but she knew her companions were not so fortunate. She hummed a gentle tune into Chester's other ear, and both the mouse and bear were comforted by it in some way they could not define.

It was a song of fighting through danger, of keeping faith and holding tight to friendship, of hope and homecoming. All the creatures felt their strength and determination reviving.

Some kind o' powerful magic there, thought Chester, though he was too exhausted and busy saving his breath to say it aloud. It was something to think on after they were safe once more. He'd never experienced magic before, though he'd often heard tales of it—second-hand and third-hand stories of curious doings, both dark and light. Yes, it was something to think on when he had a moment.

But for now, he kept his mind on weightier matters. The stag picked up the pace, and his mate and children ran swiftly after. The bear was no slouch at running when called upon, though he preferred lazing by the river with one paw drifting in its cool waters. What he wouldn't give to be there, away from this heat and smoke.

Stout-hearted bear! His paws smarted and stung from running through the ash-covered forest, yet he would not give up even as blisters rose and his fur was singed. He concentrated on following the flashing white tail of the deer, for if he lost sight of them—disaster!

What was that up ahead? Laughter? Yes, it was the two fawns, gurgling and giggling in relief. They had reached the river!

Chester galloped up beside them, huffing and puffing. The stag and his mate were halfway across the silver waters, but the river was running fast and deep.

They looked back in concern at their little ones. Were they too small and weak to fight the swift current?

"Fear not," said the bear. "Hold fast to my fur and I'll get you across."

He waded out and the two small deer grasped onto his coat with their strong jaws. The bear was not very tasty, and in fact, was currently a nasty mix of oil and sweat and burnt fur, but the fawns were too polite and scared to complain. Chester struck out with confidence, being a strong swimmer, and pulled them along with him.

Celestyna got a good dunking much to her dismay, for she was not fond of water. She snaked herself up as high as she could from the bear's head to stay as dry as possible. Nightshade rolled themself into a tight ball and slid even farther down the bear's ear. What a day they were having! The mouse had begun to think adventuring might not be all it was cracked up to be, but it was far too late to turn back.

At least the air was growing cooler as they retreated from the fire. The smoke still drifted, but that awful heat and flame was behind them. The stag and doe touched the far bank first, scrambling out of the water and shaking themselves as dry as possible. They looked on anxiously as their offspring did their best to swim, pulled along by the bear. Great was everyone's relief when the shallows were reached and they could stand and wade onto shore.

The wyrm climbed down from Chester's neck, seeking higher ground. The bear gave a mighty shake, flinging water in every direction. He'd forgotten about the mouse and had a bad moment thinking he'd sent his passenger flying, but Nightshade was nowhere to be seen.

"Eeeem shtuuuuuc."

"What's that?" Chester asked, turning his head this way and that to see who had spoken.

"I'M STUCK!" It was Nightshade from deep inside the bear's right ear.

"This is a fine how do you do," said Chester. He tried gently poking one claw down the hole but it did no good. His companions looked on helplessly, at a loss as to how to assist.

A high-pitched voice spoke up. "Allow me, allow me!" It was a prickly hedgehog, standing at the bear's feet. Chester lowered his head to get a closer look.

Before you could say Chester Charles Farthington, the hedgehog jumped up, reached into the bear's ear, and plucked out the mouse.

"There you are! Safe and sound, you are, you are. Come! Come! We've a feast set up in the forest. Those who escaped are rejoicing. All enemies are allies today! Be not afraid!"

The hedgehog trundled off. Our party wandered after, dazed and not yet over the dreadful fright they'd just experienced.

What a sight awaited them! Forest creatures of every kind gathered in a large clearing. Wolf and rabbit, fox and squirrel, kestrel and shrew. Natural adversaries, yet they had set aside their instinctual conflict for this short time to celebrate their survival.

Nuts and seeds and fruit were heaped high, with more arriving every moment, brought by industrious squirrels and beleaguered badgers.

Chester shook his shaggy head in wonder. He'd never seen anything like it and thought he never would again. Soon these creatures would go their separate ways, return to their old enmities, hunt and be hunted, but for this one moment, there was a shared relief and a joy unbounded in the knowledge they had cheated death, that day at least.

CHAPTER 4

THE HOOT OF AN OWL

A WAX-TINGED NIGHTSHADE SPOKE from their recently recovered perch on Chester's head (but most definitely not from inside the bear's ear) to the great stag of the forest. "We are much in your debt, sir, for guiding us out of danger."

The stag bowed low, his antlers leaving soft furrows in the earth. "And we to you, for bringing our children across the river safely."

Chester beamed. "Told you it'd work out, didn't I? Things mostly do, I've found. Nowt to fret about after all, was there?"

The mouse had their own thoughts on this. It had begun to dawn on them that the bear's philosophy of survival bordered on the careless. Perhaps it came of being such a large creature and having very little to fear in the world. For a tiny mouse, such recklessness in going about one's day-to-day activities was out of the question. Chester was a lively companion with a generous spirit, but Nightshade couldn't help wondering if it was quite *safe* to be around him.

It was rather late to be considering this, as the mouse had now traveled so far from home, it would have been impossible to return there. Not only was the distance too great, but there was a raging fire in between them and their cozy, quiet hole in the ground. They thought of the little treasures they'd left behind. A warm scrap of pink flannel found caught on a branch. A smooth pebble shaped like an acorn. A downy feather they used as a fan when the weather turned warm. All lost forever.

To think of everything that had happened in less than a day! Starting with the hoot of an owl overhead, an old familiar foe. Then the infernal machine, the sibyl, news of the terrible Keeylas, eating a peppery stew, meeting a monster under the bed, surviving an inferno, crossing the silver river, and now, joining in a feast with the animals who had escaped a smoky fate. Nightshade couldn't help trembling at the recollection of these unexpected events.

Chester called up to his quivering passenger in concern. "There, there, my friend. What seems to be the trouble?"

"Very likely they are hungry." It was Celestyna. Having rolled and twisted her way through some dry leaves to blot off as much of the river water as possible, the wyrm rejoined her companions. "We always find food chases away a fright. We should join the feast."

"A right good notion," the bear agreed.

Regrettably, their arrival caused an unfortunate stir. Though he could not help the way he looked, there was no doubt Chester was an overwhelmingly giant and formidable creature. That might have been overlooked in the general amnesty between natural enemies, but when Celestyna snaked into view, a general panic broke out among the celebrants. They had never seen such a thing before and assumed the worst. A chaotic exodus ensued, leaving the bear, mouse, wyrm and deer family alone in the clearing.

"I am sorry," said the doe sympathetically. "We would have spoken up for you. Told them you mean no harm if only we'd had a chance."

"A right hasty crowd," Chester observed, "but take no offense, Nightshade, my friend. I am sure it is nothing you did."

As Nightshade agreed with this assessment, they remained silent.

"We're afraid it was us," Celestyna lamented. "A wyrm will always be viewed as a monster wherever we go. It is our doom, our destiny, our heavy burden to bear."

"Eh?" asked Chester. "I am a burden o' a bear? I shouldn't like to think so."

It occurred to his companions for the first time that perhaps their friend was slightly hard of hearing. Maybe this was why he often disregarded advice—too embarrassed to admit he hadn't caught the words. Or perhaps the mouse's sojourn in his ear had simply gummed up the works.

"Not you!" Nightshade said, speaking very clearly. "Celestyna worries everyone is afraid of her."

"Ah. Well, 'tis true you are a thing of wonder to look upon," the bear admitted. "But they've only to get to know you better to realize you aren't a bit dangerous. Much like me, I suppose. We've that in common. 'Tis why I've learned never to rush to judgment. Why, I could've eaten up this young mouse as a snack in one bite when first I laid eyes on them and wouldn't that have been a shame?"

Again, as Nightshade could only agree fervently with this observation, they remained silent.

"You are an unusual bear," said the wyrm. A comment which everyone present felt to be entirely accurate, including Chester.

"Thank 'ee kindly! I do my best!"

The fawns giggled, dancing around the bear in a bout of silliness. Their mother nosed them aside and bade them behave.

"'Tis no bother," said Chester. "It's good to see young 'uns being young 'uns. I've none of my own, and unlikely ever to, being as I am the only bear left in this forest."

"That's not true," said the stag. "We've seen one other. A gentle black bear with an unusual spot of white on her back and missing one of her hind legs. She was shy of us and climbed a tree. We respected her privacy and walked on, thinking her injury made her cautious of strangers."

"Now, now, now! That is a thing, that is! That is a thing!" The bear's heart raced at this tale of another of his kind. He'd long ago resigned himself to never having a bear-to-bear conversation and thought he'd made peace with his fate, but his long-buried hopes fluttered to life at this news. "And where was this?"

The doe answered. "This side of the river. It was before we had these ones." She nodded her head at her children. "A quiet, dark part of the forest where few of us go. We were only passing through ourselves. There is said to be..." She looked around, as though fearful of being overheard, before whispering, "...*magic* there."

"Hush," her mate said. "It is forbidden to speak that word."

"Does such a thing really exist?" asked Nightshade.

"I don't know and have no wish to find out." The stag shook his antlers in such a way to indicate his dismissal of any further discussion of the topic. "There are enough perils in these woods without seeking out others."

Chester, being a somewhat contrary bear, was inclined to disagree. "I don't know about perils as such. There's not so very much to be afraid of."

"That might be true for you, but your small friend may disagree."

"They needn't worry as long as they're with me. What could possibly happen with me around to protect them?"

The sharp screech keening over their heads came as if in answer to the question. It was a call Nightshade knew only too well and had every reason to fear, but before they had a chance to react or hide, strong talons scooped them expertly from atop the bear's head, and just like that, the mouse was gone.

Chester stared upward in complete and utter astonishment as Nightshade disappeared into the far above amid a flurry of powerful wings.

"What's this? What's this?" the bear cried, patting the top of his head as though to assure himself the mouse was truly gone. "What's happened?"

"Eagle owl got 'em." It was a slinky, bright-eyed stoat with red back, white belly, and a splash of black on the tip of its long tail. "Billibo, by name. Nasty, bad-tempered gal, that eagle owl."

"But is it an eagle or an owl?" asked Chester, both dismayed and bewildered by the newcomer's apparently contradictory information.

The stoat puffed out its cheeks with a decided noise of irritation. "An owl, of course. It's right there in the name. What a question!"

"I'm so sorry for the loss of your friend," said the doe, bowing her head in sorrow. "It is treacherous being a small creature."

"We must hasten to catch up with any of our herd that survived the fire, but you have my condolences as well," the stag offered. He was generous enough not to point out that he'd done his best to warn the bear against over-confidence in his ability to protect the more vulnerable in his care.

The deer family took their leave, bounding away with their little ones in tow, to find others of their kind. Celestyna approached the stunned bear, slithering and winding herself around his neck and resting her head on top of his. "What a tragedy! Nightshade, valiant young mouse, we shall never forget you." Slow tears fell from the wyrm's eyes and oozed down the bear's face.

"Well, well, well, well, well," Chester blustered. "Well, well, well. A small set-back, I'll admit. Nothing that can't easily be remedied, I'm sure. We just find this owl eagle thingy and ask her to return Nightshade to us. Nothing simpler."

The stoat could hardly speak for laughing. "Ask... Billibo... for it back..." it wheezed, holding its stomach with one paw and slapping its knee with the other. "Ask... for... it... back. That's the... the funniest thing... I ever heard."

"Ain't nothing funny about it to be sure, in so much as one o' my company is in a right pickle," the bear replied testily.

"In a what?"

"A pickle. It's a hooman thing. Never mind. We've no time. Must get a move on. Where's this bob-bib-elo to be found?"

The stoat got on tippy-toe, stretching its long torso out to get a better view of the bear's face. "You're serious, aren't you? You really mean to ask her for her meal back?"

"Meal? What can you mean? What use has she for a wee mouse? Nightshade wouldn't make so much as a crumb for such an immense bird."

"Maybe, but I happen to know she has a couple of nestlings. Just the right size for one of them, or perhaps both, if they are of a mind to share and she tears it in two."

Chester felt a chill deep in his heart and fear crept into his mind—not for himself, but for another, so much smaller and less powerful than he. This bear, who had run bravely through a forest fire, thought nothing of boldly chasing down men with guns and rambling about his territory in a carefree and assured way, suddenly realized how fragile a thing was a life.

And not just any life, but one who had entrusted themself to his care. The faintest inkling he might have been a tad reckless in his dealings with the mouse twinkled to life, but this only strengthened his resolve.

"Where is this nest?"

The stoat shook its head. "It would be far too late by the time you got there. Might as well forget about the mouse and move along."

"Forget about them? Never!" The bear picked the stoat up by its tail, swinging it painfully through the air. "You've seen where this owl lives. Show me the way or *you'll* make a nice snack for *me*!"

Celestyna intervened. "Chester, I know you are not a cruel one. There is no need for such behavior even when we are upset."

Abashed, Chester set the seething stoat on the ground. It made haste to attempt a mad dash into the woods. Quicker than the eye can see, the wyrm hurtled through the air, twisting and turning as its frills helped it glide down and around the weaselly animal. "However, we do need your help, and this is an emergency," she said, subtly tightening her coils around the stoat. "Would you not wish to aid us?"

As she spoke, she stared into the stoat's eyes, mesmerizing it by bobbing her head to and fro.

Another bit o' magic, thought Chester, for the animal soon capitulated.

"It's no skin off my snoot if you wish to go on a fool's errand. I've nothing better to do and it might be amusing, like all lost causes."

The wyrm let loose of her prisoner. "We will hope it is not so, friend, but what shall we call you? If we are to travel together, we should at least learn your name. We are Celestyna, and this one is Chester."

"Chester Charles Farthington," the partially chastened bear mumbled under his breath.

The stoat smoothed down its fur, ruffled and rippled by its late adventures. "Not that it is any of your business, but I am called Bramble."

"Bramble," said the wyrm, rolling the sound around in her mouth. "A prickly name for a pleasingly prickly person."

Chester thought pleasing was pushing it, but the stoat looked content with the unusual compliment.

"My ma raised her children to stand up for themselves. It's a cruel life and a short one for those like us if you don't. But what are you? An overgrown snake? I've never seen anything near your size or color before."

"We are a wyrm with a y, and this size is nothing to what we will be. We've grown a thousand scales since yesterday and shall grow a thousand more today and every day until we are full-grown."

"And when will that be?"

"When we are full-grown, of course. When else?"

Both Bramble and Chester were left none the wiser by this answer and exchanged their first look of being in sympathy with one another since they'd met. I find there is nothing like feeling equally ignorant on a subject, but being too embarrassed to pursue the matter, to bring folks closer together.

"We should hurry if you're serious about going after your friend. Billibo will be back at her nest any time now. Her young ones will snap up the food she brings without a second thought. They are bottomless pits at that age."

Celestyna broke into fresh tears at this intelligence as she curled her way around the bear securely. Bramble bounded away at great speed, but Chester kept up. Even though his paws were bruised and blistered from their escape through the inferno, he was determined to follow the owl's flight. What they would find at the end of it, he shuddered to think, but one thing he knew: you never give up on your friends.

CHAPTER 5

A RAVENISH OMEN

HOW FAR AWAY THE ground looked to Nightshade as the eagle owl rose into the air, her talons tight around the unfortunate mouse. She brushed along the tops of the towering pines until her home came into sight. Two feathered nestlings that had not yet lost all the downy fluff of infancy squawked to see their mother nearing with another tidbit for them.

The talons loosened their grip and Nightshade tumbled, landing with a *thump* in the branchy nest.

A voice of complaint. "Only one?"

"And so small!" cried another.

Billibo flicked her wings in annoyance. "There is disorder in the forest. Animals on the run from a fire across the river. I braved a bear and some snake-like creature to get this for you, ungrateful spawn. I will hunt some more. In the meantime, behave and *share*." A bustle of feather and wind, and she was off again.

Nightshade peeked out to find the round, golden eyes of two young owls staring at them in a most unsettling manner.

"This is mine," exclaimed one, reaching with gaping maw in the mouse's direction.

They were shoved aside by the other. "I'm the eldest. It's mine."

"Mother said to share." The younger owlet snapped at the mouse, before being buffeted with a wing to the head.

The eldest sneered. "Mother isn't here now, is she?"

"You nasty, sneaking bully!"

The siblings began a comically clumsy brawl. Much head butting, pulling of feathers, and red scratches from angry claws ensued, as well as more than a bit of fowl language.

Nightshade took advantage of the commotion to peer over the side of the nest, thinking they might crawl away while the owlets were distracted. Having never been so high before, the mouse had never realized they suffered from acrophobia (which is a fancy word for fear of heights), and their poor head swam with dizziness.

They cowered back into the nest. Even if they could steady their nerves to crawl down the rough bark of the tree, it would be a long and treacherous journey. The mother owl might come back and catch them at it. A swifter escape was needed.

A pale blue something caught their eye. It was a crumpled piece of paper used to help line the bottom of the owls' home. The mouse had never seen paper before, but it looked strong and sturdy.

An absurd idea entered their head. They had watched a spider once, jumping onto the forest floor while holding an unusual contraption woven of silk. Nightshade had struck up a conversation and learned it was a parachute, used to ease the spider's passage from high places by slowing its descent. What if it were possible to use this square of paper in a similar fashion?

They gathered the four corners of the paper around the tip of their tail and tied the whole thing together with a piece of pine straw, making the knot as tight as they could and twisting their tail around it. Perched on the edge of the nest, the mouse stared out into the forest. To willingly fling oneself from a great height with an untested design seemed as impossible as riding on a star. They might have sat dithering far too long if the owlets had not suddenly noticed their prey had been busy while they fought.

"It's getting away! Grab it!" cried the older one.

The younger owl leapt with all the gangly awkwardness of a not-quite-adult, tripped, and accomplished nothing more than to push poor Nightshade right over the side of the nest whether they were ready or not.

The mouse was not prepared for the strength of the wind in their makeshift sail. It threatened to pull it right off their tail. They curled round and grabbed on to the pine straw binding with their paws, hanging on for dear life to keep it from flying away.

What a giddy feeling, plummeting through the air! And yet the paper did seem to be working. Nightshade glided at a far slower rate than they would have done without the parachute. Whether it was slow enough to avoid injury upon landing remained to be seen.

An ominous sound came from overhead. The faintest *sssk, sssk.* The mouse looked up. A rip was forming in the paper, insignificant at first, but it grew long and longer. A sinister development. Nightshade could do nothing but stare in horror as the paper above their head, that thin barrier between life and death, tore in two, leaving them plunging helplessly to the ground.

They barely had time to appreciate the exquisite melancholy of their impending doom when they felt the pine straw that bound them to the torn paper parachute go taut. Instead of falling, they were now flying through the air at a rate of speed that was scarcely less terrifying than their downward descent had been. Before they had time to adjust their thinking to this turn of events, they were set down none-too-gently on the sturdy branch of a spreading oak tree.

"Squawk!"

Trembling, Nightshade looked round to find a large black bird perched on the branch next to them. It had a wickedly long beak and tilted its head to one side, the better to fix one dark beady eye on the mouse. "A strange treasure. A funny creature. A flying long tail. What are you?"

"Just a mouse," answered Nightshade.

"Nope, nope, nope. You are mistaken. Mice do not FLY, ergo you are no mouse."

"Well, I was not so much flying as plummeting."

The bird paused to consider this, shaking its head and smoothing out a few misplaced feathers with its beak. "I suppose if a mouse was to find themselves in a high place—SUPPOSING, mind, because it is entirely unlikely—they might plummet if circumstances and conditions were RIPE for plummeting. I suppose that might happen, but it would in no way explain your HAT."

"My hat?" Nightshade asked, astonished. They felt around on their head and realized part of the blue paper from their failed parachute had settled there upon landing. "Oh, this isn't a hat. It's my parachute."

"A pair of SHOOTS? You do realize that sounds quite mad, but then we are all mad here. A writing desk told me so once."

It was difficult for the mouse to decide what to say in response to this extraordinary creature. Its mind seemed to be running along lines the mouse found hard to follow—almost as though it was speaking in riddles. Where had Nightshade heard mention of riddles before? Ah, yes, the tortoise sibyl had warned them about it.

"You aren't by chance a raven, are you?"

"Of course! What else would I be?"

"I thought at first you might be a crow."

"A CROW! A CROW!" The raven began to hop around in an agitated manner, flapping its wings and causing such a stir that Nightshade feared they were about to be shoved off their second tree of the day, which would have been at least two trees too many. "I have rarely been so insulted in my life and I have been insulted often, most commonly by CROWS."

"I'm so sorry," said Nightshade. "I wouldn't have offended you for the world."

The raven stopped its wild fluttering. "Not for the world? The WHOLE world? Really? I mean, I would gladly offend you or anyone if someone offered me an entire WORLD. It would be foolish to stand on principle with such a prize at stake. Unless..."

The bird eyed Nightshade suspiciously. "You aren't one of those Do-Gooders, are you?"

"A what?"

"Do-Gooder. You know, going around DOING GOOD."

"Is that a bad thing?"

"Cause an awful lot of trouble, Do-Gooders do. Always interfering. Scolding you for stealing shiny trinkets to decorate your nest. Waving their ridiculous stick arms at you for taking corn from the fields."

"What kind of creature has arms made of sticks?" Nightshade asked, trying to picture such a thing.

"Scarecrow, of course! There's a horribly RUDE one wearing a purple sun-bonnet with daisies on it, though to be honest, it is a much nicer hat than the one you're wearing."

"A scare-crow," the mouse mused, pulling the parachute from their head in an attempt to forestall further commentary on it. "I don't suppose you're scared of it then if it is meant to scare crows."

"Of course, of course, of course. What type of SILLY BILLY of a bird would be scared of something meant to scare crows. Ha ha ha... hee hee hee..."

The way the raven's laughter trailed off nervously and its eyes darted around from side to side was less than convincing, but Nightshade, being a very polite mouse, declined to press the issue.

"I have been remiss in not thanking you. You saved my life and I will be forever grateful to you."

"Did I?" asked the raven. "Didn't mean to. Sounds like the kind of thing a Do-Gooder might do," it added, looking troubled at this realization.

"I'm not sure doing good is as bad a thing as you seem to think. I have made many friends today who were so kind and helpful to me."

"You have friends? What's it like?"

"Wonderful! Well, mostly," Nightshade felt obliged to amend, remembering the mixed blessings of Chester's impetuous nature. "There was a bear that took me on an adventure, a tortoise who gave me advice, a stag that led me safely through a fire, a wyrm—"

"A WORM!" The raven guffawed, a bizarre croaking noise as though it was being strangled. "You made friends with a WORM? I have never in my life heard a more preposterous thing. Worms are notoriously anti-social after all."

"Aunty what?" Nightshade asked before deciding it wasn't worth waiting for an explanation that would undoubtedly only be confusing. "It's not that kind of worm. This is a large, snake-like thing."

"You mean a wyrm with a y. Why didn't you say so to begin with? Making me look foolish. I don't think you are a Do-Gooder after all. What were you doing with a wyrm?"

"We were on our way to find a safe place for her. Somewhere high and far-off, above the clouds where she won't be bothered by anyone who is frightened of her."

"Firstly, all wyrms are male. That is a FACT. Just as all vultures are female, red beetles taste like gingersnaps, and wolves can often be seen standing on their heads. Also FACTS. Secondly, there is nothing above the clouds except more clouds and the Great Raven God that will one day descend to eat us all."

There was rather a lot in the raven's assertions Nightshade wished to challenge as perhaps not being strictly accurate, but they did not get a chance. The bird suddenly went into a kind of a trance and its eyes rolled back in its head.

"THREE TIMES THREE

THE ANSWERS BE

FOUR BY FOUR

KNOCK AT THE DOOR

WHERE STARS ALIGN

YOU'LL SEE A SIGN

A FEATHER DESCENDS

MAKE AMENDS

ALL MUST DIE

DON'T WONDER WHY

BETRAY YOUR FRIENDS

A QUEEN ASCENDS

WHEN DANGER IT SCRIES

A RAVEN MUST FLY

GOODBYE"

On that ominous note, the raven departed awkwardly, having got the remains of the parachute tangled around one leg.

The sibyl had advised paying attention to ravens because they are wise birds, so Nightshade dutifully repeated in their head the words of the prophecy, regardless of their doubts as to the wisdom of the unusual fowl. It wasn't exactly comforting. Talk of everyone dying and betraying friends, and they weren't sure what "scries" meant exactly, but danger was a word that is all too familiar to a very small mouse. What had caused the raven to flee so suddenly?

A shadow fell over Nightshade in answer to their question. The mouse quivered. First the owl, then the raven—what fresh flying fright might this be?

They peered up at an outlandish sight. The head was that of a cat, though since Nightshade had never met a cat, the mouse had no words to describe it other than extremely fuzzily brown-striped with whiskers and pointy ears and a fine pair of green eyes. The body was that of a lizard, though since Nightshade had never seen a lizard, they could only say it had glowing green scales that matched its eyes and long-fingered hands that grasped at the air as though seeking something that wasn't there.

The tail of the thing was something like a rat's tail (which Nightshade was familiar with) only there were five of them twirling around each other restlessly. A pair of bat-like wings completed its distinctive form. It was both the weirdest yet loveliest thing the mouse had ever seen, for it was beyond comparison to any other living creature, and unique things have a beauty that comes from being rare and therefore precious.

"Hello," said the thing. "You're an uncommon one, aren't you? So small and grey and furry and small."

"I am actually quite common," Nightshade replied.

"Are you?" The creature sniffed delicately with a light pink nose. "You smell nice. What are you?"

"I'm a mouse."

"Are you good eating?"

Nightshade shook their head vehemently. "Not one bit. Mice have an unpleasantly sour taste and will give you a belly ache."

"Good to know. I have a delicate stomach and must be mindful of it. Kind of you to warn me."

"Not at all," the mouse replied, feeling such compliments were not entirely deserved as they had only been acting in their own self-interest. Turning the conversation away from the dangerous subject of food, Nightshade inquired, "And what are you, if you don't mind my asking?"

"I am a whirligig. We are also not good for eating. At least, so I was told by a sturgeon who swallowed me whole only to spit me out again. Insulting but since it resulted in my not being eaten, I suppose I shouldn't complain."

"What's a sturgeon?"

"Strange fish. Monstrous big and so absurd to look at, I hardly dare describe it. You would think me a liar or worse. Hard to believe such a weird thing exists in the world."

Nightshade was thinking exactly the same about the whirligig but didn't wish to be rude. "Are there many of you?"

"Many of me? There is only one of me. Why should there be many of me?"

"I mean, are there many whirligigs in the world?"

"Of course! We are surrounded by them. There is one over there and there and there again!" The thing pointed its slender fingers around from tree to ground and back again.

This was a disconcerting turn of events. Either there were whirligigs around that Nightshade couldn't see, or this whirligig was seeing things that weren't there. Both possibilities were unsettling but when in doubt, the mouse decided friendliness never hurt.

"My name is Nightshade. What is yours?"

"My name? What is that?"

"What do others call you?"

"Whirligig."

"That is what you are, but don't you have a distinctive word that applies only to you?"

The thing's eyes opened wide, its pupils round and black. "You mean I could have a word of my own? How extraordinary! None of the other whirligigs ever told me so. WHY DIDN'T YOU TELL ME?" it shouted to its invisible friends, tilting its head to one side as though listening to an answer only it could hear. "Oh! They say they never heard of such a thing either. How does one earn a name?"

"You don't have to earn it. Your parents give it to you."

"Parents? What is that?"

"Those that brought you into the world."

"The wizard, you mean? He never said anything about giving me a name, but then he was distracted at the time by beholding me in all my splendor. Between you and me, I'm not sure I came out exactly as intended. I have since heard rumors the wizard is not as skilled in necromancy as he likes to believe."

"What is necromancy?" Nightshade asked with a shudder. The sound of the word gave them an uneasy feeling.

"The art of creating a whirligig, naturally. What did you think it was?"

Every question in this conversation seemed only to lead to another question. Nightshade was hungry and tired and their nerves were wrung out. It had been a long day and fuller of startling events than was strictly comfortable.

"Why don't you pick a name for yourself?" they suggested in an attempt to move events along. "There's no rule against doing so I've ever heard."

The whirligig looked much struck at this idea. Its whiskers twitched as quickly as its many tails. It blinked rapidly and stretched its leathery wings while tapping its long toes on the tree branch. This went on for an unconscionably long time before it declared, "I like to eat walnuts. Could I name myself Walnut?"

"I don't see why not," Nightshade said. "Many animals are named after things of the forest, for we are things of the forest ourselves."

"Walnut the whirligig. I like it very much." It made a deep thrumming sound which if Nightshade had been familiar with cats they would have recognized as a contented purring. "I have a name! You are a delightful mouse. Are all mouses so delightful?"

"I don't know about other mice, but this one is exhausted and too far from my friends."

Walnut grew agitated. "This won't do! This won't do, will it?" it appealed to its whirligig friends. Whether they agreed or not, Nightshade, of course, couldn't tell, but Walnut nodded its head as though they did. "Yes, we should help this mouse. They have done us a great favor by telling us about names. Well, I'm sorry, but you must each pick your own names. I can't do it for you."

Another pause, wherein Nightshade was debating whether to try and creep away quietly and make their own way down the tree to solid ground at last, but before they could act, Walnut turned back to them with a catty grin. "Sunshine, Leaf, and Mold! We all have names now! Isn't it delightful? What can we do to repay you for this gift?"

"I want nothing more than to be reunited with my friends, but I wouldn't have the least idea how to find them."

"That's no problem!" Walnut grasped the mouse gently with its lizardy fingers and flapped its batty wings. Yet again, Nightshade found themselves flying. For a mouse who had never held ambitions of flight, this was becoming a habit and not one they were very fond of.

"Where are we going?" they squeaked.

"To the one who knows all! We're off to see the wizard!"

CHAPTER 6

THE DARK WOODS

WHILE NIGHTSHADE WAS HAVING their fur-raising adventures, a rescue party was well underway. Bramble slunk stoatishly through the forest on the owl's trail, ducking under fallen trees, while Chester leapt over them with bearish enthusiasm. Celestyna hung on a while before deciding she could enjoy a much less bumpy ride by disembarking from the bear and gliding on her own.

The wyrm was an elegant creature, her amethyst and emerald scales flashing like jewels in the afternoon sunshine that fell through the tree canopy here and there. Her softly strong neck frills expanded and contracted to push brush aside and ease her passage.

The forest creatures who saw her go by whispered amongst themselves in wonder at a sight they had never seen before and were unlikely to ever see again. A tale to tell their children on dark nights of a monstrous snake, a galumphing bear, and a slinky stoat embarked on what mysterious mission, none could say, though many a legend sprung up around the trio that they would have been amazed to hear.

Chester's eagerness to recover Nightshade and make amends for his careless guardianship sustained him at first, even though the pain from the burns on his paws grew from a whisper to a shout the farther they went. But he was by nature an impatient sort and soon grew weary of the seemingly neverending journey.

"Surely we are nearly there by now?" he asked the stoat.

"Not yet," answered Bramble.

"Now?"

"No!"

"How about now?"

The stoat stopped abruptly and turned to face the bear. "You're never going to stop asking, are you?"

"Only wondering. Like to keep abreast o' current events. Been my experience that being an informed bear is better than being an uninformed bear."

Bramble snorted an unusually loud sound for such a relatively small animal and got a martial look in its eye.

Celestyna decided it might be wise to intervene. "Perhaps you could give us a general idea of how much farther it is? We are naturally anxious for our friend."

"It scarcely matters whether the distance is short or long. The owl's already crossed it by now and the mouse has been eaten long ago. Why I agreed to come on this fool's errand, I can no longer remember, but never let it be said I am not a stoat of my word."

Chester howled an unbearish howl and sat heavily down upon his haunches. "Nightshade, my friend! Nightshade, my friend! 'Tis my fault, indeed, you've met a bad end."

"That rhymed," Bramble noted.

This ill-timed observation might have provoked the bear to some intemperate action if the wyrm had not again interceded. "We have no way of knowing Night-shade's true fate until we know it. A thousand and one happy accidents might have intervened to save them. Instead of wasting time speculating, we suggest continuing on, but is there perhaps not a shortcut which would get us there faster?"

"Only through the Dark Woods," the stoat replied with a shudder.

"The dark woods?"

"No, the Dark Woods," Bramble said, emphasizing their importance by capitalizing the words. "It is a place of *magic*."

"Such as the deer spoke of, mayhaps?" asked Chester. "They saw another bear there. I should like to come snout to snoot with another of my kind one o' these days."

"Haven't heard about any bears, but there is talk of many an eldritch personage with arcane knowledge and even necromantic tendencies."

There were quite a few words in the stoat's explanation which Chester did not understand but instead of being sensible and simply admitting this, he decided to bluff his way through. "Sounds delightful! Let's go!"

Celestyna cut across the exasperated huff of the stoat. "We are sure we are more than up to the task of protecting you from any dangers. As a mostly magical creature ourself, we are not without some tricks of our own." The wyrm slunk her head down to Bramble's level and performed her weaving dance again. "Wouldn't you like to take us the shortest way to the owl's nest, even if it is through the Dark Woods?"

"Ye-e-e-s, follow me..." The stoat took off at an angle to the path they had been following and Celestyna glided after.

Only Chester hesitated. He couldn't exactly put it into words, but there was something about the way the wyrm had convinced the stoat to act contrary to its natural instincts that didn't sit right with him.

It was all very well, he supposed, if such tricks were played on others, but what if Celestyna should decide to use it on *him*? Who knew what she might make him do, whether it was in his best interests or not? Although he normally had a trusting nature, he decided to keep a weather eye on the wyrm, because even good creatures may behave badly from time to time.

They weren't long on this new track before they entered a decidedly different part of the forest. Bear and wyrm realized what the stoat had meant about the Dark Woods. Not only was it murkier here, the trees growing thick and twisted, blocking out the sky, but there was a humming and a hiss in the air like the electricity that buzzes after a tree has been struck by lightning. Only instead of dissipating quickly, it hung about them, causing the fur on the stoat and bear to stand on end and the wyrm's scales to shiver, clicking and clacking.

"You s-s-see what I mean n-n-now, don't you?" Bramble asked, teeth chattering.

"It is a mite uncomfortable," Chester admitted. "Makes me feel prickly all over, like the time I had a disagreement with some bees over the rights o' ownership to honeycomb found just hanging about in a tree. Perhaps we should turn back."

"Nonsense!" cried Celestyna, writhing and twisting her coils in ecstasy. "We have never felt so alive! It is like bathing in a river of sizzling lava!"

Chester did not know what lava was but after his experiences earlier in the day, he'd had enough of fiery things to last a lifetime. Besides, whatever was in the air seemed to be having a most unfortunate effect on the wyrm. She was flinging herself about wildly, regardless of the damage she was doing to the plants and even small trees in her path.

"WATCH IT!" a tiny voice called out.

The bear stood amazed as Celestyna was not only stopped in her tracks but rose about three feet into the air, levitating there like a hummingbird hovering at a flower.

"HOW DARE YOU COME INTO THESE WOODS AND CAUSE MAY-HEM!"

Bramble dashed behind an unusually big mushroom in fright, only to come eye-to-eye with an extraordinary sight: A remarkably large black beetle (which is to say, not large in the general scheme of things, but large for a beetle) dressed in a purple cloak and hat.

"What on earth are you?" the stoat asked in bewilderment as Chester stooped down to get a better look as well.

The beetle waved its pointed hat in their faces as though that was answer enough. When they continued to look mystified, it plunked the hat back on its head with a mighty sigh.

"WHAT AM I? I AM A WIZARD, OF COURSE!"

Bramble and Chester stared hard at the beetle. While it was true it was larger than your average beetle and wearing a purple cloak and hat, unlike other beetles they had met in their lives, they were both reluctant to acknowledge it as a wizard—Bramble because the stoat was naturally skeptical, and Chester because he wasn't entirely sure what a wizard was.

"We're terribly sorry for our recklessness," Celestyna said from mid-air, apolo-gizing for her earlier unbridled writhing. "We are unused to the wondrous feeling of being surrounded by so much magic. Though we are a magical creature, we have only known a mostly mundane existence until now."

The wyrm found herself lowered gently to the ground, where she endeavored to maintain her composure even though every scale still quivered in reaction to the invisible forces around her.

The beetle floated over to her, hovering as it examined her more closely. "A WYRM?! EXTRAORDINARY! I THOUGHT YOU WERE ALL EXTINCT!"

"We are not," she answered, "though perhaps we are rarer than once we were. Humans have an unfortunate antipathy toward our kind and are apt to behave rashly when encountered. This is why we are seeking a safe haven so we might live out our days in peace."

"A HAVEN? GOOD LUCK WITH THAT!" the beetle snort-shouted.

Celestyna's face fell at the wizard's unkindly discouraging tone of voice.

Bramble, while not concerned with the wyrm's feelings but being an easily annoyed sort of creature, asked the obvious question. "Why do you keep shouting at us?"

The beetle zoomed over to the stoat. Its mouth moved but there was no sound.

"What?" said Bramble.

"I SAID, I SHOUT BECAUSE IF I SPOKE IN A NORMAL BEETLE VOICE, YOU WOULDN'T BE ABLE TO HEAR ME!"

"Oh, I suppose that is a drawback to being a beetle, even one bigger than ordinary. How did a beetle become a wizard anyway?"

"THE CORRECT QUESTION IS 'HOW DID A WIZARD BECOME A BEETLE'?"

"Okay, answer that one then," the stoat demanded with a huffy impatience.

"A SLIGHT MISCALCULATION WITH A TRANSFORMATION SPELL. NOTHING I CANNOT EASILY REMEDY!"

"Then why don't you?"

The beetle looked nervous, which was no small feat since beetles' faces are not terribly expressive. "I WILL GET TO IT BY AND BY."

"Why not now?" asked Chester, for the bear could not imagine remaining such a lowly, insignificant, unbearish thing if one didn't have to. "Can you turn into any creature you want? It's tremendous fun being a bear, you know, and then I should have company."

"I WILL REVERT TO MY NATURAL FORM."

"Which is?" asked the wyrm.

"A MAN."

"We wouldn't if we were you," Celestyna advised. "A man is a vain and selfish creature. The world would be far better off without them."

"I COULD TURN MYSELF INTO A WOMAN INSTEAD."

"That is no better. All humans are cruel, unnatural things who live only to kill others, sometimes simply for the sport of it."

"Not every hooman," Chester objected, remembering the kind woman of the cottage and her grieving mate.

The wyrm seemed to follow the bear's train of thought, for she nodded her head solemnly. "I suppose you're right. Are you a good human or a bad human?" she asked the wizard.

"I AM A VERY HUMAN HUMAN AND BEING HUMAN MEANS MAKING MISTAKES SOMETIMES, SUCH AS TURNING MYSELF INTO A BEETLE. AN ERROR I WILL CORRECT NOW SINCE IT IS INCONVENIENT TO KEEP SHOUTING. STAND BACK!"

The wizard pulled a small stick out from under his cloak—an object students of the magical arts would recognize as a wand but that to the creatures watching, who had drawn back in apprehension at the beetle's warning, seemed both ordinary and anti-climactic.

"Let us shiver in terror, for it has a stick." Bramble only just had time to make this satirical observation before the wizard touched himself on the head with the wand and was enveloped in a purple glowing haze.

In truth, the sight was alarming. The beetle shimmered and shimmied in such a disturbing fashion that even the stoat had to admit it was impressed and not a little fearful. The beetle's hard shell cracked and crumbled, falling to pieces around his feet. Strange appendages shot out here and there—a flashingly fishy tail, a hairy spider leg, the spines of a hedgehog, and the sharp, yellowed teeth of a wolf. The watchers barely had time to register these manifestations before a final form was reached.

If Celestyna had hands, she might have covered her mouth with them to try and suppress the titter that escaped despite her best efforts.

Chester was not nearly so polite, for he enjoyed a good laugh. He chortled so uncontrollably, he fell to the ground and rolled around in a decidedly undignified manner.

Bramble alone was unamused. "You're not good at this, are you?"

"Why?" the wizard asked. "What have I become? *Gobble, gobble...*" The wizard's wings flew to his beaky mouth as he strutted around in circles, moving his wrinkly head and beady eyes around as he attempted to see his new form.

"You're a turkey," the stoat replied.

"That's rather rude. I was simply asking a question. No need to be insulting."

This exchange only made Chester laugh the harder as he beat at the ground with his paws and tears of joy fell from his eyes. Celestyna, having a sympathetic nature, sobered up, realizing it was unkind to be amused by the wizard's plight.

"I'm afraid Bramble was being literal," the wyrm explained. "You are a fine example of a tom turkey. Most handsome. Magnificent array of feathers and colors. A noble form," she added, encouragingly.

The wizard was rendered speechless at this news. His beak opened and closed and a soft gobble escaped now and again, but beyond that, he seemed too overcome by this turn of events to carry on a rational conversation.

This state of affairs might have continued indefinitely if Chester had not suddenly sat up, clutching his stomach. "Oh, my, that was a right belly laugh, that was. Left me feeling awful peckish tho', no offense."

The turkey awkwardly lifted one foot. They saw his claw clutched the magical stick, which the wizard waved high in the air, causing the unwieldy bird to fall over onto his side as a huge wicker hamper appeared in front of them. Celestyna snaked over to do what she could to right the bird as the bear and stoat opened the basket and examined its contents.

It held an array of delights. Tiny cakes covered in thick icing of every color of the rainbow. Sandwiches piled high with layer upon layer of tasty goodness. Exotic fruits such as they had never seen in the forest but which gave out deliciously tangy and tantalizing odors.

"You can conjure a thing such as this," marveled Bramble, "yet cannot return yourself to being a human? How is that possible?"

"Transformation is one of the higher arts and as such, requires as much practice as say, necromancy."

"What is necromancy?"

"The art of creating a whirligig, of course!" This startling statement came from the weirdest being any of them had ever seen. It had landed softly in the clearing while they were distracted.

At any other time, their first concern would have been what in the world was a whirligig, but Chester and Celestyna had noticed something far more important. Clutched in the thing's long fingers was a very small, grey, and terribly limp mouse.

CHAPTER 7

ANOTHER PROPHECY

"Nightshade!" Celestyna and Chester cried, fearing the worst, for their friend's eyes were closed and their grey-furred body wilted over the whirligig's slender, green lizard fingers in a distressing fashion.

Walnut set the mouse down gently on a toadstool and fanned at them with its batty wings. To everyone's relief, Nightshade opened first one small eye then the other, peering out in wonder at the crowd gathered round.

"Hello," they whispered.

Chester pushed his black (and, it must be admitted, unpleasantly drippy) nose down as close to the mouse as he dared and took a deep sniff. "I do believe they be still alive."

"Obviously," said Bramble, ever impatient with anything that felt like a waste of the stoat's precious time.

"Told 'ee so, didn't I? Told 'ee all would work out in the end!" the bear crowed, pleased his optimism had not been ill-founded. "Twas you thought Nightshade was already et, but they are not et—not even been nibbled on that I can see."

A wiser bear might have spent some time reflecting on the likelihood things could just as easily have turned out much more tragically, but Chester was only emboldened in his belief that nothing truly catastrophic could happen to one of his companions while he was in charge.

"And where have you been?" the wizard demanded of his unlikely creation.

"Wandering and wilding and whither-thy-willing like a will o' the wisp," the whirligig replied, rat tails swishing and shining cat eyes blinking. "We found this thing in a tree. It is called a mice and they helped me get a name and then the other whirligigs got names too! I am Walnut, and these are Sunshine, Leaf, and Moss!" Walnut cocked his head to the side, pointy ears flicking. "Wait, I am reminded it is Mold and not Moss. Interesting choice."

The turkey strutted close to Walnut and gave it a nasty peck on its head, which fortunately was hard enough to take the blow with no ill effect. "How many times have I told you there are no others like you? You are unique. One-of-a-kind. A mistake. A cruel joke."

"Hold tight there," said Chester, pushing the wizard back with one blistered paw. "That ain't a nice thing to say!" Though the bear had only just met the whirligig, his natural inclination was to stand up for any bullied creature, even if all the formal introductions had not yet been completed—an oversight he was quick to correct. "My name is Chester. I'm a bear. And these are my friends, Bramble the stoat and Celestyna, a wyrm, but not the kind that burrows into your garden."

"Goodness!" Walnut cried. "And they call *me* strange! Look at that thing!"

"We do beg your pardon, we're sure," said the wyrm, drawing her ever-lengthening coils around her in offense.

"Not you!" the whirligig cried. "You are beautiful beyond compare, but look at this slinky, shabby, squirmy thing!"

It pointed one long finger at Bramble, who being, as we have seen, short-tempered, wasted no time in biting it clean off. Walnut gave out a feline screech and fainted dead away.

Chester rarely found himself at a loss for words, but even he was not sure how to react to such a stunning turn of events. The wyrm, however, had no such hesitation. She turned on Bramble with an angry waggle of her head and a single word. "GO!"

Furious at not only being insulted but coerced (as it felt) into helping with a benighted rescue operation and entering the Dark Woods against its common-sense, the stoat was more than happy to oblige. It paused only long enough to shut the picnic hamper of delightful treats so it could grab the handle and drag it away with a surprising amount of strength and determination. Those left behind were too shocked and concerned with the injured Walnut to protest or care.

"What a dreadful thing!" cried Nightshade, fully alert and awake now. "Walnut restored me to my friends. This is hardly a fair recompense. Isn't there something you can do?" they asked the wizard.

"Such injuries are nothing for the part of it that is lizardy. It will regenerate on its own in time."

"But until then, such suffering," said Celestyna, bobbing her head at the wizard in a dancing fashion that Chester was becoming all too familiar with. "Don't you want to help?"

The turkey stretched his neck up very tall, shaking his head so hard that snood and wattle quivered most comically. "None of that nonsense with me, young lady. I am not some easily suggestible nobody! I am a wizard. Such tricks won't work."

"Not even if I say the magic word?" she asked.

"Do you know one?"

"Of course! Flip-a-doodle!"

The wizard looked taken aback. His whole body started to quiver and he squeezed his eyes shut tightly. The turkey fell over onto his back, rolling around and flapping his wings in an alarming manner. The others looked on in dismay, afraid he was having some kind of fit but when a gurgling gargling gobbling noise emerged, they realized the wizard was laughing very, very hard.

"Flip... a... a... doo... dle! FLIP-A-DOODLE! I never! Flip-a-doodle!" In his ecstasy of mirth, the turkey waved the magic stick around wildly with his foot, accidentally poking himself in the belly with it.

A rapid-fire series of transformations followed. A black wolf, a jumpy cricket, a mischievous squirrel, more different kinds of birds than could easily be enumerated here, and even a confused-looking dolphin—though none of the onlookers knew what it was, only that it made some terribly unusual noises.

Just as they were despairing of the wizard's fate, a final form was reached: a short, pleasantly plump human with brown eyes and skin and a shock of shining auburn hair that mimicked the turkey's bright coloring. The man was still chuckling as he struggled to right himself. Chester kindly leant him a paw.

"Thank you, dear bear. You shall be rewarded." The wizard touched the tip of Chester's nose and the various burns and blisters and hurts he'd endured since the run through the forest fire were healed instantly as though they had never been.

"Ain't that a thing?" the bear marveled. "And can you do the same for poor Walnut?"

"I suppose so, now that the wyrm has spoken the magic word. *Flip-a-doodle!*" This had the unfortunate effect of setting the wizard to chortling again so mightily he was in danger of hitting himself with the wand a second time. Luckily, he recovered before disaster struck. Instead, he touched the whirligig on the nose lightly.

Walnut sat up immediately, looking in wonder at its restored finger. "I had the oddest dream. More of a nightmare, really. There was this weird creature." The whirligig looked around fearfully, relieved to see the sharp-toothed, stoatish being had apparently been a figment of its imagination.

"How generous of you!" Celestyna congratulated the wizard. "You are not such a bad human after all."

"I must apologize for my previous behavior," the man replied. "Being stuck as a beetle for so long only to then turn into a turkey was quite exasperating. I'm afraid I lost my temper with you all. Please forgive me. Is there anything else I can do to make it up to you?"

"We were looking for a safe haven for Celestyna before this ruckus," said Chester. "Mayhap you can point us in the right direction?"

"I've read of a place far above the clouds where wyrms once lived in great numbers, but there is only one way to get there I'm aware of. You must harvest zingery seeds from a mouth that never closes and plant them farther beneath the surface than any creature can dig. Water them with the fresh tears of an animal that has never existed and sing to them the song of a dying star. Only then will a vine beyond measure unfurl itself into the sky, ready for climbing, but beware, it has thorns that drip poison and red mites that will chew your noses off if you're not careful!"

"Not another riddle," Nightshade complained, sighing mightily at the wizard's dread-inducing counsel.

"Another?" asked the wizard.

"Yes, I met a raven..."

"Say no more. There's nothing like ravens for ominous omens and preposterous prophecies. I should pay it no mind if I were you. My advice on the other hand is solid as solid can be. I read it in *The Entirely True Book of Entirely True Magic* written by the wisest of wizards, Trudie Trueheart Trueliver. She is a legend."

"Is she?" asked Chester. "I never heard o' her."

"Well, maybe you've heard of me?"

"Mayhaps, but as you ain't volunteered a name, it's hard to say exactly."

Flustered at this reminder of his failure to observe the polite niceties, the wizard hastened to correct his mistake. "I beg your pardon. My name is Mercipolis, a wizard of the Old School."

"Is there a New School?" Nightshade asked.

"Not as such. Sadly, wizardry is a dying art. Takes years of study to learn the most basic magic, and few these days have the patience. A pity. Once the world was ruled by wizards and everything worked perfectly, harmony abounded. A time of plenty and prosperity."

Celestyna slid her long coils closer. "But that is not the way of things now."

"No, my dear wyrm. Just as humans turned against your kind, they also turned against those who wielded magic, for if there is one thing humans excel at, it is hating things they do not understand. One by one, we were driven from power and forced to retreat here into the deepest, darkest part of the forest. We lost interest in the affairs of humans and instead spend our time in experimentation with our powers. You can feel the residual magic in the trees from so many of us concentrated in such a small area, practicing those skills that most need improvement."

"Hence your transformations?" she asked.

"Ah, yes. Not my strong suit. Nor necromancy, apparently," Mercipolis added, glaring at the whirligig, who was living up to its name by whirling in circles, trying to catch one of its many tails in its mouth. "Truth be told, I was always more of a scholar. Made perfect scores on my written exams but barely squeaked by the practical ones. My teachers despaired of me."

"So there are others o' your kind here?" Chester said, looking around as though the woods must be full of magical folk hidden just out of sight.

The wizard ran his fingers anxiously through his red hair, causing it to stand on end in a most outlandishly charming fashion. "In theory there are, but I've not run into them. I wasn't popular in school nor after, so perhaps they are somewhere having a soiree to which I have not been invited?" he suggested with such melancholy that the others couldn't help but feel sorry for him.

Chester was relieved to hear Nightshade ask the question he was too embarrassed to ask himself. "What is a SWAH-RAY?"

"A party, a gathering, a get-together for the popular wizards, the in-crowd, the cream of society."

"Oh, do they serve cream there?" asked the bear, greatly interested. The woman of the cottage had made him fresh scones with strawberries and whipped cream once—it was one of his fondest memories.

"Less a literal party then a society of like-minded magical practitioners."

"I see," Celestyna said, bobbing her head wisely. "And you are unlike-minded," she added, as though this was the most natural thing in the world.

"Um, yes, I suppose you could look at it that way."

The wyrm used the tip of her tail to smooth down the wizard's unruly locks. "It is as well, for then you would have not been here to assist us. Now we know how to find our place above the clouds!"

"Zingery seeds from a mouth that never closes," said Nightshade. "Where do you suppose that might be?"

Mercipolis shook his head. "The book didn't say. There is an art to the interpretation of such things, of course, but if I were you, I would head west."

"Why so?"

"Because it is farther away from human lands. Magic is always strongest when no humans are near to disrupt it. But you must be prepared for a long journey and unexpected escapades. That is always the fate of those on a quest."

Nightshade couldn't help but feel they had already had an unreasonable number of escapades for one day. The idea of traveling farther still along uncertain paths was daunting, and they hadn't been of much use to the others. "Perhaps it would be better if you went without me. I am too little and too weak to be of much assistance."

"But you ain't much bother neither," said Chester, adding tactlessly, "excepting the time I had to carry you through the fire and that other time when you got stole away by an owl and set us to searching which delayed us quite a bit."

This observation did not make Nightshade feel any better about the situation, but neither did they know how to return home. They felt lost and lonely and useless. Surprisingly large tears for such a tiny creature overflowed their eyes and puddled on the ground.

"Don't fret," said Mercipolis, "this is exactly the kind of thing magic is good for." And before any of them could inquire what he meant or stop him, the wizard booped Nightshade on the nose with the magic stick.

A purple flash. The mouse gave out a pained squeak as their tail grew to enormous size, so big, they were unable to drag it around.

"Whoopsie!" The wizard tapped Nightshade with the wand again. Their ears grew so big they flopped over onto the poor thing, threatening to suffocate the mouse under the weight.

Mercipolis was not easily discouraged and tried again and again. The ears shrunk, but one foot grew elephantine. The foot shrunk but the nose grew as big and round as a cantaloupe. Celestyna watched in dismay and Chester in utter fascination as the poor mouse's body was contorted into a dozen different monstrosities.

"Maybe you need to say the magic word?" the bear suggested.

"What? Flip-a-doodle?" asked the wizard. He burst into laughter again, striking the mouse in his enthusiasm.

A last burst of purple light revealed the mouse in correct proportion, but so many times larger than normal, they were now nearly as big as Chester was himself.

"Interesting!" Mercipolis cried. "Perhaps laughter is the key. I have been taking myself too seriously. I need to relax and allow the magic to flow through me."

"Ain't that a thing?" Chester sniffed at the mouse. "Nightshade, is it really you?"

"I think so," they answered in a boomingly deep voice very unlike their normal one, startling themself and those around them, but it went perfectly with their new appearance. Their sharp teeth looked formidable at this size and their claws even more so.

Celestyna coiled and uncoiled her long body in a kind of applause and approval. "How delightful! You are large enough to be one of the party without worrying about being a burden to your friends. Although you were no such thing, of course," she hastened to add, being more sensitive to others' feelings than Chester.

The bear chortled. "My friend, you needn't be a bit scared now. What would dare attack a monster mouse?"

A thrashing sound through the forest made them all turn their heads. A white cat of enormous size, with antlers as tall and widespread as many a small tree, six legs, and three tails bounded into the clearing, took one look at the unusually large rodent, snatched them up in its jaws and ran away.

"There, what did I foretell," said the wizard. "An unexpected and alarming event. One might even say a harrowing escapade! It's always the same with quests, isn't it?"

CHAPTER 8

THE SUMMONING VOICE

"WHAT WAS THAT?" CRIED Celestyna.

"Methinks 'tis the Keeylas," Chester replied to the wyrm. "A wise tortoise tried to warn us. A cat o' unnatural dimensions and style. I suppose Nightshade is the right size now for such a one. We do be having a run o' bad luck, don't we?"

The wizard shook his head gravely. "Worse than bad luck, for none survive an encounter with that fabled creature."

"You know o' it then?"

"Yes. I minored in magical beasts at school. It has not turned out to be terribly useful as I have never encountered any before. Now I have both met a wyrm and witnessed the fabled white cat of ancient lore. This has been an unusually exciting day even though it started out so poorly what with me being a beetle and then a turkey. My fortunes have looked up since I ran into you. The least I could do is help you to track your friend, though I fear we may be too late, and I also have no clue as to how we could defeat such a monster."

"As to being too late," Chester said, "we've learned our mouse friend seems to have the talent o' cheating death. As for defeating the Keeylas, my philosophy is to not try and cross a bridge before you've built one. Let's go!"

Mercipolis and Celestyna exchanged a glance full of meaning. That is to say, neither felt chasing after an enemy of immense size and strength without having a well-thought-out plan in advance was advisable, but before they could communicate this to Chester, he was off on the trail of the Keeylas, crashing away through the woods with bearish enthusiasm.

"We must follow," said the wyrm. "There is no telling what he will do. He has an indomitable spirit but not an equal amount of common sense. We fear for him and Nightshade if we do not try to assist."

The wizard gripped his magic wand tightly to hide the trembling in his hands. He was not what some would call courageous, but he was loath to admit this out loud. Thus are heroes sometimes born out of sheer embarrassment.

Walnut the whirligig danced up to them. "Sunshine, Leaf, Mold, and I will come too! Four more for the rescue party means seven in all and seven is always a lucky number!"

Mercipolis obviously wished to debate the whirligig on whether its three invisible companions truly counted, but Celestyna only nodded her head. "How very kind!"

"Not at all. Come along, my friends!" Walnut flew away, bat wings pumping mightily. Celestyna and Mercipolis followed on the ground, the wyrm slithering briskly while the short and stout wizard huffed and puffed to keep up, so as not to lose his companions.

In truth, the trail was easy to follow. Flattened brush and fallen trees marked where the enormous cat had fled. Even as the wizard fell behind a bit, he had no problem seeing which direction to go. He was more preoccupied with whether he could pretend to have gotten lost or diverted onto another more important mission without losing face with his new acquaintances. He also briefly considered turning himself into something more physically imposing for the upcoming battle but was afraid he might accidentally transform into a beetle again or another form equally noble but not particularly useful for confronting a cat of unusual size.

So deep was he in thought, he did not realize he had slowed his steps considerably. He found himself alone in a quiet clearing. It was peaceful there with the faint rustling of leaves and occasional birdsong. A cool breeze was blowing in sharp contrast to the hot breath on the back of his neck.

"Is someone there?" he asked nervously, too terrified to turn around. An enormous tongue, warm and wet and as rough as the trunk of a tree, swirled around in front of his face, giving it a good lick as though checking it for flavor.

With a horrified shriek, Mercipolis twirled to find the Keeylas staring at him with enormous blue eyes that shimmered with malice. There was a deep slash across the cat's face as though it had been bitten on the nose. Blood streamed down, marring its pure white fur.

"Tasty," it said, in a deep growl that sent shivers through the poor wizard. Frozen in fear, Mercipolis could only watch helplessly as a wide-open mouth filled with razored teeth descended.

All hope seemed lost until a flying figure accompanied by a mighty *"oomph"* sent the cat tumbling. It was Chester, running into the Keeylas at full speed. Nightshade—the blood staining their mouth telling the tale of how the Keeylas got the wound on its nose—followed close behind. Both animals sat on top of the cat, attempting to keep it pinned to the ground, but it was too strong and threw them off as though they weighed nothing.

Celestyna was next, coiling her long body around the cat as it scratched and dug at her with its six deadly paws. Her hide was tough, but even she was no match for the power of the beast. Her delicate frills were torn and shredded as she writhed in pain.

Walnut valiantly tried to intervene but, being of modest size and having no other weapon than its small teeth, the Keeylas paid the whirligig no attention at all. Whether Sunshine, Leaf, and Mold also were attempting to help, well, no one could tell, could they?

All in all, the battle did not seem to be going in the rescue party's favor. Nightshade and Chester continued to make forays into the fray, biting and scratching at the seemingly indomitable enemy, but to little effect.

"Perhaps we should retreat," the wizard whispered softly, still frozen in fear.

"What?" yelled Chester.

"RETREAT!"

"NEVER!" the bear answered at the same moment as wyrm and mouse said, "Good idea!"

Celestyna and Nightshade abandoned the fight, pushing and pulling Chester after them as they tried to flee, but the Keeylas was not having it. It caught the wyrm by the tail and twirled the poor thing around over its head with prodigious strength, howling an unearthly yowl.

"Do something!" Nightshade implored the wizard, who had so far stood idly by watching the wild scene.

"But what?" he asked.

"SAY THE MAGIC WORD!" Celestyna screamed.

Simply the thought of the absurd word made Mercipolis smile even in such dire circumstances. Not only smile, but giggle, an irrepressible feeling of silliness coming over him. He got as close as he could to the mayhem and touched the cat on one of its many tails with the wand while shouting, "FLIP-A-DOODLE!"

A purple flash materialized and the Keeylas seemed to disappear entirely. Celestyna crashed to the ground and a stunned silence ensued.

"Are you alright?" Mercipolis asked the wyrm, though the answer was perfectly clear. Her scales had been ripped and disordered, and her soft neck frills were ruined. "No, I see that you are not."

The wizard touched Celestyna gently on the nose and her injuries healed in an instant, though she was still dizzy from her whirling and felt she would be for quite some time.

"Thank you, friend," she said. "You have saved us. But how did you make the Keeylas vanish? That is powerful magic."

"I wasn't trying to. Only to transform it into something less threatening. Look, here!" The wizard pointed to a wriggling thing on the ground. It was a white earthworm of unusual size, but since earthworms are not terribly big to begin with, it was infinitely less imposing than the giant cat had been.

Unlike most earthworms, this one was rather furious. Its strange mouth opened and closed as though it was scolding those staring down at it. Walnut bent low to try and catch what the worm was saying with its keen hearing.

"The audacity!" the whirligig reported. "The outrage! The sheer impudence!"

"Dear dearie me," Chester said. "It don't like being turned into a lowly worm, no doubt. Bit o' a comedown from what it was, for all that worms are perfectly respectable."

"It does seem a pity," Nightshade agreed. "The Keeylas was a magnificent sight."

The wizard stared at the mouse in wonder. "You're very generous. It would have eaten you if we had not intervened."

"Yes, but perhaps that was just its nature. Now, it must adapt to a very different life. How vulnerable it looks. Just as I must have before you made me so much larger. It is frightening and lonely to be a small thing in a big world. Maybe you should try and change it back."

"Change it back? Change it back?" cried Chester, agog at the thought. "So it might eat you up, whiskers and tail and all?"

"It might have learned its lesson. We should ask if it will behave more peaceably to us if we return it to its true form."

The worm thrashed about. Walnut reported its answer. "EAT DIRT! That's funny as I believe it is worms that actually do eat dirt or so one told me once."

Just then, a fat robin landed amongst them. It turned its greedy eye upon the oversized worm, looking delighted at such an unusually robust meal. The worm grew still and would have turned even paler were it not already as white as bones bleached by the sun.

"Shoo, shoo," Nightshade said. Startled at being addressed by an overly large rodent, the bird took flight, but the brief alarm it had caused apparently provoked the worm into a change of heart.

"The worm has reconsidered," Walnut said. "It would like to negotiate."

"What does it have to offer?" asked Celestyna, still wobbly and miffed at the rough handling she had endured at the paws of the Keeylas.

The whirligig listened again. "It says it knows every part of these woods better than any other who has ever lived. It can guide us anywhere we want to go. It says its word is its bond and promises to cause no harm to any here present, though it will not extend that mercy to anyone else we may encounter on our journey."

Chester was not impressed. "Humph! Don't need any such help. Been doing fine without."

While not strictly true, everyone else present declined to point this out to the stubborn bear.

"Maybe it understands what the mouth that never closes is," Mercipolis suggested. "Magical creatures often know more about magical things than even us wizards."

Walnut listened intently to the worm. "It does but will not tell us unless you turn it back."

Mouse, wizard, wyrm, and bear gathered to one side in conference while the whirligig kept careful watch of the squiggly Keeylas-that-was.

"I think we should give it a chance," was Nightshade's opinion.

"I could always turn it back into a worm again if it breaks its promise," Mercipolis pointed out.

"You have both gone completely barmy," complained Chester.

They looked to Celestyna to see which way she would vote, for she had suffered the most from the creature's attack. "We think there are already too few magical creatures left in this world. It does seem a pity to lose one. It would be different if you had turned it into a wyrm with a y. Are you sure you can restore it to its former self?" she asked delicately, not wanting to insult the wizard even though his magical feats had been somewhat erratic.

"As long as I have the magic word, I don't see why not, but I have a better idea." The wizard returned to the earthworm and poked it with the wand while shouting, "Flip-a-doodle!"

When the puff of purple smoke cleared, a white cat had indeed returned, but rather than having three tails, it had one; instead of six legs, it had four; and far from being enormous, it was now an ordinarily-sized feline—a beautiful one with luxuriously long white fur and bright blue eyes but underwhelming when compared to its previous incarnation.

"What is thissssss?" it hissed. "Are you incompetent?"

"Not entirely," Mercipolis replied, "but neither am I a fool. You shall remain in this form until we find the place we seek. If you fulfill your part of the bargain, I will return you to yourself. If you do not, an ordinary cat is still better than being an earthworm. Cats are much revered among humans, and you will easily be able to find yourself a comfortable berth by wandering into the nearest town."

The cat did not look pleased. In fact, it looked so enraged and dangerous, even in its diminished state, that the others were relieved the magician had come up with this clever compromise.

"Very well, I will help you, but if you do not transform me properly at journey's end, I will find a way to wreak revenge upon you all. You say you seek the mouth that never closes. To find it, we must follow the summoning voice."

"The summoning voice?" Chester scoffed. "And what is that when it's at home, I wonder."

The cat narrowed its jeweled eyes evilly at the bear. "I will assist you, but I will not be disrespected. As I have said, there is no part of this forest I have not visited. The mouth that never closes is obviously the entrance to a cave. I presume you want a magical one. There is only one such I know of, but a song so delightful it drives those that hear it mad pours from it day and night."

"If it drives the listener mad, what good will that do us?" asked Mercipolis.

"You're the wizard. Did you never learn to overcome such difficulties during your studies? What is the point of having magical powers if you let such trifles defeat you?" The cat stalked away and found a comfortable spot to curl up and chew on its claws while it awaited their decision.

"Meeting this Keeylas was a bit o' luck after all," Chester crowed. "See how things work out when I'm around? Now we can go to the cave and fetch those zubbity seeds."

"Zingery seeds," Nightshade gently reminded his friend. "I'm afraid it sounds awfully treacherous though."

"I'm sure we'll figure something out on the way," the eternally optimistic bear replied, bounding over to the cat and giving it a rather rude shove with his nose. The Keeylas hissed spitefully but, being eager to get this nonsense over with and return to its rightful form, it jumped to its paws and prowled away with the bear close on its tail.

Always ready for an adventure, Walnut took to the air with enthusiasm. The three left behind, mouse, wyrm, and wizard, exchanged doleful glances and heavy sighs. They could not help but feel no good would come of this, but one of the things you must understand about quests is they are not easily abandoned, particularly if it means leaving friends in danger.

By unspoken agreement, they turned to follow.

CHAPTER 9

THE MOUTH THAT NEVER CLOSES

THE KEEYLAS WAS NOT nearly as swift in its newly-ordinary cat form as it had been before its transformation, so the others had no trouble keeping up as it led the way to the cave. Chester raced ahead impatiently, turning around from time to time to urge them on with bearish enthusiasm.

"Come along, come along. No time to waste!"

"Perhaps we should take things more slowly," the wizard cautioned the bear. "I don't like the idea of this song that drives the listener mad. We'll never find a safe home for the wyrm if we lose our minds first."

"But you're magical folk! You must have tricks to get around such?"

Mercipolis fiddled nervously with the collar of his purple cloak. "I can't say I remember this particular topic being covered at school. I suppose I could conjure up some sort of ear protection. If we can't hear the song, surely it can't hurt us?"

The Keeylas stopped and turned to sneer at them. "That's not how it works. The song will seep into your mind whether you have ears or not. Its rhythm and melody soak the atmosphere around the cave. It will creep up through the soles of your feet and bombard your skin like a hard-pelting rain!"

"Goodness!" Nightshade said. "That does sound frightening. But how do you know so much about it? You can't have experienced it yourself or you wouldn't be so sensible."

The Keeylas had never before been called sensible or anything else so insulting. It was a mighty creature, a figure of fright and terror that inspired the deepest awe and horror in any unfortunate enough to encounter it. Sensible, indeed! It had a good mind to abandon this group of nitwits to their own devices, but it also had no intention of spending the rest of its life as a common cat, even one of uncommon beauty.

It swallowed its indignation in order to reply. "I have not been to the cave myself, but the silver river runs through the mountain. A great sturgeon lives there but travels far in search of food. We met once upon a time."

"And you did not eat it?" interrupted Chester, much amazed. "Fishies are the very best eating."

"Not this one. It's as big as I am—or was, that is—and as old as time itself. Scales as tough as tree bark and twice as wily as the cleverest thing that ever existed in all the world. I'm sure I could have bested it if I had been bothered to try, but it was more amusing to sit and talk. It is an inveterate storyteller and knows much about any part of the world within spitting distance of the river."

Walnut hovered overhead, its batwings fluttering wildly. "I wonder if it was the same as spit me out then?"

"Spit you out?" Celestyna asked. "Do you mean it tried to swallow you?"

"Tried and succeeded! Said I tasted something awful. Made me feel a bit low to find out I was not a palatable snack."

"We think that is rather a helpful trait than otherwise," the wyrm observed. "Else you might not have survived the encounter."

"So I tell myself, but it still stings a bit." The whirligig sighed and performed slow somersaults in the air as it pondered the sad fact that it was simply not delicious.

"You are a bunch of fools, aren't you?" the Keeylas sneered. "How you've made it even this far in a quest boggles the mind."

Chester hastened to chide the cat. "No need to be rude. We may be an unusual crowd, but we each have our own talents and together, I'm sure we can accomplish anything we set our minds to. Things have a way of working out for the best around me, you know."

Nightshade had grown used to their friend's boast and knew better than to challenge it. Besides, they were more interested in the cat's monstrous fish story.

"So, the sturgeon told you about the cave, did it? How does it live there without going mad?"

"Spends its time underwater," the Keeylas replied. "That is the one place the song's worst influence doesn't reach."

Chester crowed, "There you go! Easy as pie. We simply swim into the cave!"

"What is pie?" Walnut inquired.

Celestyna asked a far more pertinent question. "But can any of you swim well enough to do it? Sound carries very far, so we assume you would have to hold your breath a long time to approach the cave safely. We are not a fan of water or we would go ourself."

"Cats and water do not mix," said the Keeylas, "so, do not look to me."

"I am one-quarter cat," said Walnut, "so I guess that lets me out."

"I would gladly do it," Nightshade said, "but I never learned how to swim."

"I have swam more than a time or two," said Chester, "but I've an unfortunate tendency to float to the surface. Something to do with the way I am built, no doubt."

That left only the wizard. Everyone turned to look at him. His dark skin turned darker still as his cheeks burned under the scrutiny. He was beginning to regret whatever fate had brought him into this adventure. While it was true it had been annoying being a beetle, in many ways, it had been infinitely preferable to his current predicament. More peaceful certainly! Even his turkey form had its advantages.

These reflections gave him an idea. Transformation might not be his talent, but since he had learned the magic word (and to take himself less seriously), he had been more successful at his attempts if the Keeylas was any proof.

"I suppose..." Mercipolis said slowly. "I suppose I could turn myself into a thing that swims."

"That's the spirit!" cried the bear, slapping the wizard so hard on the back, it is a wonder he did not go flying off into the tops of the trees.

The wyrm, being naturally more empathetic, sensed the wizard's hesitation. "You should not do so for us. We would as soon go on as we have been than to risk any of you coming to harm. We might do best to turn aside from this quest before we encounter any more danger. We can seek out a quiet place on our own."

"No," said Mercipolis, remembering the wyrm had been the one to teach him the magic word and the power of a good laugh. "As a wizard, it is my duty to protect magical beings."

The Keeylas snorted at that statement as though it wished to contest it, but Mercipolis carried on. "It will be an honor to assist what may be one of the last wyrms left in the world since humans are bent on destroying all such."

"I wonder why?" asked Nightshade.

"That is the question. They are a superstitious lot and care nothing for anything they cannot understand, and they understand remarkably little. If they were to come upon our sinuous friend here, I'm afraid her life would not be worth so much as a leftover piece of pie."

"Why won't anyone tell me what pie is?" Walnut complained quietly, but the others were too involved in the more pressing problem to reply.

The wyrm wrapped the end of her tail around the wizard and gave him a gentle hug. "You are so kind. A true hero."

Mercipolis felt far from heroic when the Keeylas led them to the edge of the silver river where it looped back through the forest far from the fire that had first driven the others across it. He stared hard at the swift-flowing water and thought about what to become. Something that would never need to surface, for one misplaced breath would spell his doom if he was close to the cave and the maddening song.

A fish then, but what kind? There were so many. A vision crept into his mind of lazing by the river on a bright summer's day, the sun reflecting off the water and a rainbowed flash beneath the surface. He took one last look around at his companions, gripped the magic wand, shut his eyes tightly, and shouted, "Flip-a-doodle!"

Everyone jumped back as the wizard vanished under a flash of purple smoke. When it cleared, an unusually large fish, silver-scales flashing every color imaginable, struggled and wriggled on the riverbank.

"As fine a trout as ever I did lay eyes on!" Chester exclaimed. "Enough there for a feast and a half."

The Keeylas licked its lips as though in hungry agreement.

Celestyna pushed them both aside impatiently. "Poor Mercipolis! He can't breathe."

She wrapped her coils around the wizard and gently lifted him into the water, pulling herself out as quickly as possible. She despised getting wet, but when on a quest, one must sometimes do any number of unpleasant tasks.

The fish still bore the wizard's pointed hat and purple cloak, sporting them in a jaunty fashion that, combined with its colorful scales, made for quite a sight. He surfaced briefly, spitting a high arc of water at them by way of indicating he was departing on his mission. There was nothing to do now but to sit and wait for his return.

Mercipolis explored the power and feeling of his new body as he swam upriver. He moved swiftly, more swiftly than had been possible in any previous transformation. His strong tail swung from side to side, propelling him along as smaller fish, frogs, and other aquatic life scooted aside in fright at this giant torpedo.

As he journeyed, many a thought crossed his fishy mind: *How far was it to the cave? Would he really be immune to the maddening song as long as he stayed underwater? How was he to harvest the zingery seeds once he got there without leaving the river? What were zingery seeds anyway? And what was that pulling on his tail?*

This last question demanded an immediate answer as his forward progress slowed to a crawl. He twisted his head round, rolling his bulging eyes to catch a glimpse of what was holding him back. To his dismay, it was a fish at least twice his size that had his tail fins completely engulfed in its mouth.

I do believe it is trying to eat me! was the wizard's amazed yet astute assessment of the situation. In a panic, he thrashed about, succeeding in loosening the monster's grip on his tail and delivering a stunning blow across its face.

"Owwwww," boomed a low voice so deep it reverberated throughout Mercipolis's body like the boom of a church bell when you are the one standing under it pulling the rope to set it clanging.

The wizard turned to face his piscine adversary (piscine being simply a fancy way of saying fishy). It was enormous and grey, with bony bumps along its spine and sides and a curiously upturned snout.

"That hurt," it thrummed.

"A thousand pardons," said Mercipolis. "I was under the impression you were trying to eat me and reacted in self-defense."

"Of course I was trying to eat you. Big fish eat not-quite-as-big fish which eat fish that are smaller still. It is the way of our kind. You would know that if you truly belonged here, but your uncommon attire tells me you do not. What are you doing in my river?"

"Your river? Does it not belong to everyone? Who are you?"

"I am the Great Sturgeon, longest-lived and largest of any fish that ever dwelt within these waters. If I should not own it, who should?"

The wizard trout shook his head in a very unfish-like manner. "I don't think it is a thing that *can* be owned. No more than the trees of the forest or the clouds floating by in the sky."

"In-ter-es-ting..." the sturgeon replied ponderously, for its words were drawn out to an unusual length as though it was a strain to speak at all. Or perhaps it only wished to make it seem that everything it said was of the most profound importance. "No one has ever argued with me upon this point before."

"I've no wish to argue," Mercipolis replied. "I desire only to get on with my quest."

"A quest? Why didn't you say so? I do love a good quest. Perhaps I can assist—what must you do?"

"Swim to the cave with the song that drives the listener mad and harvest some zingery seeds. Do you know of this place? I was told you live there."

"And who told you that?"

"The Keeylas."

"Ah, the white beast that rivals even me in size. It thought to eat me I do believe, but I charmed it with my many tales instead. I have a wealth of fascinating stories and am always looking to add to my store. I do live in that cave when I am not out and about. It is lovely and peaceful there as long as you stay submerged. The song vibrates through the water, but it is not unpleasant. A slight tingling in your bones, a ripple along your scales, a gentle pressure behind the eyes. But you must not surface for even so much as one moment. I have witnessed many a fish make that mistake."

"What happened?"

"They lose all sense of themselves. Jump to the shore in a frenzy where I can only assume they flop about until they run out of breath or beat themselves senseless against a rock."

"How horrible! Where does the voice come from and what does it want?"

"That I cannot answer. I only know there is a deep and old magic at work there. Perhaps it is a spell to prevent the very thing you propose, the theft of these seeds. Are they valuable?"

"They are to me and my friends. We seek a haven for what may be one of the last of her kind. A prophecy advises planting these seeds to grow a vine to a place beyond the clouds where she will be safe."

"How lovely! How romantic!" The sturgeon seemed almost to swoon as it half-closed its eyes in delight. "This is the kind of tale I adore. What type of creature is your friend?"

"A wyrm."

"Oh, that is disappointing. I thought it would be something more magical than a worm."

"A wyrm with a y," the wizard explained.

"A worm with a why? Does it have a who, what, where, when, and how also? That would make it more special than average, I suppose," the fish allowed somewhat doubtingly.

"No, I mean it is spelled differently."

"Ah, unfortunately I never learned to spell," the sturgeon admitted.

"Never mind. There isn't much call for it down here, I would imagine. Our friend is a type of dragon without wings or claws. Something like an overgrown serpent."

"How wonderful! I have often been mistaken for a sea serpent because of my size, which is absurd as I am neither a snake nor is this body of water a sea. Humans can be so odd, can't they?"

Being a type of one himself, though not human in form at this precise moment, Mercipolis only burbled a fishy sound he hoped would be taken as agreement.

The monster fish continued. "You say 'our' friend. Are there others in your party?"

"They await me on shore. A bear, the wyrm, a mouse, a whirligig, and the Keeylas, though it is much reduced in size, vigor, and power at the moment."

The sturgeon chortled. "I bet it does not like that one bit. That will make for an enthralling tale indeed. And a whirligig? Never heard of such. You must tell me about it as we travel."

"We? So you'll guide me?"

"Yes, though you could hardly miss it. You've only to follow the river. But I wish to collect your story and see how it ends. Besides, I can be of use to you. You must not and could not leave the river to gather those seeds yourself. You will need an ally when you reach the cave and I think I know of just such a one!"

CHAPTER 10

BONES BUILT FOR FLIGHT

Tʜᴇ Gʀᴇᴀᴛ Sᴛᴜʀɢᴇᴏɴ ʟᴇᴅ the way lazily up the river. Its huge tail created such a monstrous backwash that Mercipolis struggled to fight the current even in his powerful trout body. He noticed the waters of the silver river got deeper, colder, and darker as they traveled. His eyesight was much poorer than when he was human, and he was forced to rely on his other senses: the pressure of the water against his scales; the sonar sounds echoing back and forth from bank to bank; a keen sense of smell that detected many creatures, big and small, they passed on their journey.

The feel of his body cutting through the water was almost like flying, not that he had ever flown. A missed opportunity while he had been in turkey form, though it was hard to imagine such a round and elaborately feathered body taking flight. Perhaps he should try turning into a falcon one day to experience life soaring high above? Such musings kept him distracted as he followed anxiously in his guide's wake.

Before too long, the sturgeon slowed and curled its long shape around to come nose to nose with the wizard. "Be careful! We are almost to the cave of song. Do not poke your head out from this point on for any reason."

Mercipolis shivered at the warning. He was not particularly brave, but the thought of his waiting friends urged him on. He began to sense unusual vibrations in the water. As the sturgeon had described, the wizard's scales buzzed with energy. A faint though not unpleasant pressure built up behind his bulging eyes.

He supposed this was the melody making itself known even at this depth. What must it feel like closer to the source? He hoped never to find out.

Their journey ended at a wide pool, depthless below and dark as night from the sheltering walls of the cave.

"What shall I do now," he asked the sturgeon, "if I cannot go above to fetch the zingery seeds myself?"

"We must enlist assistance from an acquaintance of mine." The fish thrummed a low booming sound, repeating it at regular intervals like the beat of a giant bass drum. The waters around them shuddered and danced.

The wizard's trout body was pushed and pulled from the motion. He had to be careful to employ his fins and tail judiciously to prevent himself from drifting upward. He was feeling proud of his control until a sudden splash directly in front of his face nearly undid him from the surprise. The sturgeon's mouth grabbed his tail and prevented him from floating up into the cave.

"Careful, careful," warned the fish. "It is only Bartholomew."

"And who or what is a Bartholomew?"

"Not quite a mouse nor yet a bat. I fly, I dive, and like to chat!"

This unexpected answer was delivered in a high, squeaky voice. Its owner was a pale creature, about one-tenth the size of Nightshade since they had been enlarged by the wizard's spell, but not unlike that mouse in appearance except for the addition of two wings, so delicate looking, it seemed impossible they were not torn apart by the movement of the water. Instead, the thing used them much like a fish uses its fins to swim gracefully around in the deep pool.

"What is that?" Mercipolis said quietly to himself but not quietly enough.

"I am simply a flitter-flutter and I do not like it when you mutter."

"Beg pardon! I meant no harm. I was only surprised as I've not seen your kind before."

"That's because there's only me, all alone in the world, you see."

The sturgeon opened its mouth wide in the approximation of a grin and let out a low chortling noise. "This is my friend Bartholomew. He is at home in the air or water and is unaffected by the cave's song. I thought he would be the perfect ally to fetch those seeds you're seeking."

"What seeds are these? Do tell me, please," the flitter-flutter requested.

The trout-wizard shook his head to try and clear his thoughts. "Um, they are called zingery seeds. I'm afraid I'm not sure what they look like though."

"Good thing I know! They glisten and glow."

Mercipolis's heart beat faster at this revelation. "How wonderful! Do you think you could fetch me some? There is a magical being who has need of them. She's in danger from humans who fear her and would seek to do her harm."

"Humans hate magic, a fact oh so tragic," Bartholomew agreed.

"I... I cannot help but notice you speak in rhyme. Do you speak so all the time?"

"Ever since I was a hatchling, but do be careful, it is catching!"

"Oh, er, yes." The wizard would have pulled at his cloak collar in embarrassment if he was in human form, but as it was, decided to concentrate on his mission. "So you could bring me some of these seeds?"

"I suppose I might as my bones are built for flight. But the cave may not approve daring attempts to remove."

"The cave won't? Whatever do you mean? How can a cave object to something?"

The sturgeon explained. "Bartholomew and I have often discussed this cave and its unique properties. He is of the opinion it is very much alive. A creature of some sort, trapped here by magic. The song it sings is a lament about its fate. It has no wish to harm others, but the extreme melancholy it feels drives those who hear it mad with grief."

"How extraordinary!"

"Quite. I don't believe it for a moment, but Barty is an imaginative fellow. Comes from spending too much time here by himself. I've encouraged him to go out and about and see more of the world."

"To leave this place, I cannot face," the flitter-flutter interjected.

"It must be lonely," the wizard sympathized. "I was alone myself until recently when by chance I met up with a fellowship on a quest."

"What is a quest when it's at rest?"

"That's just the thing. Quests rarely are at rest, at least not until they are accomplished. They are rudely hectic, forcing one to career from one unlikely and not entirely safe adventure to another. I never thought when I awoke this morning I would be here now, an oversized trout speaking with a sturgeon and a flitter-flutter in a cave with a deadly melody playing over my head. Quests are unnerving and even untidy, I'm sorry to report."

The sturgeon objected. "But there is nothing so romantic as a good quest. Why, every tale worth telling has a journey and a mission at its center, else what would be the point? Can't have folks wandering around to no purpose. Quests are noble and fine. I'll no doubt be telling of your exploits hundreds of years from now."

"Hundreds of years? Surely you cannot live so long!"

"What a thing to say! Why shouldn't I? Are you saying you wish me to die?" It fixed one twitching eye on the wizard, who was reminded again of the immense size and strength of the fish.

"No, no, of course not!" Mercipolis hastened to reassure the offended sturgeon. "It's only I never heard of any being living so long. It is a remarkable thing."

The flitter-flutter begged to differ. "I've been here since time began; all things shall my life outspan."

The wizard was not sure how he had entered into a discussion about which of his companions was most ancient. The day was winding down and the others must be wondering where he was and if he was ever returning. Would they wait for him? As loathe as he had been to get caught up in adventures, the novelty of having—dare he call them friends?—waiting and worrying about him, set some long-neglected part of his soul on fire. He must do his best for them.

"You are both extraordinary! I am honored to be in your presence. I do most humbly ask whether it would be possible to harvest some seeds. Perhaps if we asked the cave very nicely?"

"I don't mind if I do, I'll just say toodle-loo!" A burst of wing and water, and the flitter-flutter disappeared.

Bartholomew the flitter-flutter (who was known as Barty to his friends, of which you are one) flew up into the shadowy embrace of the cave, shaking the river from his wings and babbling to himself.

"They needs, they needs, they needs, the seeds, the seeds, the seeds…"

He thought he knew exactly the seeds the wizard trout had been speaking of, for Barty had explored every inch of the cave and its many chambers. His oversized eyes, big and pale and round as dinner plates, had adapted so well to the darkness that he was able to navigate confidently among the twists and turns, stalagmites and stalactites, meandering streams and the drippy-droppy roof.

He sought a small cavern at one of the farthest bends of the labyrinth where there was a still, clear pool. It was full of slippery frogs that blurped and blarted, and tiny fish so transparent you could see right through them to their delicately graceful bones. Around the edge of the pool grew flowers so bizarre that if I were to describe them to you, you would never believe me. Their most significant features were the bright glow they emitted and the dazzling seeds that made up a large pod in the center of each, something like the spiraling heart of a sunflower.

Barty could not have explained exactly how he knew these were zingery seeds, as no one had ever told him so, but he often had a sixth sense about such things and had learned to trust his instincts. The maddening song of the cave was loudest here of anywhere he had visited, but as he was unaffected by the tune, he did not hesitate to enter the grotto. He had noticed the frogs and fish were also indifferent and wondered if any creature that was native to the cave, as he was, were naturally immune.

The flitter-flutter hummed along in his high-pitched squeak as he made his way over to the flowers. The melody of the cave was haunting, full of the most beautiful lamentation. He wondered again, as he had every day of his life, where it came from. It seemed to emanate from everywhere and nowhere. A mystery destined never to be solved, or so he believed, little realizing how soon he was to be proven wrong.

He reached one of his feet toward the seeds, thinking to pluck some out with his toes to take to the wizard, but as soon as he touched the flower, the song in the cave rose in pitch like a voice crying out in pain. Barty retreated a moment, then tried again. Once more the song reacted as though in agony.

"Is someone there and do you care if I pluck a seed or will you bleed?"

There was no reply.

The flitter-flutter employed a scientific approach to life and felt an experiment was in order. Before the song could protest again, he grasped a seed and pulled it free from its mooring. The flowers pulsed with light and the seed burned his toes so fiercely that he flung it into the waters of the pool in shocked surprise. The seed sank into the depths, and the intensity of the song dwindled into a quiet hymn, sorrowful and scolding.

Of a sudden, Barty felt ashamed of himself for his bold attempt at theft. He had wanted to help his old friend, the sturgeon, and the magical creature the wizard spoke of, but perhaps the seeds were not his for the taking, even in a noble cause. He pondered the calm water as though looking for some sign. As if in answer, a large, slow bubble worked its way to the surface and popped in his face, splashing him with the chill waters.

The neverending song ceased. All was deathly quiet in the cavern. Barty shivered. There had never been a time in his life without the melody as a constant companion. He was bereft and lonely in the silence and wished for any sound to take its place.

After an excruciatingly long wait, his wish was granted by a voice that could only be described as broken: scratchy and hoarse, thin and wavering, yet commanding just the same. "What have you done?"

"I plucked a seed for those in need. Meant no harm. Have I caused alarm?"

The pool lit up brighter even than the zingery flowers, and a small orb, no bigger than your fist, floated up from the depths and into the air. It pulsed with light in a pattern mesmerizing to see, but even as Barty watched in fascination, it dimmed and sputtered like a guttering candle until its glow was no more constant or intense than a firefly in a garden on a hot summer night.

"I've seen you here many times," spoke the orb so softly that the flitter-flutter had to lean close to catch its words. "You've never harmed any of my flowers before. Why should you want one of my seeds? And none of your rhyming nonsense," it admonished as Barty opened his mouth to reply. "Speak plainly or not at all."

Well, that was quite a flummox! Poor Bartholomew's brain whirled round in confusion at this instruction. Rhyming was as natural to him as breathing or fluttering, not to mention flittering.

"I met a trout who was quite stout—"

The orb objected. "What did I tell you?"

"No more rhymes at this time. That is to say," he hastened to correct himself, "I must away with the foolish sway of clever wordplay."

The orb sighed heavily as did the flitter-flutter. Barty had no desire to be further chastised, but the habit of a lifetime was not easily broken.

"I'll try again," he said slowly, thinking carefully about what to say next. "I met an unusually large trout. There, I didn't rhyme!" he crowed, infinitely pleased with himself.

"Good for you, but encountering a sizeable fish hardly explains why you are stealing my seeds."

"*Your* seeds? But who are you?"

"I am the remnants of a star that fell a thousand thousand years ago. I rolled into this cave, shedding bits and bobs of myself here and there until all that remained is what you see before you. These flowers are sparks of mine that grew and flourished in this bleak place. They thrive while I am wasting away. Soon they will be the only things left to show I once burned brightly."

"It's you that sings, isn't it?" asked Barty.

"A dirge to ease my passing and mark the time. Dying is a lonely business."

Tears sprang to the flitter-flutter's eyes. "I am so sorry. I'd never have bothered you if I'd known. I only wanted to help this trout who also happens to be a wizard."

"What use are my seeds to a wizard?"

"He spoke of his magical friend who is in danger from humans. The seeds are supposed to assist their cause, though I'm afraid I neglected to ask how."

"A magical friend? I should like to have one such. How do you make friends?"

"Helping is one way. You have so many seeds, could you not spare a handful?"

The orb glowed quietly, like the coals in a fire that is slowly going out, and seemed to be diminishing subtly in size from moment to moment. "If a part of me went into the world and did some good, perhaps I would not be forgotten?"

"You would be a hero! They sing songs of heroes, and your own song could live on in legend, for I have heard it so many times, I could teach it to everyone I met."

"A hero?" The star seemed much struck at the thought. "And my song would live on? How delightful. That would be a comfort."

The orb was now not much larger than a grape and its glow was very weak. "Take the seeds and take me with you too. I will be nothing more than a dull lump of clay, but I should like to leave this cave all the same. Will you promise?"

"I do, most solemnly," Barty replied.

The star danced about in the air for a moment as though in celebration. Then, with a sizzle, its light fizzled out and it dropped into Barty's hastily outstretched foot, a small pea of dark matter. He caressed it, so smooth and cool to the touch. Its song was extinguished too, but that at least would survive if the flitter-flutter had anything to do with it.

He pulled a large leaf from one of the zingery flowers, wrapping up the star and five of its glowing seeds carefully within. Grasping the parcel firmly with his feet, he took to the air. He had a most precious package to deliver and a whole quest anxiously awaiting him. Never in his life had he left the safe familiarity of the cave, and he couldn't help but wonder, both with excitement and trepidation, what adventures awaited.

CHAPTER 11

RULER OF THE MISSHAPEN MOUNTAINS

DEEP BENEATH THE SILVER river's surface in the pool in the cave, Mercipolis and the Great Sturgeon felt both shock and consternation at the sudden cessation of the sensations provoked by the once constant melody.

"How strange," remarked the sturgeon. "I do believe the song is over. It was an uncommonly long one, for it has sounded all the many years of my life. How very strange," it repeated, moved in some indefinable way by the loss.

"Do you think that means it's safe to go above?" the trout wizard asked. "I could see what the flitter-flutter is up to."

"Suppose it were to start up again? Not gonna chance it at my age. You don't get this old by taking foolish risks."

The two fish waited a while, holding their places in the chill waters with lazy swishes of their tails and fins, but the song did not return.

The wizard noticed flashes of white above their heads, as though something were diving down close to the water but retreating before getting wet. "What do you think it is?" he asked the sturgeon.

"Don't know. Might be dangerous though. Wouldn't risk finding out." The giant fish continued to loll about, seemingly content to bide away an eternity rather than investigate anything out of the ordinary.

Mercipolis thought of the others awaiting him back on shore. He'd lost any sense of time and how long he'd been gone, but he thought they might be worrying. It isn't kind to leave friends wondering about your fate on a possibly dangerous mission any longer than absolutely necessary.

Screwing up his courage, he cautiously turned on his side and lifted one bulbous eye above the surface. The fluttering form was none other than Barty.

In his surprise, Mercipolis flopped himself onto shore where he hastily cried "Flip-a-doodle!" while rolling around on the magic wand in his cloak's pocket. He wasn't sure it would work, but the magic word is very powerful. Where a large trout had been, there was an excessively damp wizard, returned to human form and dripping noisily onto the cave floor.

"At last, at last! I've been trying to get your attention for ages!" Barty cried, not a bit taken aback at the wizard's transformation since it had already experienced much weirder things.

"Why didn't you simply dive below the water if you wanted to find me? And why aren't you rhyming anymore?" Mercipolis asked, for both facts seemed equally bewildering.

"I didn't want to get these wet," Barty replied, holding up the leaf packet containing the star's remnant and the precious zingery seeds. "And the star was vexed with my way of speaking. I'd never thought about it before, but I wonder if I haven't been annoying everyone I meet, only they were too polite to say so."

"It's not a common way of speaking, but it was your own. What is this about a star?"

Barty carefully unfolded the leaf to reveal the glowing seeds and the small, dull pea. "All this time, the song was the lament of a star that fell and ended its life here, slowly fading away. This is all that is left of it. Before it died, I promised to carry both the star and its song out into the world, though in truth, I am frightened. I've never left this cave before."

"You can come with me. New things are not so scary when you have company. I must bring the seeds to my friends. And the song is exactly what we need, for it says in the prophecy we must sing the song of a dying star to the seeds after they are planted. How fortuitous it is, but then that is often the way of prophecies. They are meant to predict the future after all."

"Does that mean your quest will be successful no matter what happens? There is no suspense to it if everything is foretold."

The wizard pondered this. "An interesting question. What if I had not been brave enough to seek out the cave? Would the quest have ended, or would another way have been discovered? We still have choices to make, I believe, and I choose to carry these seeds back to the others and do whatever I can to help them."

"Then I will too! How shall we travel? I can fly out of this cave and meet you outside if you wish to swim. There is no path to walk."

"I've a better idea. *Flip-a-doodle*!" Mercipolis disappeared. In his place, an eagle stood with golden head and eyes, fierce talons, and sharp beak that let out a piercing shriek that would've thrilled you to your bones if you'd been there. "I've been wanting to try flying! Now's my chance. Climb aboard!"

Barty carefully refolded the leaf package to secure his cargo, then settled on the eagle's shoulders, wrapping his delicate wings gently around Mercipolis's neck.

"Hold on tight!" The eagle took a running jump and a hop, stumbled a bit, ungainly in his new body, but then took flight. He was lucky the cavern was indeed cavernous or else his wingspan would have been too wide to fit. They exited out into the late afternoon sun, Mercipolis reveling in the power and lift of his magnificent wings whooshing through the air.

"Too bright, too bright!" Barty cried, for he had spent his entire life in relative darkness.

The wizard screeched the magic word. A pair of wire-rimmed glasses, perfectly sized and fitted with smoky lenses, appeared on the flitter-flutter's head.

"Better?" Mercipolis asked.

"Much! We can see the whole world from up here!" They were soaring high above the forest, following the meandering form of the silver river as it wound its way among the trees. "What is that above us?"

"The blue is the sky and the white are clouds."

"What is blue and what is white?"

"Colors, of course."

"And what are colors?"

That was a puzzler. Everyone knew what colors were, didn't they? They were just... colors.

Mercipolis glided lower so they were skimming along above the tops of the trees. "See, those whirling things falling from the tall things? The tall things are trees, and the twirling things are their leaves which they lose as winter approaches. The leaves are different colors. Red and orange, yellow and brown. Can you see how they vary?"

The flitter-flutter actually could see little difference in the leaves, for unbeknownst to both of them, he was color-blind and wearing dark glasses besides, but he didn't like to admit it. "I... I think so. How curious everything is. I have so much to learn," Barty lamented. "I didn't realize how little I knew of the world even though I have lived so long."

"Don't worry. There is more in this world than any of us could discover in one lifetime. That's what keeps it interesting."

"True. We wouldn't want to get bored, would we?" Barty agreed.

The wizard secretly thought a nice boring day was infinitely preferable to the kind of harum-scarum doings he'd been caught up in. To be fair, everything had gone more smoothly than he'd any right to expect. By chance, he'd run into the Great Sturgeon, who'd helped connect him with the flitter-flutter, who'd gathered the seeds. Soon, they would be reunited with the rest of their questing party.

Really, things have gone remarkably smoothly was his last thought before he was caught round the middle by talons ten times as large and sharp as his own and whisked away into the clouds.

The wizard eagle and his flitter-flutter passenger both blinked in dismay as they looked up to spy a gigantic orange shape towering above them. Wings so long they could not see the tips of them whomped forcefully through the air. They were trapped in a prison of scaly claws as thick as an elephant's leg and as strong as ironwood. River and forest disappeared far below as the hapless prisoners were dragged skyward.

"What do you think it is?" Barty asked.

Mercipolis's voice quivered in fear as he answered. "I've no idea. It seems impossibly large whatever it is. I don't believe it has any business whatsoever in being so large. Not to mention the immense rudeness of diverting us from our quest."

"To be fair, perhaps it didn't realize we were on a quest."

"It could have asked."

Barty thought it a bit unreasonable to expect everyone they met to inquire whether they were on a quest or not. After all, most creatures were usually not involved in magical quests, so it would have been a waste of everyone's time to constantly be asking. The flitter-flutter also thought its first foray out into the wider world beyond its cave was perhaps not going as swimmingly as he'd hoped.

"Does this sort of thing happen a lot when you are on quests?" he asked the wizard.

"Too much for my liking. That's the problem with quests. Unpredictable, messy, and dangerous to boot. It's no wonder sensible folk avoid them."

"Where do you think it is taking us?"

"At the rate we are ascending, I wouldn't be surprised if we ended up being marooned on one of those distant planets far beyond the stars."

"What is a planet?"

"A big spinning ball in the sky," answered Mercipolis. "The sky is full of them. In fact, the world we live on is one such."

"We live on a spinning ball?" Barty exclaimed. "How extraordinary! How do we keep from falling off?"

"Oh, um, some kind of magic, no doubt," the wizard hedged. In truth, he was not fully prepared to answer such questions. He had skipped the astronomy section of his studies in favor of a course in romantical potions which had proven to be not nearly as useful as he'd once anticipated. "That is beside the point though. Our more immediate concern should be how we can escape from this predicament. Perhaps I should transform into something else?"

"Would that be wise when we are so high in the air? Might be better to wait until we land somewhere. Everything that goes up must come down some time or another."

The flitter-flutter's words were prophetic, for at that moment, the monster that held them started to descend. Barty and the wizard strained their necks to peer below. They were approaching a giant structure made of immense rocks and tree trunks, lined with a bed of orange feathers.

"A nest!" Mercipolis cried in surprise. It was nearly as big as the Lamentable Lake (as much renowned for its size as it was for the tear-inducing saltiness of its waters), but it was as unmistakable in its form and purpose as the humblest twiggy abode of a sparrow.

Before he had a chance to properly appreciate the remarkable feat of engineering, the wizard and Barty were unceremoniously released from the taloned grip of the beast. They tumbled violently into the unforgiving jumble of its home, and Mercipolis cried out as one of his wings caught on the rough surface with an ominous *snap*.

Barty's protective glasses fell off. The setting sun was still bright enough to hurt his poor eyes, so he shut them tightly, calling out to the wizard, "Are you alright?"

"Most decidedly not!" was the answer, followed by a somewhat concerning, "Get away! Get AWAY!"

The flitter-flutter scrambled around and was fortunate to stumble upon his glasses. When he put them on and opened his eyes, he wished very much he hadn't.

How to describe the beast that perched on the edge of the nest harassing Barty's golden eagle companion? Its head was much like a vulture with wrinkled pink skin and enormous, piercing red eyes. Its wings were also birdlike to an extent, though the sharp claw at the end of each orange feather was not. Its body was shiny and scaled like a snake, and indeed, ended in a long coil that draped around the entire perimeter of the nest. Its taloned feet have already been described so we won't dwell on those. All in all, a formidable creature even before you took into account its overwhelming proportions.

It was using the tip of its serpent's tail to annoy Mercipolis by flicking the wizard's beak repeatedly.

"I do wish you'd stop that! Get away!"

"HA HA HA HA!" The thing's booming laugh nearly knocked both Barty and the wizard backwards from the sheer force of air it projected. "IT IS A BIRD THAT TALKS! HA HA HA HA!"

"Firstly, I am technically not a bird, and secondly, you *are* a bird and *you* are talking so I'm not sure why you should be so surprised."

"I AM NO BIRD!"

"Are you sure? You have wings and a beak. You fly and have a nest. These are all rather birdy things."

"I AM PISHPOSH THE SQUISH, RULER OF THE MISSHAPEN MOUNTAINS!"

Barty piped up. "Why are they misshapen?"

"PARDON?"

"The mountains—why are they misshapen?"

"SOME SORT OF MIX UP I SUPPOSE. WHAT A SILLY QUESTION!"

The flitter-flutter flew up close to the squish's eye. "Seems a reasonable thing to ask to me. Just like this one: why are you shouting at us?"

"I AM NOT SHOUTING!"

"You most certainly are. Didn't anyone ever tell you it was rude to shout at others?"

"That's right!" Mercipolis agreed hastily, remembering how he had been chided for that exact failing while in his beetle form.

The pink skin around the beast's head blushed as red as its eyes and slow tears leaked down, dropping onto the poor wizard's head, threatening to drown him.

"We'd best stop upsetting the thing!" Mercipolis cried. "I've enough problems with my broken wing. How we'll ever get back to the quest at this rate, I don't know."

Pishposh bent its head low. "A QUEST, ER, UM, that is," it continued in an exaggerated whisper that sounded much more like a normal speaking voice, "a quest? What sort of quest?"

"I'm not sure I should tell you. After all, you did kidnap us and you've broken my wing. We've no reason to trust you."

"A mere accident, I assure you. You were in my flight path. And it's not my fault you got tangled up in my feet nor that you are so clumsy at landing."

"Well, I never!" The wizard hopped about angrily, dragging his damaged wing behind him. "You dare to blame us for this mess?"

"It is an easily upset sort of bird, isn't it?" the squish asked Barty.

"He is not a bird. He's a powerful wizard!"

"Likely story," Pishposh replied, chortling in a most annoying manner.

Mercipolis awkwardly pulled his wand from his cloak pocket with one foot and nearly poked himself in the eye with it while shouting, "Flip-a-doodle!"

A flustered human appeared in the eagle's place, clutching his left arm and gritting his teeth against the pain. "I most certainly am a wizard and I'm on a very important quest to help a wyrm find a safe haven. My friends are waiting for us back by the river—"

The squish's eyes narrowed as it interrupted the furious wizard. "Did you say a wyrm? Is that a wyrm with a y?" it hissed.

"Er, yes," Mercipolis admitted, cursing himself for letting slip so much in his agitation.

"A WYRM WITH A Y? A WYRM WITH A Y? THIS DAY OF MY WRATH SHALL KNOW NO BOUNDS! I WILL FINALLY HAVE MY REVENGE!"

With that, the beast launched itself from the nest with such a stirring of wind that Barty and the wizard were knocked about most frightfully.

When he was able to recover himself, the flitter-flutter made his way over to poor Mercipolis. "Well, that wasn't ominous at all, was it?"

CHAPTER 12

THE BEING OF LIGHT

NIGHTSHADE AND FRIENDS HAD grown weary waiting for the return of the wizard. The sun was sinking low and there was no sign of the giant trout they had seen off on a mission to gather zingery seeds. Chester was sitting, leant against a tree trunk, determined to stay awake, but his head nodded forward with a sudden jerk so often, the bear was in danger of doing his poor neck an injury.

Walnut was talking to its three invisible whirligig companions. No one else could make sense of the one-sided conversation, but it must have been amusing as Walnut paused frequently to giggle. The Keeylas was curled cat-like into a tight ball and slept. Even in its greatly reduced form, it assumed no harm would come to it, so used was it to being the mightiest of creatures.

This left mouse and wyrm. Nightshade was still trying to get used to being so much larger than normal, and Celestyna was fretting over the fate of the wizard. As much as she wanted to find a safe home, it was much against her nature to allow others to venture into danger on her behalf.

"Perhaps it would have been better if we had never come out from under the bed," she lamented. "More and more are being caught up in the risks of this quest that benefits only ourself in the end."

Nightshade objected. "That isn't true. Helping others brings its own pleasures and blessings upon the helper. Besides, I've never had such an interesting day in my life. I've met a dozen creatures, had adventures I'd never have dreamt of, and now I'm a hundred times the size I once was. It is a life of constant anxiety to be a small creature in a big world. I've never felt so confident and ready to take on any challenge we are faced with!"

That was fortuitous, for at this moment, a huge shadow appeared over them, blotting out what little light was left in the day.

"A RECKONING IS UPON YOU, FOUL WYRM!"

"We beg your pardon?" Celestyna replied icily, for even though the creature confronting them was many times her size, no one appreciates being called foul by a complete stranger. One should really become better acquainted before trading insults.

The squish landed, its long snaky tail taking up the better part of the riverbank where the party was gathered. Chester sprang up, awakened from his dozing state by the commotion.

"What's this? What's this?" he cried, charging the monster in impetuous Chester fashion.

Pishposh swept the powerful bear aside with a casual swish of its tail, knocking him into the Keeylas, which woke with much hissing, spitting and clawing. While they sorted themselves out, Walnut approached the squish, fluttering in the air in front of its red eyes.

It seemed taken aback momentarily by the weirdness of the whirligig. It is not every day you are confronted with a thing that has a cat's head, lizard's body, five ratty tails, and a pair of batty wings. Being a weird creature itself, however, it soon lost interest in this novelty in favor of its impassioned vendetta.

Spreading its orange-feathered wings wide and drawing its body up to an enormous height, it bellowed, "A WYRM WITH A Y IS RESPONSIBLE FOR MY HIDEOUS FORM AND I HAVE VOWED VENGEANCE AGAINST EVERY ONE OF YOUR KIND! PREPARE TO DIE!"

"We don't think so," Celestyna replied calmly.

"WHAT?!?!"

"We doubt a wyrm made you what you are but even if it did, that is no reason to hurl yourself about threatening innocent creatures, not to mention the shouting, which is so unnecessary. We all have perfectly good hearing. Most of us, that is," she amended, remembering Chester was slightly challenged in that department.

"I AM NOT SHOUTING! I AM SPEAKING NORMALLY... er, that is," it continued with a loud whisper, "I am speaking normally, and of course a wyrm did this to me. I was instantly transformed into this monster when one bit me."

"Oh? Bit you? Like this?" Celestyna gave the thing a mighty nip on its tail with her spiky-sharp mouthful of teeth.

The look of complete and utter surprise on its vulture-like face was short-lived as Pishposh's body began to writhe and squirm, shudder and heave. The others retreated hastily to avoid being whipped by the squish's long body as it struggled against some invisible force.

"Dearie me," cried Chester. "The thing looks to be in pure agony, don't it?"

"Good," said the Keeylas, incensed at having its pleasant nap interrupted.

"What do you think is happening?" asked Nightshade.

"We've no idea," replied the wyrm, feeling abashed she had let her emotions get the better of her, betraying her into acting so rashly.

"*Changing, a-changing,*" sang the whirligig. "If a wyrm turned it into a monster, maybe a wyrm will turn it back again."

"But into what, I wonder?"

"What's that?" Walnut cupped a lizardy foot to one ear as though listening closely to something unseen. "Ah, Leaf says only time will tell. Sunshine and Mold agree."

"We see," replied Celestyna with a sage nod of her head, for how else could you respond to such an observation?

It was a dreadful sight to see a creature suffering such torment even if it had been discourteously threatening their lives. Scales big as serving trays were shed and scattered. Orange feathers flew. Low moans punctuated by agitated shrieks filled the air.

Nightshade shed quiet tears as they were very sensitive to the pain of others. Their eyes were so full they almost didn't notice a late addition to their party. A floaty, white, bat-like thing wearing dark glasses had flittered into their midst. In its feet was clutched a green leaf wrapped up like a birthday present. Even more extraordinarily, a beautiful pink and green moth with one crumpled wing rode on its head. Upon close inspection, the insect wore a tiny purple hat and cloak.

"Mercipolis?" Nightshade squeaked in hopeful amazement.

Barty (for of course, the bat-like thing was he) landed on a large rock as far as possible from the rumble-tumble of the transforming monster. The wizard (for of course, the moth was he) tumbled from the flitter-flutter and hit himself with a tiny wand.

The wizard appeared, human again, but clutching one dangling arm in obvious distress. "What is happening?"

"It looks like the squish," said Barty.

"Squish? Squish?" repeated Chester, equally astonished by the reappearance of the wizard when they were giving up hope of ever seeing him again (not that the bear was, but he wouldn't be surprised if the others were), the strange flitter-flutter creature, and the word squish, which was a new one for him.

"Yes, Pishposh the squish, Ruler of the Misshapen Mountains."

"Why are they misshapen?" asked Walnut.

"Exactly my question!" Barty cried, looking upon the whirligig with delight for getting right to the heart of the matter.

"That hardly seems important at the moment," the wizard chided them. "Whatever did you do to it? We were afraid it meant to cause you a mischief and flew after it as quickly as my friend, Barty, here could."

"We are afraid we bit it," Celestyna admitted. "It claimed a wyrm had bitten it and turned it into that creature. It was being rather rude, but that is no real excuse for our actions."

"I think you did the right thing. It is a formidable foe. Look at my arm!" He showed them the broken, useless appendage.

Chester grimaced. "Can't you magic it back together? I thought wizards knew all kinds o' tricksy tricks."

"We can heal such wounds, but we are not allowed to do so on ourselves. It is against the rules."

"Why?"

"Because it is against the rules. Isn't that reason enough?"

"Seems a silly type o' rule to me. Why shouldn't you heal yourself?"

"We are meant to use our magic to help others, not ourselves. It is in the Code of Magical Conduct."

"But you're not gonna be much use to us on our quest if you're hurt, are you? So, you could say you'd actually be helping us out by fixing it up good and proper."

Mercipolis and the others stared in wonder at Chester. This seemed an unusually sophisticated and considered piece of logic from the normally rash and thoughtless bear. They had no time to dwell on it, however, as whatever change the squish was undergoing reached its climax.

In a final burst of energy and cloud of feathers, the enormous beast shrunk down into a being of light, about the height of Chester when he stood on his hind legs, but slender and graceful as a willow. It wore a gown made up of the glossy orange feathers that also lay around its feet, with a long train and high collar that framed its head.

It was a thing of the greatest beauty, and one by one, the others knelt in whatever fashion their body type allowed, for they felt they were in the presence of a wonder beyond anything they had ever experienced.

It spoke to them in a voice that sounded like the sweetest bird song you have ever heard:

"I am Meera. Rise up, children. You are free creatures and should kneel to no one."

Its gentle voice soothed them and lifted their spirits as they raised themselves from their various poses of prostration. Even the Keeylas, nasty-tempered as it was, gave a catty grin. Its eyes grew big and black and round with awe as it watched the softly glowing figure intently, white tail twitching.

Ever blunt and impulsive, Chester blurted out the question on everyone's mind. "What are ye?"

Meera laughed, a sparkling melody like the sweet jingle-jangle of fairy bells (if fairies existed, of course). "I am many things and nothing at all."

Mercipolis did not like the sound of that one bit. The wizard felt there were far too many enigmatic creatures in the world who liked to speak in riddles and rhymes and who knew what other nonsense. It was rather exhausting, even for someone trained in the magical arts and thus steeped in the arcane and obscure.

"Can't you speak plainly?" he asked in quarrelsome fashion. "It's been a long day full of adventures and misadventures, and we are very, very tired." He clutched his broken arm as he spoke, wincing at the pain of bone scraping against bone.

A soft beam of light pulsed out from Meera. It wrapped itself around his aching limb, bathing it in a feeling of both fire and ice at the same time. It was a weird sensation, but the terrible agony ceased, and the wizard could feel his wound being knitted back together until it was though it had never been.

"Th-thank you," he stuttered, abashed that his ill-tempered remark was met with such a kindness. "And I'm sorry for speaking out of turn."

"Don't be," Meera replied, flashing soft pulses of the palest pink, blue, and lavender light. "I have lived so long that nothing offends me. I can see you are true to one another and that is what matters most in this world. Except you, little one. You do not belong with these others, do you?"

Another beam of light enveloped the Keeylas. Its white cat form stretched and writhed until it was returned to its former monstrous glory. It butted its enormous head against Meera's hand like the most domesticated of house cats and curled itself at the being's feet, purring loudly.

"You've tamed it!" cried Nightshade, amazed to see the terrifying beast so docile and content. "Are you a magician?"

"Not exactly no, but not exactly yes."

No one knew what to make of this inscrutable answer, but Barty had more pressing queries.

"You are so powerful! How did you get turned into a squish? And more importantly, why are the Misshapen Mountains misshapen?"

"Excellent questions, my flitter-flutter friend. You are an unusually astute creature."

Barty preened a bit, looking around at the others for their approval. After all, who doesn't enjoy a bit of flattery?

"Although I am long-lived and have certain talents, that does not make me immune to vile intent. A wyrm without heart, without a soul wished me ill. They injected the evil inside of themself into me, turning me into the outward projection of their rage and inner foulness. It affected my mind as well. I apologize for any hurt I caused while in that form. Healing your injury was the least I could do," Meera added, bowing slightly to the wizard.

Celestyna slid closer, horrified at the being's words. "One of our kind turned you into that thing?"

"I am afraid so, dearest. They are a lost one. But you have counteracted their poison with your own sweet nature."

"But we meant to harm you at the time," the wyrm admitted, abashed at her rash and violent action.

"Perhaps your head did, but you have a pure soul. I comprehend your desire. A high place where you can be yourself without fear of what others may think of you. A safe refuge. And you have gathered these good folk to your cause. Is there anything I can do to assist you?"

Mercipolis took the leaf packet from Barty and carefully unwrapped it. "We harvested these zingery seeds as told in a prophecy. Now we must plant them farther beneath the surface than any creature can dig. Would you know of such a place?"

Meera stirred through the glowing seeds with one long, delicate finger. "How beautiful!"

"The seeds are lovely," the wizard agreed.

"Yes, of course, but I meant this." Meera lifted out the star pebble. As the light of the being touched it, the star began to glow again, pulsating softly.

Meera cupped the star in its hands as it grew and grew. When it seemed impossibly large and too heavy for even a magical being to support, Meera hurled it high into the twilight air overhead.

"Thank you, thank you!" it called, as it rose into the heavens. It began to sing again but an entirely different tune than before. This one was no lament, but instead an exultation of the gift of new life among its twinkling comrades.

"Now there's a thing, ain't it? There is a thing!" exclaimed Chester, both astounded and moved by this rebirth and launching of something thought dead. "A hooman I knew talked of a goddess of the forest with power over life and death. Is it you?"

Meera shone with its gentle light. "A goddess, a god. These are only words. I am other. A thing apart. Yet I am a part of everything like each of you. We are taught to admire and adore the unique, the strange, and yet each of you are special in your own ways."

Chester scratched his shaggy head, looking around at their party. A wizard, a monstrous cat, a wyrm, a flitter-flutter and whirligig, even a mouse of unusual size. There was no doubt in his mind these were all unutterably special, but he was only a very ordinary bear. However, when he ventured this opinion, Nightshade was quick to set him straight.

"An ordinary bear?! One who befriends humans, learned how to cook and ride a machine, escorted us to safety through a roaring forest fire, and is most loyal and brave. Has there ever been another bear in the history of the world like you?"

Chester would have blushed if he was capable. As it was, he ducked his head and turned away, overcome with emotion.

Walnut and Barty, being of similar single-minded temperaments, flitted up to Meera demanding an answer to the question they considered more interesting than all this philosophical talk.

"Why are the Misshapen Mountains misshapen?" they cried in unison.

Meera laughed again, delighted. It held out its hands. Walnut roosted on one while Barty hung, bat-like, from the other.

Mercipolis scoffed. "Always with these ridiculous questions!"

The being of light scolded him gently. "There is no such thing. Curiosity is a valuable trait. When we cease to take an interest in the world around us, it starts to wither and die. I will tell you, my friends. The Misshapen Mountains are actually the spine of a dragon that lived so long ago that I alone remember her. When she flew, her wings blotted out the sky. When she landed, this planet shook. When she sighed, the winds whirled like a tempest. And when she grew impossibly old, her bones wracked and misshapen with age, she lay down and died."

Barty and Walnut blinked back tears at the thought of the death of such a magnificent creature.

"Do not weep," said Meera. "For from her bones, small plants sprouted. They grew and grew. Some became trees, new forests. Animals came. The mincing, creeping things of the earth and the soaring, winged creatures of sky. She lives through them for she gave them a home and sustenance, and there is no greater gift."

"We should like to have such a home," Celestyna said wistfully. "Do you think there is one in the Misshapen Mountains for us?"

"This I cannot foresee. But there is a deep hole there at the heart of the dragon. Deeper than could ever be dug by any creature. If you are looking for such a spot to sow your seeds, there would be none better."

"But how could we ever hope to find it?" Mercipolis bemoaned, exhausted with this neverending quest and a day that also seemed to have no end.

"I will take you there, of course!" With that promise, Meera's form exploded with every color of the rainbow. A weariness overcame each member of the party. They lay down where they were and fell into the deepest slumber of their lives.

CHAPTER 13

A MOST INFAMOUS CURSE

NIGHTSHADE, A GREY MOUSE grown to unusual size, was dreaming. A tangle of a river that burned with a lavender flame. A white kitten that caught at their mousey tail and showered it with kisses. A brown bear that sprouted enormous wings and lifted into the sky while chortling and waving madly with sharply beclawed paws.

It was not unpleasant, but then Death arrived in the form of an owl. Its yellow eyes, unblinking, burned with the light of the sun at midday, and a talon trailed along the mouse's spine, parting their soft fur. The mouse froze in their tracks, unable to move or escape as is often the way in nightmares.

Fortunately (or unfortunately, or perhaps a bit of both), a thump against Nightshade's skull woke them and broke the spell. Jumping to their feet while tenderly rubbing the lump that was rising on the back of their head, the mouse looked around wildly, but no owl was in sight, only a round and very hard stone which they assumed had awoken them.

Nightshade was alone in a barren field of plowed dirt, scattered seeds and broken stalks of harvested wheat. Your first thought in this situation might have been something along the lines of *how strange* or *where am I?* But Nightshade's was that they were starving and the seeds looked tasty. Once, a single seed would have been a feast, but in their new size, they had to gather handfuls to make the slightest dent in their hunger.

When they'd eaten their fill, Nightshade examined the barren landscape again curiously. The sky overhead was a pure, honest blue with a single white cloud floating lazily across the field toward the mouse. As Nightshade skittered here and there exploring, the cloud followed and sheltered them from the bright sun, which was quite helpful, but soon enough, the cloud became grey and dense with moisture. It let out a small grumble of thunder as though belching from being overfull.

Nightshade felt a single drop of rain on the tip of their nose. They licked it off, relishing the wetness against their dry tongue. More drops fell and more, until it was a positive deluge. When Nightshade's thirst was satisfied, they tried to move out from under the storm, but the cloud tracked the mouse relentlessly no matter how quickly they ran.

Feeling a bit more drenched than was comfortable, Nightshade sat down in a puddle and a deep depression swept over them. They were alone, as alone as any creature had ever been. There should be more. What exactly, they couldn't remember, but more *something*. This left them feeling bereft, as though they had lost friends they'd never met. They began to weep, and their tears mingled with the rain on the ground.

A small sprout formed before their eyes. A mere tendril of a thing, only two fragile leaves. The mouse leant over and watered it with their tears. The sprout grew and grew and grew some more. It stretched its leafy arms up to the cloud in the sky which parted in two and let the sun burst through. The welcoming rays warmed both plant and mouse.

Nightshade felt their spirits lift. They were no longer so alone as they watched leaves and curled strands, vines and stalk unfurl toward the heavens. The thing grew so tall that the mouse felt as an ant must at the foot of the tallest tree in the world—a wee, insignificant thing, but adventure was calling and they itched to answer. They set one paw upon the woody stalk and began to climb.

Chester, a bear of normal bear size, was sat on a surface like none he'd ever seen, all dusty and grey. The landscape was far from smooth, with hills and craters appearing exuberantly here and there with no sense of order whatsoever. (Not that the bear minded as he was a rather untidy creature himself.)

What *was* bothering him, however, was the fact he could not remember how he'd gotten here nor where *here* was. A light in the distance caught his eye. A marble of blue and green was peeking over the horizon. *Beautiful*, he thought, and was moved to rise and galumph towards it on all four paws with surprising speed for such a weighty and (it must be said) occasionally clumsy beast.

He felt unusually light on his feet, each bound taking him farther than expected. It was tremendous fun, but no matter how far he ran, he got no nearer to the object. In fact, it rose higher and higher into the sky. He soon gave up the pursuit and sat down again on his haunches, watching the sparkling ball floating above him.

"A lovely luscious looming light, is it not?"

Startled by both the suddenness and oddness of this communication, Chester leapt to his feet, looking to his left and his right, but there was no one to be seen. He flicked absentmindedly at his ear, which had grown ticklish as though being brushed by a feather. Being a bear of great power, his flick was unfortunately as strong as a blow.

"Ow! What the what was that?" A bird materialized from nowhere in front of Chester's eyes. It was nearly as tall as the bear himself, and its feathers were pale green. It had a long tail that dragged along the ground and curly fronds rising from its head like the most fashionable hat you can imagine. It also sported two beady green eyes, one of which was reddening from having received an unexpected poke from a wayward paw.

"A thousand pardons!" Chester exclaimed abjectly. "Didn't see you there."

"Naturally. Hiding in plain sight is one of my many talents, along with juggling and being able to recite over three hundred poems backwards."

"Is there much call for that?" the bear asked, thinking a poem recited from back to front might be an extremely perplexing thing as poems read the right way round were often confusing enough.

"Of course," said the bird, not exactly catching Chester's drift. "Juggling is one of the oldest and most honorable of the creative arts."

Stooping to the ground, the bird caught one small pebble after another in its beak and threw them up into the air, where they hovered, then spun in circles in a breeze created as the bird flapped its enormous wings. It was by far the most surprising thing Chester could remember ever witnessing, but then he was reminded he could remember very little. He applauded politely nonetheless, his giant paws making the sound of a booming bass drum in the relative quiet.

"Thank you ever so, I'm sure," the bird said, allowing the pebbles to drop and taking a deep bow as it folded its wings behind it. "But whatever are you doing here? We so rarely get visitors."

"We?" the bear asked, looking around nervously, afraid other invisible birds were lurking nearby.

"Yes, myself and the moon."

"The moon? Do you mean the ball in the sky that lights up the night?"

"No, it is the blue planet that lights up the sky. See?" The bird pointed its beak skyward to the marble above their heads that shed reflected light upon them.

"Where is the moon then?"

"You're standing on her. She is all around us."

"This... this is the moon?" Chester was overcome with dizziness. He felt his own world had turned topsy-turvy and sat down again with a bang before he fell over. What should be up was down and what should be down was up—a most baffling and even upsetting thought to have thrust upon one with no warning.

"Of course! And I am her sister, Luna, though the moon doesn't know it."

The bear felt a headache coming on. "What do you mean the moon don't know? How can you not know whether you've a sister or not?"

"Do you know how many brothers or sisters you have?"

"Naturally," Chester replied stoutly, then was immediately stung by the shame of realizing he not only couldn't remember whether he had siblings or not, but that his other memories were sparse at best. "That is, not right this moment. I seem to have a touch o' the thing where you have trouble recollecting this and that."

"Amnesia? How positively thrilling!" Luna squawked, dancing back and forth on her long, knock-kneed legs with excitement. "What can you recall?"

"My name is Chester and I'm a bear."

"And is that all? Nothing else?"

"Not really. I've a vague notion I was traveling, mayhap with friends. There was something important needed doing."

The bird started hopping around in circles. "Ooh, ooh, ooh, I bet you anything it was a quest. It sounds exactly like a quest. Do you think it was a quest?"

Chester scratched his forehead with one long claw. "I suppose it might've been one o' those. If it was, I must've failed at it, or else, how came I to be here? Perhaps I was shot like a ball from a cannon. Seen hoomans setting those off once upon a time. Sparks flew and the balls went awful far."

"Very likely, I should think," Luna agreed, nodding her head with enthusiasm, "though I've no idea what a cannon is, much less a hooman. Or possibly, it was magic. I am a magical creature myself, so I understand about such things." The bird preened its feathers with the tip of its sharp beak as though to say, *aren't I a very fine thing, indeed?*

"If you know about magic, could you send me back to where I come from? My friends are bound to be worriting their heads o'er me."

The bird fixed her uninjured eye on the bear. "I doubt that. They probably don't even realize you're gone. You don't seem like the sort anyone would miss."

Now Chester was by nature optimistic and cheerful. He rarely felt down or that things were impossible or that everything would not work out for the best. But for the first time in his life, a serious depression dropped over him, like the snuffing out of the warm and welcoming light of a candle in the dark.

Luna began to circle him, performing a weird ritual that involved twirling her tail feathers, puffing out her chest, and twitching her wings back and forth like she was conducting an orchestra. "In fact, I think you are the most useless, incompetent, inept, and foolish thing I've ever met."

These cruel words might have crushed poor Chester completely only he happened to be distracted by a green tendril snaking along the ground toward the awful, bullying bird. It wrapped itself around Luna's feet and wings until she was completely immobile.

"I was only kidding!" she cried desperately from her leafy prison. "Such a joker, I am! You are a most noble bear."

"He certainly is," agreed a familiar voice.

Chester's heavy heart lifted instantly at the sound. "Nightshade?"

"Yes, my dear friend."

As they embraced in joyous reunion, memories flooded into both of all they had endured and all they meant to each other, and in that moment, they were as happy as they could ever remember being in their lives.

Despite their rejoicing, they still had many unanswered questions. How had they both come to be alone in two very different places? What odd chance had brought them back together? Where were the others of their party? And, not least importantly, what to do with the squawking bird who was trussed up in the snaky green vine upon which the mouse had made his startling reappearance?

"I'm afraid this has been a most hilarious misunderstanding," said Luna, turning her beady bird eyes this way and that as she struggled against her binding. "I neglected to warn you I have a naughty sense of humor, but my sister can confirm."

"Who is your sister?" asked Nightshade, twisting their head around and seeing no one else.

"We are standing on it," Chester whispered to the mouse. "She thinks the moon is her sister, silly moppet."

"We're standing on the moon? How is such a thing even possible? It's so very far away."

"Don't know, don't care," replied the bear. "All I want is to get down from here."

"I could fly you down," interjected the bird, looking sly, "but only if you release me."

"How could you fly two creatures as big as us down from the moon? Are you daft?"

"Not a bit of it. What a horribly rude thing to say!"

"Like you weren't running rings round me hurling insults only a wee minute ago—"

Nightshade hastened to intervene as this debate was not advancing their cause or the quest one bit. "Let's calm down and talk sensibly. Chester has a point. Are you strong enough to carry us?"

"Course not!" Luna scoffed. "Never said I was. We'll use the glider. Wait for the planet to sink below the horizon, take a running start, and jump. Untie me and I'll show you. Or we could stand here forever arguing about it. If I was on an important quest, I wouldn't waste time being disagreeable to such a lovely and useful bird as me."

"She's right," said Nightshade to the skeptical bear. "It is of no benefit to us to leave her as she is, and she might be able to help us."

"I suppose," said Chester reluctantly. "Though you missed the part where she was making a right fool o' herself calling me names. Do you promise to assist us if we untangle you there?" he asked the bird.

"Abso-positive-lutely! You will be ever so glad you did. Won't they, Sister dear?"

The moon declined to comment.

Nightshade raised an eyebrow inquiringly at the bear, who shrugged and began to pull at the strong vines with his sharp claws. The mouse used their teeth to chew through the plant. It took some hard work on both their parts, but finally the bird was free.

"So long, you mugs!" Luna cried as she took off amid a flurry of pale green feathers and with immense satisfaction at the despicable feat of having taken advantage of two honorable souls.

Bear and mouse could not help feeling a little bitter and hopeful the bird might meet her rightful comeuppance one way or another, but they had more pressing problems.

"Didn't think we could believe that one, but I'm just as glad to be rid o' her," said Chester. "Nothing but a troublemaking nuisance, a bully, and a liar to boot."

"Do you think she was lying about the glider?" Nightshade asked.

"Wouldn't be a bit surprised, but as I don't know what one is, we could be standing right next to it and none the wiser."

They looked around again, and a twinkling far off caught their attention. By unspoken agreement they turned to walk that way, leaping tall bounds through the air in the curious weightless fashion that one journeys on the moon.

Before too long, they came upon a contraption shaped something like a bird, with long wings attached to a broad body of two seats just the right fit for a large bear and a mouse of unusual size if they didn't mind leaving their back paws dangling in mid-air. It was painted with black and yellow stripes like a hornet and shone as though buffed to a high gloss by a loving hand.

"How did such a thing come to be here?" Chester wondered.

Nightshade shook their head. "It is yet another mystery. I'm beginning to think there is more magic on our world and off than I ever would have dreamed of before meeting you and the others."

"I suppose we sit there," said Chester, pawing the chairs doubtfully, "but how do we flap the wings?"

"We don't. They are meant for gliding, like a falcon floating on the winds aloft. I don't think Luna was lying about that. We take a running jump over the edge of the moon and drift down to our home when it has moved below us."

"Sounds mighty dangerous to me. Supposing we miss?"

Nightshade laughed gently. "It is a huge target. Besides, what else can we do? If we wait to be rescued, we might be here a very long time and there's no food and water. We could starve before the others found us."

"Do you think they're even looking?"

"Of course! It's the first thing we'll do if we manage to get ourselves down, isn't it? They might be in trouble like we are."

"It's a rare disappointment, ain't it? I took Meera for a good 'un, yet it sent us all off on our lonesomes instead o' to the heart o' the dragon as promised."

Nightshade looked thoughtful. "I wonder if this is actually its doing. Perhaps some other magical being interfered. Or maybe it is a residual effect of the curse that ill-intentioned wyrm put upon Meera."

"That would be most infamous, if true!" Chester cried. "'Tis a hard thing when we are trying nothing more than to help a friend."

"I suppose it is the nature of a quest. If it was safe and easy, Celestyna could have done it herself in no time. Shall we give the glider a go then?"

"I reckon so, though I never heard o' a bear that could fly. Ain't natural! But mayhap whatever magic is at work will protect us."

Having no other option readily available, bear and mouse seated themselves in the weird machine. They figured out that a system of leather straps and brass buckles was meant to secure them in their chairs and fastened the restraints as tightly as possible, as neither relished the thought of falling from the glider.

Taking deep breaths in to calm their nerves, they used their dangling feet to run as hard as they could toward the horizon. It seemed to go on forever but suddenly, the ground fell out from beneath their paws. They were in flight.

CHAPTER 14

THE FATHOMLESS DEPTHS

CELESTYNA WAS A MOST unhappy wyrm. In fact, she thought she must be the most miserable wyrm who had ever crawled upon the earth. That was because at this moment, she was not crawling, but swimming with an awkward grace (for she was incapable of doing anything truly clumsily) through the fathomless depths of a dark and cold body of water.

Above all things, she hated being even the slightest bit damp. Now, not only was she wet through and through, but she had no idea where she was or how she came to be there. She found to her surprise but great relief that she could breathe easily enough and was in no danger of drowning. If she could lay aside her dislike of being excessively moist, it was even pleasurable moving her body sinuously through the water.

Her curves were ever longer as she had grown considerably in just the day in which she had been traveling with… somebody… to somewhere… for some reason she thought was important but escaped her like a trout wriggling off the hook of a disappointed fisherman. She wasn't sure why a trout of all fish had come to mind as this water was too deep to be a river. Though she couldn't see far in any direction, there was a weightiness to it which convinced her it was at least a large lake.

The water had a peculiar taste, briny and sour. Nothing like the fresh waters she was used to. It puckered her scales and caused her lovely frills to wilt. She remembered a woman with kind eyes telling her about the ocean, where waves broke upon a rocky shore and salt coated everything like a second skin. Perhaps she was in that ocean and need only swim far enough to reach that rocky shore.

Which direction to go in though? With no markers to guide her, it seemed likely she might swim round in circles forever. She turned her head frequently, frustrated with the encroaching darkness. But wait, what was that? If her eyes didn't deceive her, it was the teeniest prick of light, flitting about like a firefly would on land.

She swam toward it powerfully, covering the distance in no time, to find that rather than a single being, there was a swarm of them: petite jellyfish, no larger than a thumbnail, with long trailing tentacles as thin as a human hair and bells that glowed pale blue. They danced in loose patterns, forming shapes that seemed meaningless until she got closer. They were making letters, words!

How extraordinary! Celestyna thought. At least it was a friendly message (and yes, she was that rare wyrm who had learned to read. Another gift from the woman of the cottage.)

"Greetings!" the jellyfish spelled out. They were humming too, a pleasant, vibrating sound though tuneless. When she listened carefully, Celestyna realized they were all speaking at once, over top of one another.

"Hulloo!" "Hi!" "Howdy!" "Hello!" "Felicitations, pip pip!"

This last unusual salutation was from a jellyfish that was not like the others. It was glowing bright green and its tentacles, instead of being orderly and straight, were curly and frenetic as though buzzing with an energy that was only poorly contained.

"Shhhhh," Celestyna urged gently. "One at a time please. We are not able to understand you if you speak all at once. What is your name, little one?" she asked, booping the green one ever so gently with the tip of her tail.

"Skibbiter-lit-lot-ballydish!"

"That is a mouthful. Perhaps you have a nickname?"

"Nickname? What is that, toodle-le-pip?"

"A shortened version of your name that a friend may call you."

"Are you a friend, tippity-pip?"

"We hope to be. We seek to be friends with all we meet," the wyrm replied. "We could call you Pip as it seems to be a word you enjoy using."

"I have no idea what you mean, pip-arino."

One of the other jellyfish spoke up. "They mean the annoying habit you have of adding nonsensical words with the syllable 'pip' in them to the end of everything you say."

The green jellyfish turned an ugly shade of puce. "I didn't realize I was doing that, and I certainly didn't realize it was annoying. How humiliating, pip pop... er, this is embarrassing, full stop with nothing at all added onto the end."

Celestyna would have hidden her smile behind her hand if she had one, but as it was, the jellyfish could see she was amused, which only made his color deepen into a most alarming mulberry. The wyrm was sorry to see the delicate creature so discombobulated, for it is very rude to make a new acquaintance feel ill at ease.

"You must excuse us," she said. "We are out of our element here. We belong on dry land. How we came to be so deep beneath the surface, we cannot remember, but we have no wish to cause you any discomfort."

"I don't suppose you mean to eat us," the jellyfish said, its color lightening slightly.

"Of course not!"

"Excellent. We are highly poisonous and would give you a bad stomachache, but that would do us no good if you had already eaten us."

"Sounds like it would do neither of us a favor. Besides, we are vegetarian. We only eat plants."

"Plants? There's a lovely patch here." The jellyfish, returned almost to its original bright green, led the swarm down. Their glowing bells lit up the waters enough for Celestyna to see a beautiful forest of dark green leafy kelp and long strands of a wine-red seaweed flowing in the current. She took a mouthful of each. They were delicious—salty and sweet—and mysteriously, tasting exactly like your favorite dessert.

She ate her fill, having only just realized how hungry she was. As she dined, she looked about her with interest. The light from the jellyfish revealed there were many creatures living even at these depths. Fish with mouths as large as their bodies and glowing lures to attract unwary prey. A cave full of eels, darting out and backing up again like a many-headed monster. A school of rays, flapping by like a flock of birds.

An octopus scurried up, wrapping itself around the wyrm's tail. Its skin turned to amethyst and emerald, blending in so seamlessly with Celestyna's own pattern, it could hardly be seen. It tickled and made the wyrm giggle, a sweet, burbling sound that drew still more creatures.

Soon, she was surrounded by a representative of every inhabitant of deep water you can imagine. They were curious for the most part, with only one sea cucumber that gave her the side-eye and an ill-tempered squid that squirted dark blue ink which did the wyrm no harm.

A kind of sea shanty started up:

Tell us more, tell us more
Speak us a fable and unlock the lore
What in the world are you down here for?
Tell us more, tell us more!

Celestyna nodded her head in time; it was addictively catchy. The green jellyfish prodded her to answer their plea. "They really want to know!"

"So do we!" exclaimed the wyrm. "Our memory is not what it was. There was a party—no, a group of some kind full of unusual allies, and yet they were our friends and were trying to help us, we believe, but we can't remember anything more. We miss them awfully though, for all we could not name them if we tried."

"You may call me Skibby," the green jellyfish said. "As a nickname, friend."

"Thank you. And we are Celestyna."

"Is that your nickname or your name name?"

"It is our name. We have never had a nickname, but you may call us Stella, which means star, for our mother named us for the stars in the sky."

"What are stars and what are sky?"

"You know, above the water."

There was much whispering and consternation among the sea creatures.

"Above the water," Skibby said. "There is nothing above the water. There is only water. Water is all."

"WATER IS ALL," intoned the others in a way that invited no argument.

Celestyna had no wish to upset her hosts. "Yes, indeed," she soothed them, moving her head back and forth in a mesmerizing way. "Perhaps you could simply point us to up?"

As one, the crowd around her drifted away toward what was for them the limit of their world, but for the wyrm, was the blessed sight of the surface. Her head broke through the waves, which also broke the spell she had cast over the creatures below. They scattered away, back to the depths from whence they came.

Happiness filled Celestyna at having some part of her body out of the water. She turned on her back and floated, watching the heavens. How bright the stars were! One in particular was burning with unusual intensity. In fact, it seemed to be coming nearer and nearer. If she wasn't mistaken, it was falling straight at—

Celestyna threw her sinuous curves to the left, half-diving under the water again to avoid a collision. The waters churned with a violent eruption as a heavy object hurtled into the water, narrowly missing the wyrm. Imagine her astonishment to see a brown bear and a mouse of unusual size caught in a contraption that was breaking into pieces except for the straps that held them prisoner in their seats.

There was fear in their eyes as they plunged into the depths. Without hesitation, Celestyna dived after them, catching the thing they rode in her long, sharpish teeth and dragging it up to the surface. While she hoisted it, the bear and mouse worked furiously to free themselves from their harnesses. By the time the wyrm crested the surface again, they had managed to break away and were soon bobbing along, paddling mightily to keep their heads above the saltwater waves and coughing from their near drowning.

"Nightshade! Chester!" the wyrm cried, her memories returning in full force the moment she saw their dear, familiar faces. "How glad we are to see you again! But do tell us how you came to be falling from the sky."

Both mouse and bear would have liked to answer their friend but were stupefied by their precipitous journey from the moon and spluttering from the effort it took to keep afloat in the choppy waters. Seeing their predicament, the wyrm encouraged them to climb upon her back. With some grunting effort, they succeeded in doing so. This solved their immediate problem of being vulnerable to sinking but it proved to be a standoff, as they quickly fell off and were dunked again when Celestyna attempted to swim with her passengers.

As long as she stayed still, floating, Chester and Nightshade could cling without sliding side to side. They traveled this way a while, at the mercy of the tides as to which way they drifted. Mouse and bear recovered their breaths enough to recount their adventures, and the wyrm offered her own tale.

"Bad doings," said Chester when they were caught up. "I thought Meera was a right 'un and bound to help us, but it split us all asunder and stole our memories. That's not the actions of a friend. 'Tis only merest happenstance brought us together again."

"A very strange chance," Celestyna observed. "The vine that took Nightshade to you and the glider that brought you down right to us? They seem as magical in nature as the small jellyfish that helped me."

"What is a jellyfish?" asked Nightshade.

"Lovely glowing things."

"Like that?" said Chester, pointing one claw at a bright green light that was floating along toward them.

"Skibby?" the wyrm called out, thinking it was her friend returned to check on them, but as it got closer, it became obvious it was much too large.

They watched in fascination, and not a little trepidation, as the light grew nearer, wondering if it was friend or foe. It spread out over the surface like an oil slick. Celestyna would have swum away from it if she could, but bravely held her ground so Chester and Nightshade would be spared another dunking.

A million, million tiny twinkling green stars winked at them. Beneath, an immense shadow loomed. Suddenly, an enormous beast broke through the surface, mouth agape, swallowing as many of the stars as it could in one huge gulp. It breached from the water, as tall as the tallest tree in the forest, and slammed back down with a splash so mighty that wyrm, bear, and mouse were soaked through in an instant. Celestyna fought to maintain her balance and her passengers, but it was a near thing.

A huge eye popped up beside them. "Pardon, pardon! My sincerest regrets! So intent upon my meal was I, I did not realize I had neighbors." This was all said by the thing's mouth which was still underwater, so it sounded more like "blurb blurble blurble-lee-loo" than anything else, but somehow our friends caught the intent of the apology.

"But what are you?" asked Chester.

A long shape that stretched as far as they could see emerged. Its gorgeous color reminded Nightshade of the deepest blue of a twilight sky as the sun disappears below the horizon. Its back was covered with white spots that matched the white along its belly. The creature lazed along on its side so that one fishy fin towered into the sky. A powerful tail, barely in motion, kept it afloat.

Its massive mouth opened and a voice as low as low emerged. "I am a leviathan. *The* leviathan, to be exact, for I am the only one of my kind to the best of my knowledge. I feed upon the emerald algae here in the Lamentable Lake and compose romantic operas in my spare time."

This was a lot to take in, but Celestyna, being a practical wyrm, focused on the part that seemed most pertinent to their current plight. "The Lamentable Lake? Is that where we are?"

"Of course! Do you mean to say you had no idea where you are? How is that possible? Surely when you entered these waters, you must have known? How extraordinary!"

"It is even more extraordinary than that. My companions and I were magicked away to three separate locations. We have only recently been reunited, having no idea what body of water this is or how to get to dry land again, for we are none of us aquatic by nature."

"Oh, *magic*!" the leviathan said with a sharp shudder that sent gentle waves swirling in every direction. "That explains it. There is never any telling what mischief will occur when you get yourself mixed up with magic. I resolved long ago to have nothing to do with it, and my life has been most peaceful since."

"That's well and good for you," said Chester, grown grumpy from being wet, tired, and hungry. "But our friend the wyrm here is a magical creature herself, looking for a safe home, and the only way to reach it is by magical means."

"What a pity! I am sorry to hear it. No good will come of it, mark my words, but to each his own."

Nightshade was sympathetic to the leviathan's point of view, having had some very unpleasant experiences with magic, but they were no less determined to get the quest back on track if possible. "Can you help us get to shore? Not being water creatures, I fear we are out of our depths here in more ways than one."

"I don't see why not as long as no magic is involved. Can you climb upon my back?"

Celestyna managed to wind herself up the side of the leviathan but lost both her passengers in the process. She lowered her tail into the water so bear and mouse could grab hold and climb up using the wyrm's scales as footholds. They collapsed on the broad blue back and lay panting as the leviathan's tail ruddered, pushing them forward through the salty waters.

The leviathan swam, and as it swam, it sang a haunting tune unlike anything they'd ever heard before. No words as such, but the melody spoke of lost love and longing. Nightshade thought it the most beautiful song they'd ever heard.

After what seemed like an unconscionably long time (the Lamentable Lake being absurdly large), a beach appeared, sand shining white in the moonlight and ringed round with dark cliffs that loomed, blocking out the stars above. The leviathan was too much of a giant to approach closely into the shallows, so its passengers summoned their last reserve of strength to make a final swim.

"Good luck! And watch out for that magic. Tricky thing, magic!" their new friend called after them, diving back into deeper waters with such a splash that the wave it generated pushed wyrm and bear and mouse to shore, throwing them out onto the warm sand. They lay still as the quiet sounds of night pulsed around them in gentle lullaby, easing them into an exhausted sleep.

CHAPTER 15

A BEAUTIFUL TRANSFORMATION

THE WIZARD MERCIPOLIS AND Meera, a magical being of light, stood on the banks of a silvery-watered river staring at each other in surprise and a certain amount of consternation. Their band of companions, comprised of one visible and three invisible whirligigs, a flitter-flutter, wyrm, bear, mouse of unusual size, and the Keeylas had disappeared in a puff of oily black smoke that looked foul and smelt worse.

"Where did they go?" asked the wizard. "Did you send them to the heart of the Misshapen Mountains? Why didn't you send me with them?"

"I meant all of us to go," Meera answered. "Something has gone wrong with my magic. I could feel it as I cast the spell, but too late. There is a sour feeling within me like I've eaten something rotten."

"Look at your hands!"

While still gowned in the dress of orange feathers, Meera's glowing skin was slowly turning orange as well. Sharp spines poked out here and there, the quills of feathers forming a new shell around its body as Meera's eyes turned an alarming shade of red.

"It is the evil wyrm's curse!" Meera cried. "There must have been a bit left in me after all. I'm afraid for the others. Who knows what effect it may have had on my traveling spell?"

"But why weren't you and I transported?"

"We two are wielders of magic. Perhaps our powers prevented it? Oh, no!" A sharp beak broke through Meera's nose. Pushing at it with both hands and mumbling under its breath, it managed to push the birdy appendage back beneath the skin. "I don't wish to become that creature again. It was filled with spite and intent on nothing but causing pain and turmoil."

"Can't you control it?"

"Not in this form. It remembers what it was and seeks to be that thing again. Perhaps if I was *other*..." Meera paused and looked at the wizard.

Mercipolis broke out in a cold sweat. "You don't mean you want me to transform a being as powerful as you? I'd be frightened to death. What if I made a mistake or couldn't undo it? To be completely honest, I have been known to bumble my spells."

Meera placed one hand gently on the wizard's shoulder. "Anything would be better than becoming that evil creature again. Even the humblest of forms. I seek only to do good in this world. That is the most precious thing to me. More precious than this container I wear."

The wizard trembled at the idea of attempting to change such a magnificent being. His magic was of the most pedestrian kind, learned by rote in school and little improved upon until his recent discovery of the magic word and the power of a healthy sense of humor. But as he watched Meera straining and fighting against the shifting that was intent on taking over its body, a small seed of courage sprouted.

He pulled out his wand and tried to think of something beautiful, charming, and as unlike the evil squish creature as he could imagine. Bowing low and tapping the hem of Meera's gown, he whispered a tentative "flip-a-doodle," crossing the fingers on his other hand for luck.

A purple cloud appeared, and Meera vanished. Frantic, Mercipolis ran around in circles on the riverbank, waving his arms wildly on the verge of completely losing his head in terror that his spell had flopped.

"Calm down, calm down," a high, whirring voice called to him. "Here I am!"

Something glittering on a nearby tree branch caught his attention. It was a tiny hummingbird that looked like it was made of clear crystal. Its many facets caught the moonlight, spreading a rainbow of reflected color around it, and its wings beat furiously with a clinking, tinkling sound that was delightful to hear.

"How do I look?" it asked.

The wizard produced a small mirror from among the many useful objects contained in his voluminous pockets and held it up.

Meera preened this way and that. "How wonderful! You are a talented wizard, aren't you? I feel myself though I am not myself, and no stain of evil can there be or we would see it through this translucent form. How clever you are!"

Mercipolis blushed as deeply as he had ever in his whole life, turning his dark skin a rich plum that almost matched the color of his cloak. He was as astonished as anyone might be at the form his transformation had taken but as long as Meera was pleased, that was all that mattered to him.

"What should we do now?" he asked.

"Find our friends, of course, though that may be a challenge. Dark magic is unpredictable. There is no telling where they ended up, or even if they are all still together."

"I hope they are. It would be a lonely thing to find yourself in an unfamiliar place with no companions. A funny thought to have as I've been alone most of my life, but I find you can quickly get used to having others around. Though I've known them only a day, I miss them and hope they're safe."

The hummingbird fluttered down and flew lightly against the wizard's cheek in a kind of caress before hovering at a comfortable distance in front of his face. "Do not despair. I have a thought. My magic has less reach in this form, but I think if we work together, we might be able to assist them. I have a spell that will send those you think about something magical that will help them out of any danger they may be in."

"What does it send them?"

"That is the most delightful part of the spell! It provides them with whatever they need to escape their current situation. I've even known it to draw together those who are separated when they use the magical object, like a kind of magnetism. I think it would be most suitable in this situation since we have no way of knowing where or in what trouble our friends are, but you must help me to cast it."

Mercipolis was wracked with tremors again from head to toe. What extraordinary magic he'd been called upon to perform since he met up with the questing party! He had a low opinion of his skills, and not even his recent successes could convince him he was not a very poor partner for a miraculous being such as Meera. But he was mightily worried about Nightshade and Chester, Celestyna and Barty, and even the frivolous and flighty Walnut with his imaginary friends. (You will note he left the Keeylas off his list as he had not forgiven its impetuous and haughty ways.)

"I will do everything I can," he offered, and though his voice shook and his nerves jangled, he meant every word.

"Brave-hearted wizard!" the hummingbird cried approvingly. "Pop me under your hat!"

"Under my hat?"

"Yes, I will nest in your hair and whisper the words of the enchantment. You must think about each of our friends. Keep their images in your mind and at the right moment—you'll know when—wave your wand and say your magic word."

Though dubious (to say the least), Mercipolis followed these instructions to the letter. It was weird to feel the little crystal bird shifting around in his auburn curls under his pointed wizard's hat, but the spell it wove was much like a song, though interspersed with clicks and buzzes, hummingbird-style.

He concentrated very hard on recreating the faces of the friends he had so lately made, pretending he was drawing each of their portraits on a blank canvas in his mind. When he had finished, a painting of their familiar selves, grouped together as though they were reunited on their quest, stood clear in his imagination. He could only hope this illusory reunion would soon become reality.

Meera's song reached a crescendo. Mercipolis felt a thrill move through him from the tips of his hair down to the scraggly ends of his toenails. He waved his wand grandly and shouted "FLIP-A-DOODLE" with all his might.

"Did it work?" he asked, lifting his cap to allow the hummingbird to escape.

"I hope so. I think so. But I'm afraid it may be ages before we find out. Whatever they have been sent should help them, but if they are scattered far, it may be a long while before we are all together again."

"What must we do in the meantime?"

"Keep faith. Be patient. Stay alert and remain true."

Wizard and hummingbird wandered slowly down the riverbank, hopeful the magic of their spell would guide their steps and draw them near to their friends once again.

CHAPTER 16

FULL OF HOT AIR

THE KEEYLAS IS A legendary creature. A white cat of enormous size, its majestic head sports antlers as tall and widespread as many a small tree. Six legs and six paws blessed with eleven claws each (for it is polydactyl, which means having extra toes on each foot just for good measure). It also has three fluffy tails that when coiled together would make an extra-comfy bed for anyone brave or foolish enough to snuggle there.

Many the tale of close (and for some doomed creatures, too close) encounters with this ferocious beast are told and retold in den and hole, nest and warren. So renowned is the Keeylas for death and destruction, the mere sight of anything large and white in the distance will cause wise creatures to scatter and vanish.

Now imagine anywhere you went, everyone ran at sight of you and disappeared, even if you only meant to pass the time of day or exchange a pleasant word. What a lonely existence! Perhaps the Keeylas deserves it, you say, for being such a mean and rotten thing, but nothing starts out in this world so evil.

Once, the Keeylas was just a kitten. A ball of fluff that could fit in the palm of your hand, with the merest bumps upon its head to show where its crown of horns would one day grow. It mewled so softly and sweetly, the sorcerer who had conjured it could not help but simper and smile over the tiny thing. If you've never seen a seven-foot tall, grey-bearded and all-powerful sorcerer fussing over a wee nothing of a cat, you have missed out on a most comical sight.

Zeeylas was the sorcerer's name. He had graduated top of his class at magician's school and was one of those superior and obnoxious types who would have undoubtably led the crowd that bullied Mercipolis had they crossed paths. However, Zeeylas was far older (but I would argue, not wiser) than our friend the wizard.

Mercipolis was aware of him all the same, for Zeeylas had forged a reputation of his own for death and destruction. It is that way sometimes when people realize they have great power. Whereas you or I would try to help those less fortunate than ourselves, Zeeylas delighted in making their lives miserable. Why? If we knew the answer, my friend, many of the problems of the world could be solved.

One of the ways in which he liked to annoy people was by creating monsters that could do his terrorizing for him, as it is tiresome to have to go about terrorizing people yourself. He first created a crocodilian type thing with legs as long as a giraffe's and vermilion feathers sprouting from the end of its tail. It used its sharp teeth to snap and devour any that ventured into its swampy home. Being egotistical, Zeeylas named it after himself but changed the Z to a C for crocodile. Thus, the Ceeylas was born.

The Seeylas was a snaggle-toothed shark with wings instead of fins and feathers instead of scales. This last was a misstep on the sorcerer's part as it slowed the Seeylas significantly, the weight of wet feathers causing it to sink to the bottom of whatever body of water it swam in and thus severely limiting its scope for evil.

The Keeylas was his next invention. When it came to naming, he realized he had already used the C from cat, so he changed it to a K. We won't dwell on the conundrum this caused when the sorcerer created a kangaroo-like villain since our interest is in the Keeylas and not its maker or fellow monsters.

As I have said, the Keeylas started out as innocent as any creature born into this world can be, but the malign influence of its maker wormed its way into the heart of his creation. When he unleashed it upon the world, it knew no better than to scratch, gnash, and gore anyone it encountered. Word quickly spread throughout the forest of a white cat with sharp horns and sharper claws. Very soon, the Keeylas found that only the most unwary would even stop long enough for it to get within swiping reach.

Easy to imagine this was a lonely existence, yet the Keeylas had never known another and so did not really understand its plight. True, it was rather a novelty and almost pleasant to converse with the Great Sturgeon, the only creature un-afraid of it, but this was not sufficient to make it regret its existence.

But then, but then...

A questing party was met.

Transformations were undergone.

And a magnificent being of light appeared, so radiant and so good, that even the haughty and impetuous Keeylas was tamed like the mewling kitten it once was, and its heart, once forsaken of anything soft and caring, felt a twinge of some other life that might be lived.

What might have happened next, we will never know, as the quest companions were rudely flung apart. The Keeylas was not exempt from the corrupted traveling spell. It awoke in a desert of pink sand like finely ground glass that blew and bit in high, swirling winds. There were angular, leafless trees that blazed like torches spread out here and there, creating a choking smoke.

Everything was different from the cool, damp forest the Keeylas had known its entire life. Its environment changed in an instant, it stood in shock, closing its eyes against the grains of sand and burning haze. It twirled and flicked its three long tails in a futile attempt to wave away the irritants. The sand embedded itself in its lush fur and made walking painful. For the first time in its long life, it felt helpless and something else...

Alone.

It had never thought about it before, but even its short time amongst the quest-ing party had sparked a revolutionary idea: that one might travel and converse with and even help others. Being torn away so abruptly from its new companions hurt more than it should, or so the Keeylas thought.

"I don't need anyone else. I am the Keeylas!" it shouted to the wasteland.

"Are you?"

The Keeylas opened its eyes and looked around wildly. "Who's there?"

"Sparrow."

"Where are you?"

"Up here!"

The Keeylas rolled its eyes as far toward the sky as it could. There at the tip of one of its antlers, barely visible, was a small brown bird. Previously, the Keeylas would have been annoyed and offended at such effrontery and chased off the bird or even eaten it if it could. Now, it was a relief to not be so alone in the vastness of this place.

"Where are we?"

"It's called the Desolate Desert by some. By others, the Desert of Dreams. Depends upon your point of view, doesn't it? I say Dreams."

"Dreams? More like a nightmare. Don't these blowing sands bother you?"

"My feathers are tough and protect me. Every creature must learn to adapt to its home. You look ill-suited to live here. How have you survived so long?"

"I've only just arrived and wish to not be here a moment longer. Which direction should I travel to escape?"

"Escape the desert? It isn't possible. There's no end to the desert. The desert is the world."

"That's not true. I live in a lush forest, with green moss and ferns and a wide silver river. I always thought the forest was the whole world."

"You learn something new every day," marveled the sparrow. "You are the second strange thing I've seen today. Beyond that ninth burning tree to the left there is the weirdest gadget I've ever encountered. Would you like to see it?"

The Keeylas, having no better plan, assented. The walk was an endless misery to the big cat, but it was finally rewarded by the sight of what you and I would recognize instantly as a hot air balloon.

The Keeylas sniffed around the woven wicker basket, noticing it was lifting slightly off the ground, kept in place only by a taut rope tied to a burning tree. "I think it flies."

The sparrow chirped. "Get in then! You could soar like me high above this grit and smoke. The sky is a gorgeous blue over our heads."

A rash plan but the temptation of escaping the horrors of this place was irresistible. The Keeylas slunk into the basket—no easy task as its antlers snagged on the ropes holding the balloon to the basket and threatened more than once to pop the balloon itself. Once inside, it noticed a simple mechanism with up and down arrows. Throwing caution to the wind, it cast off the restraining rope and moved the switch to the up position.

Up and up and up it flew. And up and up and up and...

Nightshade was dreaming again. Such a jumble of things: a cloud that followed them around like a loyal puppy dog, the scarred and silent surface of the moon, dropping through a sky full of stars like a stone, a sea monster of unimaginable size. The mouse's whiskers twitched and their tail flicked. Paws paddled as though they were trying to swim. Then they felt the warm wetness of their mother's tongue grooming them between their ears...

Wait, it was too wet and dripping to be that. They opened one eye, only to have it flooded as water was poured from an outsized leaf over the mouse's head.

Spluttering and sputtering, Nightshade sat up on the sandy shore, shaking themselves to clear their ears of the obnoxious moisture. "What are you doing?"

"You've a right good coating o' salt," explained Chester. "Thought I'd help you clean up a bit. Celestyna and I found a fresh spring as nearby as nothing. Come along, come along!"

The bear rumbled off from the beach and disappeared into the narrow forest that stood at the foot of the high, dark cliffs looming overhead. The forest was not like the one the mouse was used to. In fact, it would more accurately be called a jungle. It was a tangle of vines and tropical trees that might have been impenetrable for any without the forward velocity of a determined and impetuous bear.

Nightshade followed the path carved by his friend to a burbling spring that leapt from the ground and formed a shallow pool. It was not deep enough to accommodate bathing but sufficient for cupping hands (or paws) to gather water to help rid themselves of the layer of salt from their soaking in the Lamentable Lake. When bear and mouse were as clean as they could get without a proper bath, they turned their attention to their wyrm friend.

Celestyna was suffering. The salt burned her scales and weighed down her delicate frills. Even though she despised water and getting wet, she lay patiently as Chester and Nightshade carried leaves full of water to her and tried their best to rinse away the corrosive stuff. The wyrm had grown very large and this was a most inefficient way to bathe, so they were relieved when a pleasant rain began to fall gently. The three friends welcomed the freshness and danced about, scrubbing themselves until the last of the salt was washed off.

As though aware they had no further need of it, the rain ceased and a warming sun broke through the trees and into the clearing around the spring. They basked in its warmth, fur and scales sizzling and drying. Once dry, more clouds appeared, drifting lazily but not threatening.

"Look how the clouds block the sun from burning us!" cried Nightshade. "How unusual the weather is here. Almost magical the way it knows what we need."

"We wish its magic extended to helping us get out of here," said Celestyna. "When we first awoke, we toured the beach and the perimeter of the trees all along these cliffs and found no way to escape this place without entering the Lake again." The wyrm shuddered at the thought, still disturbed by its forced sojourn in the salty waters.

"Perhaps I could climb up the cliff and look for help?" Nightshade suggested. Even in their enlarged form, their paws were nimble and well-suited for clinging to surfaces most of us would not attempt.

Chester shook his head as they stared upward at the formidable ascent. "I dunno, 'tis an awful long way up and an even longer way to fall should you slip. And who knows what awaits at the top there? Could be monsters or unfriendly folk like that Keeylas fella. You'd not want to meet that one on your own, would you?"

Of all the unusual and frankly unbelievable coincidences that had happened on their quest, the next was perhaps most surprising to all involved. No sooner had the bear invoked the name of the Keeylas than a red and yellow hot air balloon appeared floating along the top of the cliff.

"What do you think it is?" asked the wyrm.

"If I didn't know better," Chester replied, "I'd think it was an enormous white cat with antlers a-riding in a basket. But that would be a foolish thing indeed, so it can't be."

"But it is! Perhaps it can help us!" cried Nightshade. "Down here, down here!" The mouse ran along beneath the balloon, trying to attract the attention of its occupant.

"What are you doing?" Chester shouted in alarm. "That thing is no friend o' ours. It'd as like to eat as help us."

This observation gave the mouse pause, but it was a moot point as the balloon disappeared beyond the edge of the cliff and out of sight.

Nightshade sighed. "It didn't see us. I'll have to try and climb after all."

"Just as well," Chester comforted the mouse. "I'd not trust the beast as far as I could throw it—which granted is pretty far as I am unusual strong, but just the same."

"It is a pity though," Celestyna lamented. "We might have persuaded it to help us. It seemed quite tamed under Meera's spell."

"Nasty, ill-tempered brute like that? No chance! Some things are evil through and through without a redeeming bone in their body. Like the squish."

"But the squish was really Meera," Nightshade reminded the bear. "And even though its spell went awry, I refuse to believe such a luminous being is truly evil. Mother taught us no one is all good or all bad. There are many shades in between and many chances to make better choices."

Celestyna nodded. "She was wise. The world is more complicated than some would have us believe. We each contain the capacity to help and to hurt others. Most of us will do both in our lifetimes, sometimes without even realizing it."

Chester clutched at his head. "I am only a simple bear. This kind o' talk is awful complicated, but one thing I know—I can guarantee, given the chance, that Keeylas fella wouldn't lift one o' its many paws to help us out."

This emphatic assertion from the bear was punctuated by the end of a thick rope hitting him on the nose with a sharp THWACK.

"Ow! Who's throwing things?"

The trio looked skyward again to find an antlered head looking down at them. The distance was too far for its voice to carry, but the way the Keeylas was moving the rope and gesturing indicated it meant to pull them up. Nightshade grabbed the end of the rope and fashioned a kind of looped seat with their nimble paws.

"You're never gonna trust that monster, are ye?" Chester asked.

"We don't have a lot of options. I'll go first and if it doesn't eat me, you'll know it's safe!"

This hardly seemed the wisest plan, but before the bear could protest, Nightshade had secured the rope around themselves and was being pulled up. Wyrm and bear looked on in anxiety. The stone of the cliff face was sharp and cutting, and winds aloft threw the mouse around, but the Keeylas was strong and swift. Before long, Nightshade disappeared atop the cliff's edge.

More anxious moments followed until the rope appeared again and they saw Nightshade waving at them encouragingly.

"I'll go next," said Chester, "in case that beast gets a notion to eat one o' us after all."

The bear was not much bigger than Nightshade in the mouse's enlarged form, but somehow was much denser and heavier. Still, the Keeylas showed no strain as it gathered the rope to it. When bear and mouse were reunited at the top, it was Celestyna's turn.

"She's grown so much," observed the Keeylas. "I don't think I can lift her."

"We'll help," Nightshade asserted. They gathered extra rope from the hot air balloon's basket and threw down three looped lines instead of one.

Celestyna wriggled one loop around her middle, wound her tail around another, and gripped the third in her strong mouth. It took every bit of effort from those on top working together to bring her safely to the cliff's edge. There, they swapped stories of their various escapades which were full of such odd chances and coincidence.

It was Celestyna who expressed the amazement and gratitude of all. "How wondrous and strange our adventures! And most worthy of celebration is whatever we needed in our time of distress was delivered to us! There is magic at work here."

"Let's hope it ain't done yet," said Chester. "We've others to find, and a quest to complete. Let's go!"

CHAPTER 17

THE TREE OF WEEPING

B ARTY THE FLITTER-FLUTTER AND Walnut the whirligig were clinging near the top of a towering tree. A pine tree to be exact, with unusually sharp needles that poked them in indelicate and inconvenient places. Not to mention the pointy pinecones that rained down upon their heads whenever they shifted position.

"Where in the whole wide world are we, do you think?" Walnut asked Barty.

"I couldn't say as I have only recently ventured out into the wider world, but I don't believe this is the heart of the dragon. Meera said that was a deep hole in the ground and we are high in the air. And where are the others? Why were just us two sent here?"

"Us five, you mean. I'm sure you don't mean to be rude, but Leaf, Mold, and Sunshine are present also."

Barty looked about surreptitiously, unnerved to think he was surrounded, and indeed outnumbered, by whirligigs. Walnut seemed quite nice, but all in all, the flitter-flutter's first experiences outside of his cave had been startling at best and alarming at worst. He was beginning to regret leaving the cool, peaceful darkness of his former home, but one must make the best of any situation, including humoring one's companions.

"Of course. Us five. These needles are uncomfortable. Should we attempt to climb down?"

"I suppose," Walnut said, looking unusually thoughtful for that giddy creature, "though perhaps it would be faster to fly."

Barty couldn't help but giggle. "That was silly, wasn't it? I forgot we both have wings—er, that is, all five of us."

"No matter! I often forget all manner of things and it has done me no harm that I can remember, but perhaps it has and I've simply forgotten. At any rate, it seems simpler to fly than climb. Alley-oop and tally-ho and so forth and so on."

With that, the whirligig leapt from the tree, dropping like a stone until it remembered to unfold its batty wings. It coasted down to a green clearing which was ringed round with the most delightful lavender-colored mushrooms. They bowed their caps at this unexpected and unusual-looking visitor and murmured excitedly amongst themselves.

Walnut was soon joined by Barty, provoking even more delight from the circle of fungi. Their language, it must be said, was both obscure and angelic. Our friends bent low to the ground to listen and wished they could understand it.

"They are welcoming you," croaked a soft voice. It was a tiny olive-green toad that was in fact no bigger than a green olive crouched under one of the larger mushrooms. "They rejoice in novelty, and the two of you are very novel indeed."

"How wonderful!" Walnut cried, bowing to the toad and then wildly around in various directions in acknowledgement of this compliment. "Greetings! Greetings!"

"Who exactly are you?" the toad asked.

"I am a whirligig and my friend is a... I forget!"

"A flitter-flutter," Barty supplied.

The toad did not feel much enlightened by this information but was always content to meet any creature on its own terms and not be nastily inquisitive by requiring an exact definition of unfamiliar words. "That is *what* you are, I surmise, but *who* are you? Have you names?"

"Yes! Though only most recently. I am Walnut. I gave that name to myself!"

"Delightful" said the toad. "And you?"

"I am Bartholomew. Barty for short."

"Pleased to meet you both. I am Theodora."

"Theo for short?" Barty asked as he was fond of nicknames.

"Nothing for short. Please call me Theodora or nothing at all." This was not said in an unfriendly way, simply stated as fact. Walnut and Barty both nodded in comprehension, for you should always call others what they ask you to.

"And this is Sunshine, Leaf, and Mold," Walnut added with a flourish of one lizardy front foot.

The toad looked very hard at Walnut and at the air around the whirligig. It glanced over at Barty, who shook his head slightly and shrugged.

The toad grinned an amphibious grin. "I see. That is, I don't see, and it is an excellent thing to be skilled at camouflage as the woods can be a dangerous place. What brings you here?"

"Magic!" Barty and Walnut both exclaimed a bit more loudly than necessary in their enthusiasm.

"Magic, of course," the toad agreed. "What else would one expect in this enchanted place? To inquire more precisely, for what purpose have you ventured here?"

"We didn't exactly venture," Barty answered. "We were sent here by a powerful being of light named Meera. We were meant to end up at the heart of the dragon of the Misshapen Mountains, but I fear something has gone awry, for we have also lost our other companions."

"That is a pity. To have mislaid one's way and friends all at once is ill-fortune in truth. My heart bleeds for you both."

Walnut reassured the toad. "No need to worry. I'm sure it's only a temporary setback. You see, we are on a quest, and setbacks are to be expected in such a circumstance."

"A QUEST! A QUEST! NO NO NO NO NO!" The toad began to hop about wildly and the purple mushrooms shuddered. One particularly tall fellow toppled right over, losing his cap, while a horrid screeching sound arose from the fungi ring.

"I don't believe they like quests," Barty whispered to the whirligig.

"Quests are FORBIDDEN," roared the toad, puffing up its cheeks and inflating like a balloon. It was soon alarmingly larger than our friends and looked ready to pop as it chased them from the circle and out into the forest. "Get out and STAY OUT!"

Barty and Walnut half stumbled, half flew away from the angry toad as quickly as they could. They soon found themselves surrounded by a dense, misty fog that swirled around the tree trunks like a tub full of slippery eels. They tried to fly above to clearer air, but no matter how hard they struggled, the mist pinched and pulled at their wings as though it were a live thing, clawing them back down to the ground where they huddled together, bewildered at this sudden turn of events.

"I'm rather sorry," admitted Walnut, "that I mentioned the quest. The toad fellow was quite pleasant up 'til then."

"Well, you told no lie," Barty comforted the whirligig. "We are still on a quest and that must have come out sooner or later. Telling the truth is usually the best path. I wonder what they have against questing?"

"I can tell you." A gravelly voice spoke from the mist, and a squat brown beaver appeared. It sported an absurdly long pair of front teeth that gave it a charming lisp. "Last queshters shtomped all over the place in their shiny iron suits and monshtrous clip-clop horsies and trod on more creatures than shtars in the sky. Shince then, queshts have been outlawed!" Its paddle-like tail slapped the ground with a resounding SHLAP for emphasis.

"How terrible!" Barty cried, "but we are harmless, I assure you."

"Don't matter to me. I've a cozy den with the missus and our kits along the rivershide. We shtay out of foresht folks' business and they shtay out of ours so long as we don't chew down any of the Elder Trees. Take my advice, don't mess with an Elder Tree unlessh you want a good thrashing. They've wicked good aim with their branches."

Walnut looked around nervously, wondering how they were supposed to distinguish an Elder Tree from any other tree, but in whirligig fashion, was soon distracted by another thought. "There's a river nearby? Is it a silver river where a great sturgeon lives?"

"Oh, yesh. That old fellow. Often shwims by for a jaw. Nothing it likes better than to hear the sound of itsh own voice."

"Could you lead us to the river?" asked Barty. "It was on the riverbank we last saw our companions. Perhaps if we wander along it, we will find them again."

"Can't shtop you following me, I shuppose."

The beaver waddled off into the fog. So as not to lose their guide, Walnut hastily caught hold of its wide tail. Barty in turn held on to one of the whirligig's rattails, and the strange procession disappeared into the thick mist.

They did not travel quickly or in a straight line as their host stopped often to pick up fallen branches while muttering under its breath, "Nice shtick, that."

Its arms were soon so full, its waddling gait was severely impeded. It tripped often and had to stop to retrieve fallen cargo. The whirligig and flitter-flutter attempted to help but the beaver waved them off impatiently, perhaps suspicious these strangers meant to run off with its precious finds.

Barty and Walnut were no less impatient and much relieved when they heard rushing water ahead.

"The river!" Walnut cried, taking off in a flapping of batty wings that startled the beaver into dropping its entire bundle of sticks.

"What'sh this? What'sh this? What impetuoush balderdash!"

"Terribly sorry," Barty apologized. "My friend is an enthusiastic sort."

"There'sh enthusiasm and then there'sh foolishness. Let's hope we don't find your friend in a fix when we reach the rivershide!"

This worrisome observation made Barty wish to fly on ahead. Feeling it would be impolite to leave their host, however, he waited while the beaver retrieved every last stick and started its slow journey again. Before too long, they left the forest and fog behind and emerged onto a grassy riverbank. The silver waters pooled here against a magnificently built dam atop which stood another beaver.

"That'sh me missus. How de do, dear? Look at the nice shticks I found."

Mother Beaver beamed toothily in pride. "You're a right one and no mistake! Come, kiddies, and see what your da has brung us."

Three slightly smaller beavers, nearly-grown kits, emerged from out an earthy den and ran to their father, relieving him bit by bit of his burden while prattling excitedly.

"You'll never believe what we saw!" "A green bat!" "With three ratty tails!"

"You've met my friend then," said Barty, causing the three kits to stop their chatter and stare, finding the flitter-flutter no less of a curiosity than the whirligig that had passed them by. "Where did it go?"

"Thataway!" they cried in unison, pointing their paws across the river and upstream.

"Dearie," tsked Father Beaver. "Old Willow lives jusht round the bend there. Hope your friend remembers my warnings about the Elder Treesh. Of all the Elder Treesh, the Willow is the worsht. We give 'em a wide berth as their branches are unushual long of reach. Many an unwary soul's got tangled there."

Barty felt a thrill of premonition. Of all the creatures he had met since leaving his cave, Walnut was the most flighty and unwary. It seemed more than probable that if there was danger to blunder into, the whirligig would find a way to do it.

"Perhaps I'd better go and make sure there's not a problem. We do thank you most heartily for leading us back to the river."

Father Beaver waved a negligent webbed paw. "Was bound to return here shooner or later. A beaver too far from the river ish a poor thing indeed. That'sh why beavers never go a-queshting nor even want to. Home and family ish more important than gallivanting about t'foresht getting into who knows what trouble, or more likely causing it."

"But we are seeking a home for one of our companions. And my friends, though I've known them such a little time, are the closest thing to a family I've ever had. I've lived alone most of my life."

"Tch, tch," tutted Mother Beaver. "Poor thing! Pay no attention to my mister. You go find your friends and hold them close to you when you do," she added, coming down to shore and gathering her kits in her arms to demonstrate.

They snuggled together as their father also joined in. It warmed Barty's heart but made him melancholy also. As far as he knew, he was the only flitter-flutter in the world. He'd never have a family of his own like this.

All the more reason to reunite with my new friends, he reminded himself fiercely, blinking back tears.

"Goodbye, goodbye," the kits called, waving wildly as he took off into the air. When he glanced back again, the beavers were already busily weaving their new sticks into their woody home. Such a happy family.

Barty turned his face determinedly away and followed the course of the river around a swirling, swooping loop. He was astonished to find an immense willow tree growing half in and half out of the water. Its massive roots clung to the sloped bank, and its trunk tilted so far out over the river, it seemed a wonder it hadn't toppled in. Long graceful branches swept the entire width of the river like a curtain and danced in the shallows. Its sharp-pointed leaves were turning autumn yellows and golds, and many floated down to the river below, sailing away like miniature boats.

A muffled shouting and commotion near the center of the tree caught his attention. Remembering the beaver's warning, Barty approached cautiously and stopped at what he thought was a safe distance, but he hadn't counted on the immense length of the tree's branches. One whipped out in his direction and tangled around his wings, drawing him into the heart of the tree. He came face to face with Walnut who was similarly ensnared.

"Hello! I wondered when you'd show up. I tried to shout you a warning but guess you didn't notice. Not to worry—Leaf, Mold, and Sunshine are still free. I'm sure they'll rescue us."

Barty had considerably less confidence in the invisible whirligigs but felt it was not an opportune moment to engage in that particular discussion.

"What does it want with us?" he asked instead.

The most lugubrious (which simply means infinitely sad and dismal) voice imaginable answered. "Want? I want nothing. I expect nothing. I am nothing."

"That's the tree," Walnut explained, somewhat unnecessarily. "Not a very cheerful chap. Been going on like that ever since I crashed into it."

"The world is but a dream," the tree continued ponderously. "Life is an illusion. Weep, weep, for we are mere shadows and wraiths, and all is sorrow and despair followed by a slow, painful death."

Great beads of moisture rolled along the willow's bark, plopping heavily into the river below like tears.

"See what I mean?" said the whirligig. "Depressing, ain't it?"

And truly, Barty felt a darkness spread over him as he listened to the tree's low moans. Life had been undoubtedly complicated since he'd left his cave. Many catastrophes had befallen him and his companions, and they were apparently no nearer to accomplishing their goal. What was even the point of struggling and striving?

His body went limp as he ceased battling against the restraining branches. He watched as Walnut, that most irrepressible of spirits, gave up as well. Both creatures began to cry. It was soft at first but rose to such a wailing that a multitude of birds in the forest nearby took off as one giant flock, startled and alarmed by the horrendous racket.

Barty watched one of the willow's teardrops trickle down the branch that held him. It caught a beam of sunlight, gleaming like the last gasp of the dying star he had rescued from the cave. Though his mind was heavy, a few notes came to him. Star song. He hummed a bit, then sang the tune in his high, clear voice.

The tree stilled, as though listening. "What is this?" it asked.

"A star's lament. It was dying alone in the dark in a cave. I brought it out into the world where a being of light breathed new life into it and flung it back up to the heavens where it shines brightly now."

The willow wept harder than ever. "That is the most beautiful thing I ever heard!"

"There is sorrow in this world, yes, but also, beauty," Barty said, as much to remind himself as the tree. "Sometimes it is hard to see unless we pay close attention, but there is still magic to be found."

"Magic?" mumbled the tree. "What is magic?"

"Why, you are, for one! You are an Elder Tree, eldritch and long-lived. A thing of wonder."

The willow creaked and groaned as though it sought to straighten its crooked trunk and stand tall in pride. "Of wonder?" it breathed, loosening its hold on our friends.

Walnut and Barty wriggled out of their bonds, flying down to the riverbank, exhausted by their ordeal.

"You have gladdened my heart. I shall henceforth cease from weeping," the willow said, straightening its back and raising its branches in celebration.

Through the parted curtain a dark figure dressed in a purple cloak appeared. Round and round its head flashed the wings of a tiny crystal bird. Another reunion was close at hand.

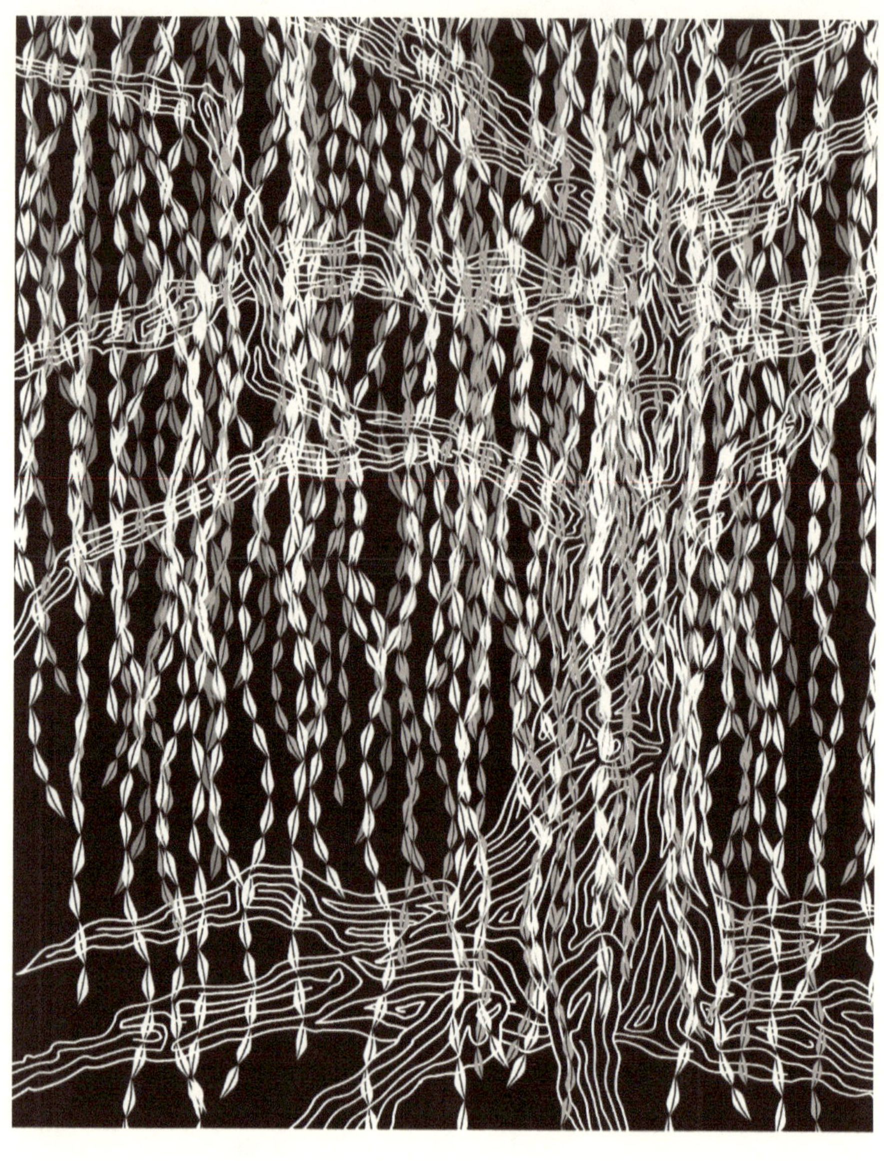

CHAPTER 18

A QUILT OF MEMORIES

"LOOK!" CRIED MERCIPOLIS AS he wandered the riverbank with Meera in the form of a lovely crystal hummingbird. "Isn't that some of our friends?"

Through the parted branches of the largest willow tree either had ever encountered, they could make out the figures of a pale flitter-flutter and the tabby-headed whirligig.

"It must be," Meera agreed. "I don't think there are another two like them anywhere in the world."

Barty and Walnut were equally excited to see the wizard approaching but wondered where he had acquired such an exquisite companion. The tiny bird flitted and zoomed, its wings moving so quickly, they flashed miniature rainbows onto the willow's leaves as it skirted through the pockets of sunshine under the tree's spreading branches.

"What a thing! What a thing!" exclaimed Walnut, instantly enamored of the delicate creature and repeating itself in excitement. "How do you do? How do you do?"

The hummingbird laughed a high, tinkling sound. "Why, we have met before, dear one! I am Meera, changed as you see by our most clever wizard friend."

"Oh—did he mean to?" the whirligig asked.

While there was no doubt the wizard's transformation skills had not always been predictable, it wasn't exactly polite to draw attention to the fact, but Mercipolis only nodded as he answered.

"Meera wished for another form, but this one is more a reflection of the beauty that cannot be suppressed in whichever state such a delightful being appears than my own poor magical skills."

"You are too modest," Meera scolded. "While it is not necessarily a bad thing to be humble, like any virtue, one can take it too far."

Mercipolis blushed under this loving criticism and the continued scrutiny of his friends. He decided it was time to change the subject. "We are relieved to find you two safe. We think Meera's traveling spell was corrupted by some part of the evil wyrm's influence that still resides within. Have you seen the others?"

"No, only some mushrooms and a very rude toad. It turns out, not everyone approves of questing," reported Walnut, still miffed that the nobility of a mission such as theirs should have been the cause of so much ire.

"There was a lovely family of beavers, though," Barty added. "So not everyone we've met has been unkind."

"True. Even this old tree let us go after taking us prisoner." Walnut slapped the trunk of the willow with one lizardy hand to emphasize its point.

A low voice, no longer quite as dismal as it once was, answered with a "Watch yourself there, youngster!"

Meera flew up and perched on one of the long willow branches, bowing in a most enchanting fashion. "Greetings, Willow! We are honored to be in the presence of one of the Elder Trees."

The tree returned the bow in its own stiff fashion. "And I am honored to meet one of the Ageless Ones. We whisper amongst ourselves of your kind, but you are the first I have ever seen. Are you the one that returned a star to the sky?"

"Yes."

"Such a gracious and generous thing to do." Slow tears rained down again from the tree. "It makes me weep to think of it."

"Uh-oh," said Walnut. "You've set it off again. Now we'll all be soaked through."

The hummingbird chimed in. "There is nothing wrong with letting go of tears, but like modesty, too much crying is not good for you. Instead, we should be happy to think of our star-friend twinkling above our heads at night. It is a joyous thing."

"We would be happier still if we could find the other members of our party. I wonder where they could be?" pondered the wizard. "They might be anywhere. What if they're not even in the forest anymore?"

"Perhaps I can help," said Old Willow. "I am the tallest thing around and can see very far. What am I looking for?"

"A large brown bear, impetuous in nature. An amethyst and emerald wyrm, something like an overgrown snake. And a grey mouse of unusual stature."

"An extraordinary crowd. They should be easy to spot given that none of them are small. I don't suppose they might be traveling with an antlered white creature who is also not inconsiderably sized?"

"The Keeylas!" Mercipolis cried. "Do you see it?"

"Yes, and these others you mention. They seem to be flying in a large basket with a ridiculous red and yellow ball attached. A charming folly! Really, the most outlandish thing I've ever seen, and I've seen more than you can imagine. Here they come. Look overhead."

The others rushed out from under the willow's canopy, waving and fluttering around to attract attention. It was indeed a remarkable sight with the four creatures stuffed uncomfortably into the hot air balloon's wicker basket. A portion of Celestyna's body and tail hung over the edge as testament that the fit was tight.

It was Nightshade who first spotted those below. They waved their paws in overjoyed greeting and alerted the others. The Keeylas guided the craft down to the ground, and the passengers, with some difficulty, extricated themselves from the basket, tumbling out onto the riverbank.

Many confused but relieved greetings and explanations followed as each reported on their adventures since last they'd met. Only the Keeylas hung back, unsure of its reception since it must be acknowledged it had tried to eat and/or attack more than one of the party.

Chester, being of both an impulsive and forgiving nature, however, gave full credit where credit was due to the Keeylas for its timely rescue efforts on the cliff.

And even Celestyna, who had been most cruelly knocked about by the Keeylas in the past, was willing to give the beast the benefit of the doubt. The others followed her lead, for few creatures are beyond redemption if they resolve to reform and make sincere amends.

When all stories had been exchanged and much wonderment expressed at the strangeness of their experiences, Mercipolis magicked up a picnic of everyone's favorite foods since many had gone too long without sustenance. While they ate, they discussed what steps to take next since Meera's plan to transfer them instantly to the heart of the Misshapen Mountains had gone so spectacularly awry.

"I suppose we must walk," said Nightshade. "The basket was barely big enough to fit us and would not accommodate any others."

"At least three of us could fly on our own," Meera pointed out, "and Mercipolis could transform into a bird as well."

"Is it far, though?" asked Barty. "I've never flown such great distances before and I'm not sure I could make it."

"Very far. It's why I had hoped to use a traveling spell, but I am afraid to try again."

"I think," Mercipolis volunteered, "I mean, I'm not sure, mind, but I might be able to make the balloon large enough to fit us all. Enlargement and shrinking spells are among the first we learned in school. I could try at any rate."

With much encouragement, the wizard retrieved his wand from his pocket. Closing his eyes tightly, he waved it in the general direction of the hot air balloon while muttering the magic word under his breath. Unfortunately, Walnut chose that moment to flit by and was turned into a Keeylas-sized whirligig. This mix-up was soon sorted, however, and on the wizard's second try, the flying craft was tripled in size. There was now plenty of room for every member of the party.

"I wish I could go with you," mourned the willow. "It sounds a most exciting time, and nothing much ever happens here as every creature is afraid of me."

"Perhaps if you stopped capturing them, they might learn to trust you," Barty suggested. "Then you would have friends to keep you company."

"Do you think so? That would be lovely. Even an old tree like me can be taught a thing or two it seems. Before you go, I will give you a present in gratitude."

The willow shed one of its longest, most sweeping branches. "Take this with you. It is as strong as any rope and has magical properties."

"Like what?" asked Chester, helping the wizard gather the branch into a tight coil.

"You shall see, you shall see," the tree teased with a low chuckling. "When most you have need, you shall see."

The questing party packed up the leftover food to take with them, not wanting to waste any of the mouth-watering delicacies. Then they packed themselves into the wicker basket, where they fit much more comfortably now it was so enormous, and the Keeylas worked the mechanism to send the balloon skyward.

If it had been a sight before, now it was a spectacle. Many a creature of the forest, even the busy beaver family, stopped whatever they were doing to goggle at the gigantic conveyance filled with the weirdest collection of passengers passing overhead. And Old Willow waved its branches in the air in blessing as long as the balloon was still in sight and even long after.

The quest companions admired the magnificent view from their high perch in the hot air balloon. The land below them was laid out like a patchwork quilt, one full of memories, good and ill.

Walnut and Barty waved at Old Willow and the beaver family on their dam as they faded away into the distance. Their side quest had not been as exotic or dangerous as a trip to the moon or being stranded in a desert or underwater, but they were relieved to be reunited with their friends all the same.

Mercipolis spotted the Dark Woods, full of the spit and hiss of magic, where he had practiced his craft alone so long. He was only now realizing how lonely he'd been. The silver river twisted like a serpent through the landscape. The wizard could make out the hulking shadow of the Great Sturgeon, lazing near the entrance to the cave where the star had sung its treacherous lament.

Not far away was the enormous pile of rocks and trees that made up the squish's nest where he and Barty had been briefly detained. Hard to imagine that terrifying avian creature who had held them captive had become the glittering hummingbird resting lightly on the tip of his wizard's hat.

Chester recognized the kind woman's cottage at the heart of the forest, and his own heart was warmed by the memory of the generosity and welcome he had enjoyed there once upon a time. The woods nearby were charred and smoking, laid waste by the ravenous inferno that had threatened the lives of so many. He shuddered to remember the panicked flight through the flames and his burning paws but beamed with pride at the memory of saving his companions.

Nightshade thought of the wild ride when they first met Chester, the Sibyl who warned of danger, and of the noble stag and his family who had guided them to safety through the fire. The happy celebration on the other side of the river had been cut short by the eagle owl Billibo, who had taken the mouse on their first, but alas, not their last, airborne voyage. How Mother would have laughed and marveled to know her very own Nightshade would have so many aerial adventures.

Far away, the endless waters of the Lamentable Lake twinkled in the sunshine. Celestyna caught sight of the leviathan, breaching the surface with a splash so mighty it would have easily soaked their basket if they had been overhead. She thought of the little green jellyfish who had helped her and was humbled again to think of how many strangers had come to her aid on this journey to find her new home.

The Keeylas eyed the high cliffs where it had made the momentous decision to throw its lot in with the quest and help those stranded on the beach below. It had never felt a part of anything in its life and it liked the feeling more than it would admit to its companions, being still a proud and haughty creature by long habit.

It was dazzling watching the landscapes passing below them. They were so busy looking down, they missed the first glimpse of the Misshapen Mountains, an awe-inspiring range that indeed followed the shape of the spine of a dragon rising from the low tip of its tail to the enormous height of the ribs and down again to where a gigantic boulder resembled nothing so much as a dragon's skull.

Meera called their attention to it. "Look, there in the center. It is the heart of the dragon. A cavern so deep that none can measure it."

They saw what the hummingbird meant as they came closer. In between two of the peaks that made up the ribs of the dragon was what looked like a modest black dot from afar but was revealed to be a hole in the ground as they neared. The Keeylas guided the balloon down to a plateau nearby and everyone disembarked to get a closer look. The entrance was small, certainly not big enough for the larger creatures in their party.

"How did that jingle-jangle go?" Chester asked the wizard.

"The prophecy? Harvest zingery seeds from a mouth that never closes and plant them farther beneath the surface than any creature can dig. Water them with the fresh tears of an animal that has never existed and sing to them the song of a dying star. A vine beyond measure will grow from the seeds and unfurl itself into the sky, ready for climbing beyond the clouds, but it has thorns that drip poison and hungry mites that will chew your nose off if you're not careful."

"Don't sound very pleasant," the bear observed.

Many of the party privately agreed but held their tongues as they stared down into the inky blackness.

"I know the song of the dying star," said Barty, "and I will fit in the hole, so I should go."

Walnut sniffed its catty nose and flapped its batty wings while its lizardy scales shone in the sunshine and its five ratty tails swished erratically. "Too bad we don't have one of those animals that never existed though. What are we gonna do about that?"

Everyone stared at the whirligig. Meera fluttered over, hovering in front of the creature's face. "But, my dear, you are just such a thing. Before the wizard created you, no such animal ever existed in all of history. You are unique!"

"You are forgetting about Leaf, Mold, and Sunshine."

"Of course, of course," Meera agreed soothingly. "Why don't you all go? It isn't safe to go alone into the unknown. The more the better."

"I'm not sure any of us can cry on command though."

"It shouldn't be too hard. Think of something either extraordinarily sad or thrillingly joyful and I think your tears will come. I have faith in you."

Walnut's eyes got big and dark. It was a flighty, frivolous thing that had not been called upon to do anything truly heroic in its brief life, though it had helped out, more by accident than design, from time to time. The whirligig suddenly felt very important.

"We'll do it, won't we?" it said, glancing to either side of it at its invisible companions. "They agree."

"I'm glad," said Barty, for he had not relished the idea of venturing into the cavern by himself. Even though he was used to dark places, who knew what they might encounter in the deep.

Once the decision of who would go had been made, discussion turned to how they might best travel.

"We'll fly, of course," said Walnut.

"But it might be a long way down," Nightshade said, "and your wings could get tired."

"We could lower them on the willow branch part of the way," Celestyna suggested. "That way they could save their strength for the end."

Everyone saw the sense in this strategy. The willow branch was retrieved from one of the wizard's magically voluminous pockets and secured to a sturdy rock for safety. Chester and the Keeylas, being the two strongest of the party that remained above, slowly lowered the flitter-flutter and whirligig into the hole.

They discovered what Old Willow had meant about its magical properties. No matter how much of the branch unwound from their hands, there was still plenty more waiting.

"I believe it might go all the way!" the wizard exclaimed. "This is such useful magic. I must return to the willow one day and learn more about it."

"But how will we know when they get there?" asked Chester, for he was already feeling the rough friction of the branch rubbing against his paws.

The Keeylas scoffed. "It'll go slack, won't it. Common sense."

The bear bristled at the creature's dismissive tone but before he could think of a properly scathing reply, the branch stopped moving. It jiggled a bit then jerked violently before suddenly retracting from the hole as though on a spring windup mechanism.

Chester and the Keeylas sprawled on their backs from the sudden release of tension. The others gathered round. The end of the branch was bright red with what looked and smelt like blood. They peered down the hole with the greatest possible anxiety. What in the world had happened to their friends?

CHAPTER 19

THE CHOSEN ONE

*H*OW *VERY DARK IT IS!*

This was the shared thought of Barty and Walnut as they were lowered into the deep hole at the heart of the dragon, though neither spoke it aloud, not wanting to alarm the other. It was already alarming enough to be swinging from a willow branch over a seemingly bottomless abyss without making much of the fact they could not even see where they were going.

Barty removed his smoky glasses but found even his dark-adapted eyes could make out nothing around them. The descent was gentle enough, well-controlled by the combined strength of Chester and the Keeylas on the other end of the rope, but with no visual cues to mark their progress, they quickly became disoriented.

"Do you think we're almost there?" asked Walnut.

"I imagine it is quite a distance," Barty replied. "We'll have to be patient. Perhaps we could tell stories to pass the time."

"Oh, I know a good one! A crow walks into a fox's den and is eaten up, *snippity snap snip snap!*"

"That's not a very long tale and it has an unfortunate ending."

"Don't all tails have unfortunate endings? Mine do," Walnut retorted, catching its own ratty ones in lizardy fingers and exploring their length. "They get caught in things and drag on the ground and are great nuisances. I'd as soon not have any."

Every so often in life, one may find oneself in the position of having said something one very soon regrets. This was the case for the whirligig as one of its tails became tangled in the branch they were traveling on. The willow twisted round the appendage in such a way as to cause agonizing pain. Panicked, Walnut used its catty teeth to try and chew through the branch but in the confusion of darkness, managed to chomp through its own tail instead.

Released from its entanglement, Walnut plummeted toward the ground, knocking the unlucky Barty off the branch in the process. While it had been disconcerting to be descending at a controlled speed through inky blackness, that was nothing compared to plunging wildly toward an uncertain fate.

The flitter-flutter's long but relatively uneventful life flashed before his eyes while the whirligig spent the time regretting it had ever spoken so rudely about its tails. After all, they were a part of Walnut just like its wings—

"WE CAN FLY!" Walnut remembered.

"So we can!" cried Barty.

Both had forgotten momentarily they could propel themselves quite nicely through the air without outside aid. The only problem was their complete confusion about which way to fly. Thrashing this way and that in the dark, they promptly ran into one another, ramming their heads so hard together, they were stunned into unconsciousness and resumed their somersaulting tumble downward.

As fortune would have it, however, the cavern's bottom (for it did in fact have one) was lined with the most extraordinary fungi. Pillowy soft and saucer-shaped, the mushrooms glowed so extravagantly with a golden light that they lit up the darkness like a beam of sunlight.

Barty and Walnut landed on the spongy mushrooms with a muffled thud, shocking them both awake, a little bruised and sore but relieved not to be splattered across the cavern floor.

"Are you okay?" the flitter-flutter asked the whirligig as he rose to his feet shakily. "Your poor tail!"

"Not to worry. I have four left which seems more than sufficient. It does sting a bit, though whatever this stuff is seems to calm it," Walnut added, rubbing the offending stub against the glowing fungi.

Before their eyes, the wound closed up as though it had never been.

"Must be magic!" the whirligig exclaimed. "Maybe it will soothe all my aches and pains."

Walnut slid around on the mushrooms with wild abandon. By the time the whirligig was done, it was glowing as brightly as the fungi. The sight was so comical, Barty couldn't help but burst out in nervous laughter.

"Who goes there?" a raspy voice called out.

A crowd of large, furry rodent-like creatures had appeared and were spilling out into the cavern from a tunnel. They each sported a pair of iridescent wings not unlike a dragonfly's that swished along the ground behind them. As they came closer, one by one they bowed their heads and whispers arose:

"The Chosen One... the Chosen One... the Chosen One..."

"What do you think they mean?" asked Barty.

"Not the slightest idea," Walnut admitted.

The creature nearest them came forward. "They speak! Teach us of your wisdom, Chosen One!"

Whirligig and flitter-flutter exchanged a bewildered glance, even looking behind them to make sure there was no one else around that could be the target of this unexpected exhortation.

"Who are you?" Walnut ventured.

There was consternation and murmuring among those gathered.

The spokes-creature responded. "Ah, this is a test of some sort no doubt. We are the womblybats, as you must know, Chosen One. Your arrival has been prophesized in the scroll that records the words of the revered Womble, founder of our clan in the long ago. They wrote of the coming of a luminous being who would lead us from this accursed place into the far above where we might roam free. And yea, you have appeared to us in all your glory!"

Barty pulled his friend aside to whisper in its ear. "They think you are this being of light because you are glowing from the mushrooms."

"I should explain then."

"I don't know. There are so many of them and only two of us. We can't be sure how they might react if they find out we are only rather ordinary."

"You mean we should lie?" Walnut said, aghast at the idea, being in possession of an honest and open spirit.

"Not exactly, but maybe play along a bit until we find out if they are friendly or not. They have unusually sharp-looking teeth."

"Is anything wrong?" asked the womblybat.

"Better let me do the talking," Barty mumbled under his breath, not at all confident in Walnut's ability to speak sensibly in this unprecedented situation, or indeed, any situation.

He stepped forward to address the crowd. "I am Bartholomew, the Chosen One's speaker. Who is it that speaks for you?"

The womblybat bowed low again. "I am Pruebelle, leader of this clan."

"Greetings, Pruebelle. We—that is, the Chosen One has come on a mission to plant some special seeds. From this, a mighty vine will grow up and out of this place."

"And we can climb this to the above?"

"Perhaps," Barty hedged, remembering the dire warnings of poisonous thorns and fearsome insects. "But you have wings, did you never try flying up and out?"

"Our wings are so delicate, and we are so pleasantly plump that we cannot fly very high or very far. Besides, we have been waiting for the Chosen One to rescue us as was foretold. We would not be so bold or insolent as to attempt to save ourselves."

This struck Barty as a poor and passive way of living, but then he remembered he had never thought to leave his cave until Mercipolis had come calling. "We shall plant our seeds and see what comes of it. If you cannot escape that way, we will try and find some other path out for you. Won't we, Chosen One?"

Walnut stared at him blankly until Barty poked the whirligig furtively in the side. "Oh, yes, yes. Good idea. We shall plant the seeds. The future has been foretold. It shall be so and so it shall be. The Chosen One has spoken!"

This speech might have been even more impressive had Walnut not tripped over its feet and fallen flat on its face, but the wombleybats seemed not to mind. They cheered enthusiastically and fluttered their wings in approval.

Barty unwrapped the zingery seeds. They were glowing as brightly as when he had harvested them and felt warm to the touch with an almost electric thrum. The whirligig and crowd of womblybats looked on with interest.

"Where should we plant them?" asked Walnut.

Barty glanced around his feet. "I assume they need some kind of soil but there's mostly rocks here. What are these mushrooms growing in?"

Walnut used its long lizard toes to pick the shimmering fungi until a small circle was cleared. Beneath was a rich, loamy dirt, moist and pungent. Barty dug small holes, dropping a seed gently in each and patting the earth back into place.

"Now we need your tears, Walnut, er, Chosen One."

"Don't know that I can cry on demand. In fact, I can't remember ever crying. Maybe we'd better have Sunshine, Leaf, or Mold give it a try?"

This was a bit of a stumper for Barty. He didn't want to upset the whirligig, but the fact was, he did not believe in Walnut's invisible companions any more than you might believe in ghosts (unless you do, of course—there is nothing wrong with that). He was relieved when Pruebelle intervened with a suggestion.

"We womblybats are accomplished criers. We think it is important to let out strong emotions at least once a day so we don't burst."

"Metaphorically, you mean," Barty said, to clarify.

"Oh, no, we explode literally. It's terribly messy and such a waste. Used to happen a lot until we started telling a daily story. Our tales are renowned as being the saddest you will ever hear. If we can't make you cry, you must be made of stone. Buckle, you are our most talented storyteller. Come and amaze us!"

A small womblybat with silver and black fur wombled out from the crowd. The others quickly sat back on their haunches, forming concentric circles, and perked up their ears in rapt attention, for there are few things a womblybat likes better than a truly heart-wrenching tale.

Buckle closed his eyes and swayed from side to side as though in a trance. His voice was soft but carried clearly in the confines of the cave, and his wings fluttered delicately from time to time with a lovely rustling, a musical accompaniment to his story, which went a little something like this...

CHAPTER 20

A TENDER KISS

ONCE UPON A TIME there was a gentle, wee maiden named Hazel who dwelt in the woods. Her legs and arms were slim lichen-covered twigs, her body a fat pinecone, and a shining brown acorn served as her head. Her hair was dried grass that shone gold in sunlight, and she wore a shimmering gown woven from spidersilk. Her voice was as beautiful and lilting as the sweetest linnet song. Fortunate indeed felt all who crossed paths with such a marvelous person as her nature was as good-natured as her words and thoughts.

Hazel was wed to a red squirrel, named Wildcap for the extravagant tufts of red hair that sprouted from his ears. Their marriage ceremony was a sight to behold with creatures both magical and wild standing by and cheering as a stately magpie officiated most solemnly. Vows of true and eternal love and caring were professed. Blessings rained down upon the couple's heads from a sea of well-wishers. The wedding cake was made of suet and honey and the many good luck toasts were celebrated with acorn cups full of nectar collected from only the tastiest flowers.

Now, Hazel had fallen in love with the squirrel's dashing good looks and charm but unfortunately, Wildcap proved to be a selfish fellow who rarely thought about anyone but himself. Many were the sacrifices Hazel made so that her husband should be comfortable, but she did not realize this was not usual in the best marriages as she had never experienced any but her own. Her mild temperament and eagerness to please were taken advantage of by the squirrel without a second thought since he felt he was entitled to all the pleasures of living without any of the hardships.

A mismatched pair, you may be thinking, but nevertheless, they got along happily enough for a few years until an unusually savage winter came upon them. Rough were the winds that blew and harsh the driving snows that piled up in drifts so high that Wildcap had trouble uncovering his carefully stored stashes of nuts and acorns that had been collected for him by his wife. He grew jealous of Hazel, who by nature of the unique makeup of her body needed no food to survive and never felt the cold.

"It is all very well for you," he grumbled one day, fed up with her lack of suffering, "to watch me fade away to a mere nothing for want of food or freeze to death for want of warmth. I have always suspected you cared nothing about me."

Hazel was cut to the quick at any implication she did not love Wildcap most ardently and wish only for his happiness. "Husband dearest, take my gown and wrap it round your throat to keep it warm," she replied, disrobing and winding the warm spidersilk around her spouse's neck.

"That is all very well," he complained, "but the rest of me is as frigid as an icicle."

"Husband dearest, take my hair to build a fire to keep you warm." She pulled out every last strand and used a piece of flint to spark a flame in her golden tresses.

"That is all very well," Wildcap griped, "but the fire will soon go out."

"Husband dearest, take my limbs to keep it lit." Hazel pulled off her arms and legs and added them to the fire.

"That is all very well," he whined, "but your twigs are so small. Look how quickly they burn. What will I do when they are used up?"

"Husband dearest, take the scales from my body for a woodpile to draw from."

The selfish squirrel pulled one scale after another from his wife's pinecone to create a little hoard of firewood.

Soon all that was left of the lovely Hazel was her beautiful, brown acorn head on the ground staring sadly at the bonfire provided by her own body. "Are you content now, dear husband?"

"I am warmer," he was forced to admit, "but so very, very hungry."

A hush fell over the forest with no sound but the crackling of the fire to break it.

Finally, Hazel spoke again, but so quietly, the squirrel could hardly hear her lovely voice. "Husband, dearest, come near."

Wildcap bent down close to his wife's face. With a look of tenderest pity and love, Hazel bestowed a kiss of such sweetness and understanding upon his brow that you might think even the hardhearted squirrel would have been moved. But he only thought how very delicious she smelled.

"Go on," she urged, though swift tears trailed down her face—

CHAPTER 21

THE SPROUTING OF SEEDS

"H E NEVER ATE HER head!?" Walnut interrupted, aghast at this tale of selfishness and cruelty.

Buckle nodded sadly. "He cracked it open and sucked out the insides."

"Poor Hazel!" the whirligig exclaimed, laying its lizard hands across its heart, which was wrung to think of such an extraordinary creature sacrificing all for such an unappreciative recipient. "This Wildcap is a complete villain—the most dastardly rogue I ever heard tell of!"

Tears sprang to Walnut's eyes. Whether they were tears of sorrow or fury or some of both, tears they were, and they fell plentifully upon the buried seeds.

Now it was Barty's turn to play his part. He opened his mouth and out poured the dying star's lament. The womblybats were fascinated by the uncanny tune and hummed along, clicking their wings in time. Soon the entire cavern was filled with the eerie music.

"Look there," said Walnut, pointing toward the dampened soil.

A small sprig of green was pushing up, shedding its earthy grave. The chorus continued to sing.

The sprout seemed to take energy from the sound, furling and unfurling curly tendrils. Soon the other seeds joined in, five shoots in all, that wound about one another, forming one stout stem which thrust itself up toward the roof so far above. As it grew, it thickened and twisted forming a trunk-like structure not unlike a mighty tree.

Hundreds of thorns as long as your arm pushed their way out from the growing vine. Balanced on the end of each one was a shining pearl of an egg within which a red squirming thing could be seen.

"Those must be the mites," said Walnut. "I wonder how long before they hatch?"

"Perhaps rather than waiting around to find out, we should start to climb," Barty replied.

A sensible suggestion, but just then the tips of the thorns began to ooze an ugly mustard yellow liquid that dropped and sizzled on the floor of the cavern.

The flitter-flutter motioned everyone back. "Careful! It's poison!"

Pruebelle examined the scene from a safe distance. "Perhaps we can avoid it if we stay toward the center of the vine and away from the ends of the thorns. Womblybat fur is thick and may also provide us some protection. The two of you are stronger flyers than we are. You needn't use the vine at all."

Barty considered. "That might work except I think we have a more immediate problem!"

He pointed a shaking finger at the eggs. They were splitting open and red mites as big as your hand were emerging. They began a skittering, scurrying, scampering rush down the vine toward the cavern floor.

Walnut, Barty, and the womble of womblybats stared in dismay at the army that was forming on the vine and swarming down to meet them. In a panic, all retreated into the tunnel from which the womble had first emerged with the whirligig and flitter-flutter bringing up the rear.

Barty looked around frantically. He noticed one of the stalactites near the entrance of the tunnel was very narrow at the top. He started to fly into it as hard as he could. Many a creature would have thought Barty had lost his senses from panic, but Walnut only thought it looked like great fun and joined him in pounding on the rock until it started to shudder and sway.

"Watch out below!" Barty cried as the stalactite gave way with a roar and rush of stone.

Debris filled the tunnel. When the dust settled, the entrance was completely sealed, thwarting the oncoming mite army but also cutting off access to the vine.

"This is a terrible predicament," Pruebelle lamented. "If we can't reach the vine, we'll never escape this place."

"Are you sure there isn't any other way out?" asked Barty. "Have you explored all the tunnels?"

"All but the haunted one."

"Haunted? By what?"

"We don't know and don't care to find out. It makes the most horrid sounds if we get anywhere near, and none of us are foolhardy enough to investigate. There are plenty of other tunnels after all."

Barty exchanged a glance with the whirligig before volunteering their services. "We'll go and take a look. If there's even a chance of getting out, we owe it to you to try."

"Very well. Far be it from me to question the Chosen One's actions. But don't say I didn't warn you if you meet with a horrible fate!" Pruebelle said, none-too-comfortingly. "Come this way."

They followed the womblybat down one winding corridor after another. Each looked much alike to them but Pruebelle wombled forward, turning confidently left or right whenever she met a fork in the path. Barty and Walnut were getting turned around and weary of the twisting journey when Pruebelle stopped abruptly at a tunnel entrance that looked no different than any of the others they had passed.

"The haunted cave!" she announced dramatically.

Walnut peered into the darkness. "Don't look haunted."

"It's not the sights, it's the sounds. Listen."

They did and heard an eerie huffing and grunting noise. It was off-putting, to say the least, and they did not wonder at the reluctance of the womblybats to investigate. They were feeling reluctant themselves, if truth be told, but having raised the hopes of the womble, our friends felt responsible for exploring any possibility of escape.

"Would you hold my hand?" Walnut asked shyly.

"If you like," Barty replied, secretly pleased to have this concrete piece of moral support himself.

Rather than fly, they crept forward slowly, thinking maybe they could sneak up on whatever was in the tunnel and do some spying without being noticed. The glowing mushrooms grew thick here, so their way was well-lit at least.

The snorting and puffing grew ever louder and gradually could be discerned as mumbling and sighing, perhaps even grumbling and crying.

"Sounds sad," Barty whispered to the whirligig.

Walnut was nothing if not tender-hearted and did not like to think of any creature, even a monstrous or ghostly one, being melancholy. "We must cheer it up!" it cried, taking flight and disappearing down the tunnel.

No longer surprised at his friend's impulsiveness, but slightly chagrined nonetheless, Barty reluctantly followed, wondering if this was his last few minutes among the living and what it would be like to be a ghost.

He followed the whirligig until he reached a den of sorts, lined with pine straw and rotting leaves and littered with eggshells and small bones—though not much smaller than he thought his own bones might be, so this was not exactly consoling.

Walnut was in earnest conversation with a silver-and-black-furred individual who sported a white face with distinguished black stripes, long snout, and in-quisitive expression. Neither Walnut nor Barty had encountered a badger before but that is what it was. And while badgers can be fierce and even ill-tempered creatures, this one looked more intrigued than angry.

"Ah, another one! Two visitors in one day! This is a notable date and no mistake!" The badger wrung its front paws together as though in satisfaction at this development. "It gets lonely here."

"Aren't there others with you?" Barty asked.

"Other badgers? There's plenty in the forest, but we're a quarrelsome lot. I've fallen out with most of them one way and another. I've heard other creatures in these caves, but none have ever come to visit me before."

"You must mean the womblybats," said Barty.

"Womblybats? Extraordinary! Never heard the like. Do they also have dens down here?"

"Yes, but they are trapped, as there is no way out."

"No way out? Nonsense! I come and go all the time!"

CHAPTER 22

A BITTER BATTLE

MEANWHILE, ON THE SURFACE, a concerned group was gathered round the dark hole down which Barty and Walnut had been lowered. The sudden retraction of the red-tinged willow rope filled their hearts with fear and trepidation.

"It's blood," confirmed Nightshade, sniffing at the distinctive bittersweet scent on the branch. "What do you think it means?"

Chester raised up on his haunches, waving his mighty paws wildly through the air. "Doom and despair! Calamity! Tragedy and misfortune. Misery and heartbreak. In short, disaster!"

"Very like," agreed the Keeylas. "Imagine you'll not see those two again," it added with somewhat too much satisfaction in its growling voice. It seemed the monstrous cat was not so quick to lose the malicious impulses of a lifetime.

"Let's not leap to any conclusions on such scanty evidence," Mercipolis chided. "It isn't terribly much blood. Perhaps just a scratch from the rough bark of the willow. And maybe they decided they were close enough to the bottom to fly the rest of the way down and let go of the rope voluntarily."

"We would like to think so," said Celestyna. "If any one of this party should come to harm from our quest, we could never forgive ourself for involving you." Tears filled the wyrm's eyes and trickled down her elegant scales.

The crystal hummingbird flew close and hovered near. "Do not cry, dearest. The wizard has the right of it. Speculation is not proof. I will fly down myself and investigate."

Mercipolis protested. "We don't know what you may find, and your magic is not as potent in your current state. Let me turn you into something mightier or turn myself so I may accompany you."

"But into what? If either of us are big and strong, we won't fit into the hole."

The wizard pondered. "There must be something that is both small and powerful. Give me a minute to think of it." He wandered away deep in contemplation.

"Listen," whispered Nightshade, head bent toward the opening. "I think I hear something. Is it a ghost? Perhaps there is a haunted soul trapped down there and it devours all who enter its lair." (It must be noted that Nightshade's mother had been a fan of telling terrifying tales to her offspring but had perhaps recounted a few too many.)

Chester joined the mouse. "Sounds more like a bunch o' voices chanting 'THE CROWS ARE RUM' which is certainly true. Crows are about the rummest birds you can imagine. I remember once—"

"The crows are rum," the Keeylas scoffed. "Have you no brains at all? They are clearly yelling 'TEN TOES ARE DUMB' which is certainly true. Superior creatures such as myself have many more."

"We believe you're both mistaken," Celestyna corrected them gently, for wyrms have a keen sense of hearing. "They are chanting 'THE CHOSEN ONE.'"

"Intriguing." Meera hovered over the dark chasm. "I do wonder what's happening. I've a good mind to zip down and see, though I wouldn't like to upset Mercipolis, but suppose our friends are in trouble?"

"Not a whole lot you could do about it if they were," the Keeylas sneered. "What could you do as a hummingbird? Buzz around their heads and annoy them? A creature of any decent size would swat you down like an insect."

"I do have some magic left, even if not as much as when I am in my usual form. One needn't be the largest combatant in a fight if one is imaginative and clever. And if Mercipolis goes with me, we can combine our powers."

"Are you sure he isn't running away instead?" the white cat asked, waving a paw toward a figure in the distance.

In his distraction, the wizard had wandered far and was in imminent danger of walking over the edge of the plateau upon which they stood. Meera flew swiftly to intercept him, startling him back from the rim by zooming in front of his face.

"Goodness me!" he cried, heart racing at his near miss. "You've saved my life, you have. But I'm afraid I'm no nearer to thinking of a small but mighty creature."

"Maybe it doesn't matter. Why not turn yourself into something small enough to fit in the hole and able to fly first. Then once we reach the cavern below, if need be, you can transform both of us into something grander and more ferocious."

"How ingenious! I should have thought of that myself. Let's go tell the others."

Once they explained their plan, the next question was what the wizard should turn into for the journey.

"Any modest-sized bird would do," Mercipolis mused. "A dove or a robin. Even a crow."

"Don't turn into a crow," Chester protested. "They are the rummest birds. Did I ever tell you about the time one tried to—"

But I fear we are never destined to hear exactly what outrage a crow once imposed upon the bear, for at that moment a rumbling beneath their feet put a stop to further conversation. None of the party had ever experienced an earthquake but if you have, it felt like that. The shaking intensified and the rock around the hole began to crumble and spit out in all directions like missiles. A hasty retreat was beaten by our friends.

When they were at a safer distance, they watched in astonishment as a giant green vine emerged from the hole and shot toward the sky.

"They've done it!" Nightshade cried in delight. "Walnut and Barty. They've planted the zingery seeds and sung the star's song and watered them with tears. They must be alright!"

"They may be, but I'm not sure we are," Mercipolis cautioned. "Look at the size of those eggs!"

"Them mites that prophecy warns of," said Chester. "You can see 'em wiggling around inside. Nasty things—I hate bugs. They're good for nothing but biting and itching," he added, scratching at his neck where one particularly determined flea was currently feasting.

"There's so many. Do you think they'll try to harm us?" Nightshade asked.

The answer came sooner than any of them would have liked. One by one the eggs split open and a fully-formed, hungry red mite emerged. While the mites below the surface rushed downward into the cavern, the ones above immediately sensed the tempting group of victims nearby and poured off the vine in their direction.

A fierce battle that was not for the faint of heart ensued. The Keeylas and Chester swatted at the insects and gnashed their teeth fiercely. Nightshade danced about pulling mites off their friends and hurling them over the edge of the precipice. Celestyna opened her enormous mouth and swallowed as many as she could, though the taste was bitter and disgusting as you might imagine. She could feel them wriggling around as they slid down her long neck, which is not a pleasant thing to experience.

"Why don't you do something?" Chester roared at Meera and Mercipolis who stood to one side in deep discussion.

The hummingbird darted over to the bear. "Don't worry. The wizard has studied entomology and knows the mite's natural enemy. Look!"

A flash of purple heralded another transformation taking place. A shadow so big that it blocked out the sun towered over them. It was an enormous lady-bug—or ladybird as they are called by some—though perhaps in this particular case we shall refer to it as a gentleman-bug. Its brilliant red shell with black spots flashed as the creature devoured mouthfuls of the hateful mites with blinding speed.

Now that the fight felt less hopeless, the wizard's companions joined in with renewed vigor, mopping up whatever insects escaped the gentleman-bug's seemingly bottomless appetite. Before too long, the plateau was swept clean of the dangerous pests.

Mercipolis transformed back into himself again, letting out an enormous burp. There is no doubt he was in for a bad case of indigestion, but that is a small price to pay for being the hero of the hour.

After being heartily congratulated by his comrades-in-arms, the wizard walked closer to the vine to examine where it was emerging from the cave. "It's blocked off the hole."

"Perhaps we can dig around it," Chester suggested. "Bears are fearsome diggers, you know."

The wizard reached out a hand to stop the bear from suiting action to word. "Careful! See that yellow goo on the thorns? It's acidic. Look how it hisses and scorches the rock where it drips. We dare not touch it. I'm afraid we'll never gain entrance to the cavern this way."

"Nor can our friends escape," Nightshade mourned. "Are we to be parted from Barty and Walnut forever?"

A familiar voice rang out. "Not a bit of it!"

Meera, Mercipolis, Nightshade, Celestyna, Chester, and the Keeylas were astonished to see their whirligig and flitter-flutter friends winging their way across the plateau at the head of the unlikeliest parade imaginable. Following Walnut and Barty was a badger, an animal which was recognizable to those of the quest who had spent considerable time in the forest. But behind that somewhat mundane creature, a crowd of the weirdest-looking rodents strode. Their brownish fur sparkled with golden highlights in the sun and their wings glittered and clicked as the womble of womblybats cavorted for the first time in their lives in the open air.

Freedom is a heady thing if you've been trapped your entire life in a dark and dreary place. The womblybats went half-mad at the sights and sounds and scents above ground. They rushed here and there in such confusion and delight, it is a wonder none were lost over the edge of the plateau. Amid the hubbub, Barty did his best to explain what a womblybat was and how they came to free them through the badger's den once they convinced the womble it was not haunted, but instead simply home to a charmingly grumpy tenant.

"Many thanks to you," Meera said to the badger, "for leading all to safety. What is your name, if it is not too forward of me to ask?"

"Of course not, most lovely hummingbird! I am Matthias, longest-lived of my littermates and too old to be much use to anybody anymore, so it has been a pleasure to be of service. If it is not too impolite, I might remark this is an unusual crowd," he said, looking around at the reunited quest party. He put one paw to his mouth and whispered to Meera, "What is that big snake-like thing?"

Celestyna picked up the question readily and gently slithered over. "We are a wyrm with a y. A type of dragon if you are more familiar with that term."

"A dragon? My!" Matthias inched away only to find himself uncomfortably close to a large bear and even more monstrous cat. "I must say, this is all a bit alarming. And what is this?" he asked, coming nose-to-shin with Nightshade.

"I am Nightshade. A mouse," they answered from on high.

"A mouse? That can't be right. Mice are wee little things no bigger than my paw."

Mercipolis explained. "Our quest has encountered many perils, so I made Nightshade larger so they might be less vulnerable to danger. I am a wizard, you see."

The badger had thought he could not be more astonished, but found he was mistaken. "A wizard and a wyrm? A mouse nearly as big as a bear and a bear as big as, well, a bear? I suppose next you'll tell me this cat is the famed Keeylas of forest legend?"

"As a matter of fact..."

"No, don't say it. I don't think I could take any more excitement today."

Pruebelle, leader of the womblybats, wombled over and was introduced around. She was less astonished at those she met than the badger had been since everything above ground was a novelty. "What joys there are to be seen! What wonderful creatures to behold! What happens next?" she asked, looking at the quest party expectantly.

"Um, I suppose we will carry on questing," answered Mercipolis. "What do your folk plan to do?"

"I don't know. It's a whole new world. Are there good things to eat? And water to drink? What about shelter? What do you suggest?"

Our friends gazed at each other in a certain amount of consternation. They had enough problems without the added responsibility of helping a previously underground society adjust to their new lives.

The badger spoke up. "I should be glad to be of use to my former neighbors. I'm old and set in my habits, but I understand the ways of the forest. If you follow me, I'll teach you what I can. It will take time to learn, but you can use the caves as shelter now that you know you can come and go at will."

There was a great clamoring as Matthias ambled through the crowd of womblybats, who made way for their benefactor and bowed their heads as though a personage of the most enormous distinction was passing, and who's to say one was not?

Pruebelle thanked Walnut and Barty heartily before following the rest of the womble. When they were gone, the plateau was quieter and calmer, giving the questing party a chance to sit and rest as they contemplated their next moves.

"The vine should lead to that place beyond the clouds where it is said wyrms gather," Mercipolis said. "But how can we climb it when the thorns drip poison?"

"Perhaps wyrms are impervious to it since it is meant as a route to our safety," Celestyna observed. "We will test it."

She slid over to the vine and touched some of the yellow gunk with the tip of her tail. The sizzle and shriek that followed told the onlookers she was not immune to the effects of the nasty acid.

"Poor dear!" cried Meera, when Celestyna rejoined them. "Let me see."

The hummingbird flew to the tip of the wyrm's tail and murmured a few words until the wound scabbed over and healed before their eyes.

"Thank you," Celestyna said, "but it is crushing to think there is no way for us to ascend the vine. We were so close to succeeding at our quest. Now our goal seems farther away than ever."

"Nonsense," scoffed Chester. "Just need to put our heads together and think o' a solution. There's not a single thing that's impossible when you put your mind to it."

Taking the bear literally, Walnut flew over and pressed his catty forehead against the bear's own. "Does this really help?" the whirligig asked skeptically, for he felt no cleverer than before.

Chester waved the creature away impatiently and would have given it what for if Meera had not intervened.

"Chester simply means we must work together to come up with an idea. We have many different talents among us. There must be a way of overcoming the poison or the prophecy would not have suggested planting the seeds to begin with."

"Unless it was meant as a cruel joke," the Keeylas commented cynically. "You are all far too trusting. Take it from one who knows, there is more evil in this world than good. Likely whoever wrote that meant to waste the time of any who stumbled across it and lead them far astray. For all we can tell, there is nothing above the skies but more danger. I've had the feeling we're being watched from there," it added, pointing to a cloud wrapped around the vine high in the sky.

The cloud was dark and ominous and looked heavy with rain though none fell. A rumbling started out low, becoming louder and louder like the roll of thunder but unending. Our friends stared skyward in anticipation that something was about to happen, but none could have predicted the giant eye that suddenly appeared.

It was bulbous and bloodshot with a pale blue iris rimmed round in black that matched the black pupil which was barely a dot in the sea of blue. Lest you think it was a floating eyeball (which would certainly be alarming and perhaps even repulsive), I will reassure you it was attached to a face of some sort that was hard to make out through the gauzy cloud. There was the hint of a sharp nose, the sweep of dark brows, and pale skin as evidenced by the eyelid that blinked lazily at them.

"Who dares disturb my slumber? Answer me at once!" a booming voice demanded.

"Who wants to know?" the Keeylas retorted insolently, as ever offended that anyone would attempt to order it about.

"THE IMPERTINENCE! THE AUDACITY! THE SHEER CHEEK!"

The cloud roiled and churned as though greatly agitated.

"Now you've done it," Mercipolis complained to the monster cat. "Can't you ever be polite?"

"It's not my way. Besides, whatever that is ain't exactly being the soul of tact, are they?"

"They might be able to help us climb into the sky though. We should at least attempt to mollify them. WE DO BEG YOUR PARDON!" the wizard shouted as loudly as he could. "WE MEAN YOU NO HARM!"

The voice growled back as the cloud parted in two. "Wish I could say the same!"

CHAPTER 23

AN UNWISE MAGICIAN

OUR FRIENDS WATCHED IN horror as a shining, black boot, larger even than what you are imagining, descended from the skies heading straight for them. They scattered quickly as it landed in their midst, squashing the base of the vine into a puddle of green and yellow goo. The rest of the towering plant collapsed from the sky like a rope that has snapped from its tether and falls into messy coils upon a ship's deck.

The questing party looked in dismay from the ruined vine to the boot and back again. All in a moment, their dream of reaching that haven beyond the clouds was crushed. Even optimistic Chester was finding it hard to interpret this unexpected event in any but the gloomiest of spirits.

Before they could express their shock and sorrow, the boot was followed by a second. Both were attached to immensely long legs wrapped in grey woolen trousers, rather nicely tailored. The top half of this colossus was still hidden by the cloud but that didn't stop the peevish voice from booming out again.

"What is this mess? Look what it's done to my boots. And I just bought them too. Whoever is responsible shall pay for this outrage! Sending spiky green plants up into my house and spoiling my new boots. Aloysius! Get down there and discover the miscreant!"

From out of the misty cloud, a small figure descended down the left pant leg, using the weave of the wool as foot and hand holds. As it neared, the onlookers saw it was what we would call a monkey, though none of the forest dwellers had ever seen the like and so lacked the vocabulary to name it.

It looked something like the adorable capuchin breed, with orange fur on its face and a fluffy black tail. It wore a most ill-fitting black frock coat with long swallowtails behind and a bright blue bowtie that contrasted attractively with its orange fur. It also sported a towering top hat that appeared to have seen better days.

"'Tis but a little bit o' a thing," Chester remarked as it neared. "We've not much to fear from that."

When one stops to think about it, one might consider it poignant how often the bear's predictions fell flat, and I'm afraid this time was no exception. As the monkey lit upon the ground and the questers made to move closer to converse with it, they realized they had become frozen in place.

The monkey hopped around examining them closely in a most impertinent manner before zeroing in on the hummingbird, who was caught mid-air in flight. It waved a paw in front of its face and Meera was freed from paralysis.

"Goodness! How did you do that?" Meera asked.

"Magic, naturally. I am the Astoundingly Astonishingly Amazing Aloysius. Please do not call me Al. Who or what are you? You don't seem to be an ordinary hummingbird."

"I am Meera. I've been given this form temporarily by the wizard Mercipolis," it said, indicating the purple-robed enchanter who was frozen in the mortifying moment of removing some bothersome wax from one ear.

"Oh, a *wizard*," the monkey sneered, contempt dripping from his voice and with a scowl of distaste.

"Yes," Meera answered, puzzled at his disdain. "Aren't *you* a wizard?"

"Don't be insulting! I am a magician which is an entirely different thing. Behold!"

Aloysius began to pull an extraordinary and fascinating array of items from his top hat. A bewildered-looking white rabbit. A fireplace poker. A four-course dinner. The life-size jade statue of a baby elephant. A rowboat complete with two fishermen. And finally, the portrait of a distinguished gentleman in a finely-tailored grey wool suit who sported black muttonchop whiskers and bulging blue eyes.

With another wave of his paw, all the items except the portrait vanished into thin air as they say (though I have never personally witnessed air that was thick, except perhaps with mystery and intrigue.)

"This is my master, His Lordship Sir Ridiculously-Named Ludicrous Preposterous the Fourth, Esquire."

It took much self-control for Meera not to giggle aloud at this patently absurd moniker as the magician seemed entirely serious. Besides, it isn't polite to make fun of other people's names when they are so often bestowed upon them as infants against their own wills or natural inclinations.

"I see," the hummingbird said. "And is this Sir Preposterous the same as the person whose leg you climbed down?"

"Of course. This vine situation has upset him mightily, and when he is upset, none of the household can be at rest. Please tell me which of you is responsible so I can turn them into a bridgorbal and we can have some peace again."

Meera wasn't sure what a bridgorbal might be but assumed from the context it wasn't something pleasant or much to be desired.

"Perhaps if we said we're sorry, that would be sufficient. We had no idea when we grew the vine that anyone's house was directly above us. We meant no harm."

"We? Do you mean you are all responsible?" the magician asked. "That is a lot of bridgorballing," he muttered, appearing discouraged at the notion.

"It is, isn't it," Meera agreed sympathetically. "Wouldn't an apology be simpler?"

"Simpler for you, but you don't know my master. He takes offense easily and often. The only thing that will mollify him is severe punishment imposed upon the offender. Nothing for it but to knuckle down and get to turning you all into bridgorbals. I'll need to gather my strength though. Give me a minute."

Aloysius clapped his top hat upon his head and in the blink of an eye, disappeared within it. He had not bothered to refreeze Meera, not realizing the hummingbird had some magical powers of its own. It took advantage of this lapse to fly over to Mercipolis and perch on the finger that was reaching into his ear.

"Can you hear me?"

With effort, the wizard blinked in reply.

"I'm hoping if we combine our forces, we might be able to break you free from this spell."

Mercipolis blinked again.

Meera concentrated and the wizard did likewise. First, the finger the humming-bird perched on flicked. Then one foot kicked out involuntarily. His knees bent and he fell forward onto his elbows with a sharp crack. "Ow! Oh, I can talk!"

"Are you hurt?"

"I don't think so. Not badly anyway. It feels good to be able to move about. I've not often had magic worked upon me without my consent. It isn't very nice. Makes you think," the wizard added, remembering the times he had used his powers as a weapon of sorts, though he had never done any lasting harm to anyone that he knew of. "What's happening? Who was that fellow in the top hat?"

"A magician."

"A magician? We wizards were taught they were mythical beings." Mercipolis strode over to the hat and picked it up, examining the apparently empty piece of apparel inside and out. "And a magician's hat! I've read about them in stories but never thought to see one. Watch this!"

The wizard slapped his hands together, crushing the top hat accordion-like into a flat disc.

"OUCH!" The hat popped open and Aloysius popped out looking extremely disgruntled. "You lot really have no manners at all, do you? Thrusting vines into people's drawing rooms and squashing them inside hats. The sooner you're all transformed into bridgorbals the better!"

Mercipolis was no wiser than Meera as to the meaning of that word, but instinctively reacted negatively to the idea of becoming one against his will. Pulling out his wand, he tapped the monkey on the nose while shouting a most heartfelt "FLIP-A-DOODLE!"

When the purple cloud cleared, a fat-cheeked and outraged chipmunk stood next to the hat. "HOW VERY DARE YOU?"

The chipmunk waved its paw over itself and returned to its monkey form. "YOU THINK YOU CAN OUT-MAGIC A MAGICIAN? LET THE BAT-TLE COMMENCE!"

Mercipolis had not trained in the art of magical combat, nor was he naturally inclined to such rudely vigorous behavior. However, in defense of his friends and in the interest of the quest not coming to an abrupt end by everyone being turned into bridgorbals (whatever that was), he had little choice but to attempt to rise to the occasion. He gripped his wand tightly and prepared to counter whatever attack came his way.

The monkey held his top hat out with one paw while producing an iron skillet from the hat with the other. With this classic weapon choice in hand, he attempted to swat the wizard on the head. Luckily, Mercipolis's pointy purple hat was made of sterner stuff and repelled this outrage. With his wand, the wizard turned the skillet into a bright-blue butterfly which fluttered around them gracefully.

Next, Aloysius produced a large anvil which, while heavy enough to cause considerable harm when dropped from on high, proved too weighty a thing for flinging about to be truly practical. After narrowly missing dropping it on his own foot, the magician abandoned that plan in favor of a magnificent hound that slobbered an unwarranted amount of drool from its sharp-toothed maw. Mercipolis touched it on its nose with his wand as it ran to bite him. From the cloud of purple smoke, an adorable puppy appeared and ran off to chase the blue butterfly.

"CURSES!" the magician screamed in traditional villainous frustration.

"Can't we talk this out?" the wizard asked plaintively as he had an inkling they might continue on in this nonsensical magical fashion indefinitely.

"NEVER!" cried the monkey, hurling an enormous ball made of thumbtacks, toothpicks, porcupine quills, and other pointy items at his opponent.

Mercipolis turned it into a hive of bees, an unfortunate choice as nothing irritates bees more than being hurled about, but you try thinking on your feet when an angry magician is chucking one missile after another in your direction.

A brief if informal hiatus in hostilities followed as Aloysius and Mercipolis ran about the plateau trying to escape the furious swarm. In the confusion, the magician's hold over the other members of the questing party was broken. They were relieved to be able to move but dismayed to find they also were being chased by angry insects. A certain amount of chaos followed.

Only Chester found time to sample the honey from the bee's hive. His thick fur protected him from stings and bears naturally find sweet things irresistible.

"Delicious," he remarked, holding up one sticky paw as the wizard rushed by him in a panic.

"Fling it over the edge!" Mercipolis cried.

"But it's so tasty!"

The Keeylas, who was as you might expect extremely annoyed and offended at being chased by something so insignificant as a bee, ran up and knocked the hive from Chester's paws and off the side of the plateau. The bees followed. Everyone was able to take a quick breath before the fight between the magician and wizard commenced again.

The rest of the quest party gathered to discuss whether they should try to intervene in the duel and overwhelm the monkey with their greater numbers. Chester and Walnut were predictably in favor of such impulsively direct action. The more level-headed among them pointed out the magician could simply refreeze them if they interfered.

In the end, they decided to settle in and observe, intervening only if Mercipolis was on the verge of injury or defeat. A long (though hardly tedious) hour ensued wherein each clever (and sometimes not so clever) move by the magician was met with a clever (enough) countermove by the wizard. Equally matched in power, Mercipolis perhaps had the advantage in being less prone to the emotional outbursts and exasperation that made the monkey recklessly careless at times.

It is no small thing to witness such a battle of wits and magic. The audience of this historic event watched in wonder and fascination as each fantastical weapon conjured by the magician was transformed into something relatively harmless by the wizard. While no blood had yet been drawn, it was still an awe-inspiring sight.

I've often speculated the only thing that could make an all-out battle between a magician and a wizard more exciting would be if a sorcerer wandered by and decided to join in. Little did I ever suspect one day my theory would be proven correct, for just when it seemed both combatants were running out of steam, a golden goose descended from the cloud above.

When I say it was golden, I do not mean its color alone. Its feathers and beak, watchful eyes and webbed feet, even its tongue and the yucky, squishy bits inside that you can't and don't particularly want to see were made from pure gold. It landed with a heavy clunk and spread its wings wide with a jarring jingle like the sound of a thousand tiny out-of-tune bells caused by its feathers clinking against one another.

"What is the meaning of this, Aloysius? Sir Preposterous sent you down here on a simple errand and as usual, you have complicated matters beyond comprehension."

"Shut up, you dirty duck!" the magician cried, perhaps unwisely, but in his defense, he was overwrought by the heat of battle.

The goose placed one feathered wing upon the monkey's head and the magician instantly turned to gold.

"Can't say you didn't ask for it," the bird muttered, tilting its head so that one impatient beady eye rested upon Mercipolis. "Have you anything you wish to add?"

The wizard backed away with hands held high in surrender. Being frozen in place was one thing—being turned into a golden statue quite another, and he wanted no part of it.

Meera, as the bravest of them, and also the one most well-equipped to quickly zip out of range if necessary, approached the goose cautiously, introducing itself and the others as is only polite upon meeting a stranger, and this one was very strange indeed.

The goose did have some manners, for it returned the favor. "I am Grizelda, sorcerer to Sir Preposterous."

"He has a magician *and* a sorcerer?"

"Of course. He collects any magical object or creature, but what he really wants is a wizard. Been looking for one for ages. Drives the monkey crazy it does. He has some idea that magicians outrank sorcerers and wizards. Completely bonkers."

"He did seem a bit hot-headed, but this is an unkind fate," Meera said, hovering hummingbird-fashion around the golden head of the monkey.

"It's only a temporary curse. It'll wear off. Always does. He'll be in a worse temper than ever then. Tiresome fellow." Grizelda sniffed dismissively. "Now can somebody explain to me what is going on here?"

A chorus of confused and confusing voices did their best to explain the events leading up to the present moment, but the goose quickly focused in on a single word.

"Did you say this person is a wizard?" Grizelda asked, eyeing the purple-clad Mercipolis up and down as though he was a specimen trapped in a display case.

Belatedly, everyone remembered Sir Preposterous was in the market for just such a thing. Having no wish for their friend to be "collected," they became notably silent. Chester even went so far as to look around vacantly into space and whistle a tuneless melody as though he hadn't a thought in the world.

Not so, Walnut, for whirligigs (if Walnut is any example and I'm afraid it's the only one we have) are by nature flighty, thoughtless creatures. "Indeed, he is! The greatest wizard that ever lived. He created me and these three other whirligigs you see here!"

Grizelda had no idea what a whirligig was or why she couldn't see more than one, but that was not the important point of Walnut's statement.

"A wizard! My master will be pleased," she crowed (or honked to be more accurate), spreading her wings wide and grabbing the purple cloak of Mercipolis in her beak.

In a clatter and flutter of golden feather and wing, both goose and wizard disappeared skyward.

CHAPTER 24

THE HOUSE IN THE CLOUDS

"THIS IS A FINE how-do-you-do AND kettle o' fish!" Chester exclaimed.

The Keeylas scolded the unfortunate whirligig. "You may have the head of a cat, but you have a brain stuffed full of damp feathers and fog. If you'd not told Grizelda about the wizard, he'd still be with us. We'll probably never see him again."

Meera reproved the cat gently. "Walnut meant no harm. While we have encountered what could undoubtedly be described as a series of regrettable events—unfortunate, even—we must not turn on one another."

"True! Besides, Walnut does its best," Barty offered, feeling protective of his whirligig friend. "It's not easy being one of a kind, as I can tell you."

"I'm NOT one of a kind! How many times do I have to say there are FOUR of us. Sunshine, Leaf, and Mold are highly offended at this constant disregard!" Walnut said, wrapping its batty wings around its lizardy body and waving its four remaining ratty tails in a huff.

"And it's past time," replied the Keeylas, "somebody told YOU that you are UTTERLY DAFT! There are no other whirligigs. They are a figment of your addled mind!"

Walnut burst into tears. Celestyna slithered over to the Keeylas and bit it hard on one of its fluffy white tails. The monstrous cat howled in pain, rearing back, spitting and swiping four of its giant paws at the wyrm. Chester roared and gave a good scuff to the cat's ears with his sharp claws. Meera darted in and out nervously, attempting to quell the violence but only coming dangerously close to becoming an accidentally-shattered crystal hummingbird more than once.

Meanwhile, Barty attempted to apologize to Walnut, but Walnut spiraled away from the flitter-flutter in a circle every time he flew toward the whirligig's face. Thus ensued a comical dance that looked something like the world's most awkward waltz.

Off to the side, Nightshade observed, pulling on their tail nervously. *What tenuous bonds bind us together,* they thought, *and how quickly they can be broken.*

The mouse could have wept to see their friends at each other's throats (in some cases, literally), but instead, they spoke.

"Silence... silence... SILENCE!"

The urgency of Nightshade's voice cut through the chaos. Everyone froze as still as the golden monkey statue which stood in their midst. Whether the Amazing Aloysius was able to witness anything going on about him was unclear, but everyone had more important things on their mind at that moment.

Having gotten their attention, Nightshade took the floor to speak as eloquently as they knew how.

"My friends, it breaks my heart to see you so. Once upon a time, I would never have thought to go a-questing. Nor that I would meet so many stout-hearted companions and have adventures that must be far beyond the scope of any mouse that has ever lived. In many ways, it has been overwhelming, but through it all, my courage has been strengthened to know I was among comrades who would remain true through any hardship. But look at yourselves!"

The rest of the party peered around shame-facedly, each caught in a slightly dishonorable, ungraceful, or simply silly act.

Celestyna glided over to the mouse and wrapped her tail around their shoulders in a gentle embrace. "You have done right to remind us we are allies and not enemies. We fear this quest of ours to find a home for ourself among our own kind has dragged you all into disorder. And to no purpose since we have failed."

"Who says we've failed?" Chester blustered. "Just 'cause that vine thingy didn't work out, don't mean we're licked. There's more than one way to skin a cat."

"I BEG YOUR PARDON?" The Keeylas howled. Of all the questers, it was least abashed by the mouse's scolding, being of the opinion anything it did was both correct and admirable. "Do you dare to imply you are in the habit of skinning cats?"

"It's only a saying I picked up from a hooman woman."

"Humans," the cat sneered. "I might have known."

Meera interrupted before further strife could break out between bear and cat. "Nightshade is right. We mustn't squabble amongst ourselves. If we stick together, I believe we can rescue Mercipolis and find the wyrm haven. Both are beyond the clouds after all. We've only to figure out a way to get up there. Barty, Walnut, and I can fly above and scout out the situation."

"Brilliant!" said Chester. "And the rest o' us can climb."

"Climb what?" asked the Keeylas, flicking its whiskers at the smooshed ruins of the thorny vine.

"These here pant legs, o' course," the bear replied, indicating the smartly-tailored grey trousers that still stood amongst them, Sir Preposterous having forgotten to retract them back into his home in the cloud one must suppose.

"You want us to clamber up that?"

"Why not? The magician came down that way, and bears are fearsome climbers, you know. But if you're too scared..."

"Don't be ridiculous. Cats are renowned for their climbing skills. Much more so than bears!"

"First-rate! What about you two?" Chester asked wyrm and mouse.

"I will go where you go," said Nightshade loyally.

"And it is only proper we make the attempt as well," replied Celestyna, "as this is for our benefit."

Chester rubbed his paws together in gratification. There was nothing he liked better than taking any kind of action regardless of the chances of success or failure.

And so it was decided. Hummingbird, flitter-flutter, and whirligig (and everyone agreed, to save argument, the three invisible whirligigs) took off on the long flight to the cloud above.

Below, Chester was the first to brave the climb, hooking his long claws into the woolen weave of the left trouser leg. Not to be outdone, the Keeylas scrambled up the right leg. An informal but deadly serious race ensued with both creatures trying to outdo the other in speed and upward progress.

Nightshade sighed a bit at this evidence of a rivalry that had not been entirely set aside, but gamely followed behind Chester at a much more sedate and circumspect pace. Celestyna came last, trailing the Keeylas up the other leg. She wound her way round and round, using her belly scales to inch along (or perhaps foot or yard along is more accurate given her ever-increasing size).

This left only Aloysius on the ground. If the climbers had looked back, they would have noticed a deep scowl on the monkey's golden face and his eyelids blinking furiously. Grizelda's spell was wearing thin. He would soon be loosed and WOE AND MISERY UPON THOSE THAT HAD DEFIED HIM! (At least, that's what I imagine he was thinking—his mouth was not yet in working order.)

Have you ever been wearing a nice pair of grey woolen trousers and had a bear, a monstrous cat, a mouse of unusual size, and a wyrm with a y climb up them? Unlikely, I know, but I thought I'd ask. Sir Preposterous was experiencing exactly this unusual phenomenon and finding it most uncomfortable.

It was scratchy and itchy and ticklish and vexing. It made him sneeze and giggle and snort and curse, none of which was overly bothersome to our intrepid mountaineering quartet. But when he decided to shake one leg after another extremely vigorously to rid himself of any unwanted passengers, that was another story.

Only Celestyna had any hope of hanging on, wound tight as she was around one leg. Mouse, bear, and cat did their best to cling, tooth and claw, but it was a losing struggle. Before you could say "His Lordship Sir Ridiculously-Named Ludicrous Preposterous the Fourth, Esquire," they were all three falling through the air to their certain doom on the unforgiving rock below.

It's funny—as in strange or odd, not funny ha ha, though you may find it amusing; there is no accounting for taste—how often certain doom turns out to be not so certain after all. In this instance, the Amazing Aloysius (having broken free of the golden goose's spell) froze the falling trio of Nightshade, Chester, and the Keeylas in the air a mere foot from the hard rock upon which he stood. The magician had no desire for his elaborate plans of vengeance to be thwarted by the untimely splatting of so many of his enemies, unless he was doing the splatting.

Still clinging on to one grey-panted leg, Celestyna was left in a quandary: continue upward to help her friends above or descend to help her friends below. While there was no telling what was happening in the sky, she could see clearly that those on the ground were in a potentially perilous situation. She decided to go to their aid first, slithering down onto the plateau just as the legs of Sir Preposterous were abruptly withdrawn skyward.

The wyrm had no time to ponder what this might signify as the monkey magician quickly turned his fury on her.

"Thought to escape my wrath, did you?" Aloysius sneered. "And where is that ridiculous wizard? Realized he had no hope of besting me in battle and ran off, I suppose."

"On the contrary," Celestyna replied tartly, for she was growing weary of the magician's rather ridiculous brand of villainy. "He was holding his own easily before he was kidnapped by a sorcerer."

"Grizelda!" The way the monkey spit out the word sounded very much like cursing. "That interfering fowl. Thinks she's so important because she's made of gold and is worth a small fortune. One of these days I'll catch her off guard and melt her down."

"We wish you luck as it was she who caught you off guard and turned you into gold. You are fortunate she did not make it permanent."

"She wouldn't dare! Sir Preposterous appreciates my worth. Magicians are far superior to any other magic practitioner."

"Who knows? He may be so enthralled with the new addition to his collection that he no longer cares about you."

"The wizard? He'll soon tire of the pathetic parlor tricks of that one."

Calling upon her wyrmish powers of suggestion, though uncertain they would work on another magical being, Celestyna shook her heavy, toothy head. "We hope you're right. It would be sad to think you might lose your patron's favor. We notice he has withdrawn himself from this place and has not called on you to return to the cloud. Perhaps he has lost interest in magicians."

If the wyrm had hoped to rile the monkey up still further, she succeeded beyond her wildest expectations. Aloysius began hopping from one foot to the other while twirling around in circles. He forgot about his freezing spell, and Chester, Nightshade, and the Keeylas dropped unceremoniously to the ground (though it must be said that falling from a foot of height is infinitely less painful than falling from many, many times that amount).

"Oof!" said the bear.

"Ouch!" said the mouse.

"This is outrageous!" said the monstrous white cat. It had certainly endured many more indignities since joining the quest than it ever had in its life before (though it is not a bad thing for the haughty to be humbled from time to time in my opinion).

"Oh, shut up, all of you!" the magician screeched. "Let me think!"

"Think about what?" Celestyna asked. "Hadn't you better return to the cloud before your master forgets your existence?"

"I will. I will. Just give me a moment."

"Ha!" jeered the Keeylas. "I bet you can't return now there is no way to climb up. It's not like you magicked yourself down here."

"I can so! All I have to do is pull something useful from my hat, like an eagle with a saddle or a rocket ship made of cheese or—"

"A hot air balloon?" Chester suggested.

"I suppose so," Aloysius agreed impatiently. "Something along those lines."

"But we already have one!"

Yes, dear readers, in all their excitement and disappointment and confusion, the quest party had failed to realize the same vehicle that had brought them into the mountains could easily take them up into the clouds. They could have kicked themselves for missing this obvious solution, but that would have been a waste of time as well as a tricky thing to try and accomplish.

Instead, everyone clambered into the hot air balloon. Room was even graciously allowed for the magician on the off chance this act of kindness might have some effect on his wrathful nature. In truth, he was unusually subdued on the ride into the sky, either concerned at what they would find above or perhaps deathly afraid of heights (or balloons or wicker baskets).

In an absurdly short time given how out of reach it had seemed before, the balloon rose through a hole in the cloud to reveal an immaculately-appointed drawing room of immense size.

The walls were papered in a burgundy damask that matched the plush velvet on several overstuffed sofas and the smooth leather on a pair of wing chairs near a roaring fireplace. An expansive tea was laid out on a low table, with finger sandwiches and fairy cakes and other mouth-watering delicacies. The smell of a fine cigar filled the air and decanters of richly-colored liquors stood upon a sideboard near sparkling crystal glasses.

All in all, the atmosphere was one of a life well-lived and lived very well indeed. A luxurious and opulent existence that no doubt suited someone called Sir Ridiculously-Named Ludicrous Preposterous the Fourth, Esquire to a T.

Seeing that gentleman in his full glory for the first time left our friends speechless. A true colossus towered over them, leaving even the mighty Keeylas feeling insignificant for the first time in memory.

A grey woolen vest and jacket and pristine white shirt were as perfectly tailored as the giant's pants. He had apparently had time to re-polish his black boots. Their shiny surface reflected the light from the fireplace in mesmerizing fashion. As recorded in his portrait, his black hair was smoothed back from his forehead, and his sideburns merged with an impressive pair of muttonchop whiskers along each side of his jaw.

His bulging blue eyes were gazing in satisfaction at a glass-front display cabinet wherein, I am sorry to report, not only was Mercipolis locked away but Barty and Walnut also. Only Meera was unaccounted for.

"A flitter-flutter and a whirligig, you say," boomed Sir Preposterous in a voice so loud, our friends could feel it reverberating through them like the sharp crack of thunder when lightning strikes uncomfortably close. "What a find! What a discovery! I shall have to write this up for the Society post-haste! Grizelda, bring me my sketchbook. I must make a few drawings of these extraordinary creatures!"

"But, Master, do look!" the goose insisted, waving one golden wing in the direction of the newly-arrived hot air balloon.

"Gadzooks, golly, and even, dare I say, zounds! What type of infernal contraption is this and what is it doing in here? Get rid of it, Grizelda!"

The sorcerer ran at the balloon with a large and wickedly sharp golden pin. Seeing what was about to happen, the passengers scrambled to exit the wicker basket in manners variously speedy, awkward, and downright undignified.

POP! went the balloon as its basket plummeted through the hole in the drawing room floor and out of sight. A sighing *plumpf* sound that wafted up to them was enough to indicate its sad demise on the rocks below. Our questing party was now truly stranded above the clouds, but they had more immediate concerns. Sir Preposterous had noticed the flurry of unusual visitors joining him.

"Is that a wyrm? By Jove and by Jingo and by Jupiter too! Been a while since I saw one of those. And this white creature? Never seen the like. Seems to have an inordinate number of legs and tails. Hmmm, an extremely ordinary bear. Disappointing. But is that... could it be... a mouse of unusual size? Delightful! What a day! Never have I added so many uniquities to my collection at once. Grizelda, capture them all!"

TEARS OF A GIANT

I ONLY WISH I had the skill to do justice to the scene of utter chaos and confusion that followed the giant's command. You will have to do your best to imagine a long and sinuously-winding purple and green wyrm, a monstrous and extremely aggrieved white cat, a disappointingly normal but eager brown bear, and a grey mouse of unusual size being chased around by a golden goose who, while no match for any of them in stature, did have magic on her side.

The commotion was complicated by the fact that the Amazing Aloysius was in turn chasing after Grizelda. He was pulling random objects out of his magic hat in order to exact his revenge upon her for turning him (albeit temporarily) into a statue. A sinisterly clown-faced Jack-in-the-box, silver candelabra complete with burning candles, and full-grown ostrich were only a few of the things being flung about amid the madness.

Tables were upended. Delicate crystal and porcelain smashed. Tea cakes and finger sandwiches went sailing and were ground under foot and paw into the expensive carpet. Valuable paintings were knocked from the walls, and the cotton stuffing from sofas ripped open by claws wafted through the air like softly-falling snow.

The noise was indescribable but above it all, the booming voice of Sir Preposterous rang out. "I say! What, what? End this jiggery-pokery! Halt this tomfoolery! Cease from being so higgledy-piggledy at once! Criminals! Miscreants! Complete and thorough scoundrels! Stop it, I say!"

Exasperated beyond bearing by the destruction of his prized possessions, the giant chose the most expedient way of gaining control over the situation by picking up his monkey magician and goose sorcerer by their feet and holding them high in the air above the fray. It took a moment, but Celestyna, Chester, the Keeylas, and Nightshade gradually realized they were only chasing one another instead of being chased.

The sofa fluff settled as did the befuddled and overwrought ostrich, who crumpled into a heap, tucking its head under one wing and going to sleep. All of the questers—except the Keeylas, who could not have cared less—looked around in dismay at the devastation. While they didn't think it was their fault as they'd only been defending themselves and trying to escape capture, they couldn't help but feel a trifle responsible for their part in the general mayhem.

Sir Preposterous collapsed into a leather wing-backed chair—one of the few items to have escaped damage—and began to weep copiously at the ruins around him. He still had hold of Aloysius and Grizelda, one dangling upside down from each hand, which left him unable to wipe his face or clear his eyes.

Nightshade approached quietly, climbing up upon the giant's knee, and pulling a handkerchief as big as a sheet from Sir Preposterous's suit pocket to gently wipe away his tears. "I'm so sorry. Your beautiful things! But it really isn't right to catch and lock up those that are meant to be free."

"What do you *sniff* mean *sniff*? I am His Lordship Sir Ridiculously-Named Ludicrous Preposterous the Fourth, Esquire. If I of all people don't have the right *sniff*, who does?"

"Nobody does. That's the point," explained the mouse. "Those with free will and lives of their own must be allowed to make their own choices and go about their business, which in our case is finding a refuge for our wyrm friend, Celestyna. She grows too large to be safe down below among humans who fear her and would seek to harm her."

"Harm such a beautiful creature? The very idea! All the more reason I should keep her here. She could roam my extensive gardens freely and securely as long as she never left its walls."

Celestyna came closer, raising her elegant head to the giant's eye level. "We thank you for the kind thought, but we still have hope there may be more wyrms somewhere here among the clouds, for who doesn't wish to connect with others of their kind? Don't you enjoy keeping company with your own friends and family?"

Sir Preposterous bawled harder than ever and flung his hands about in despair. This was very trying for the poor monkey and goose, who had this discomfort added to the indignity of being held upside down like nothing more than hunks of meat on display in a butcher's shop window. Fortunately (or unfortunately), just as their brains were getting properly scrambled, the giant let go and they went flying off in opposite directions, landing with a *thump* and a *clank* respectively.

The magician was first to recover, standing and rubbing his sore posterior with one hand while waving his top hat toward the giant with the other. "Now you've gone and done it. He hasn't got any family or friends. Why do you think we stay with him? Me and the goose can't be compelled to do anything against our will. We have magic after all. We simply feel sorry for the blighter."

"Really?" asked Chester, much impressed. "That's awful kind o' you!"

The monkey looked truly furious at being accused of such a thing, but Grizelda waddled over, golden feathers clinking, and agreed. "It is, isn't it? We are both superior beings in that way as well as most others, though the magician does harbor some foolish notions."

"Chumps is what you are," the Keeylas jeered. "You mean to tell me you have all this magical power and could be anywhere you wanted to be and yet you choose to stay here and serve someone else? Wouldn't be me."

"And yet, here you are," the goose observed. "Why? When, as you say, a formidable creature such as yourself could be anywhere, beholden to no one."

If a cat could blush, the white fur of the Keeylas would have been tinged pink at this remark. "Um, uh, just hadn't anything better to do at the moment," it mumbled.

"You're too modest," Nightshade said as they continued to mop the tears from the giant's face. "You have been such a help to our quest. You are our ally and our friend."

The mouse's soft statement made the Keeylas feel exceedingly peculiar. Its first instinct was to strongly deny such a thing. On second thought, it decided to simply curl up on the enormous hearth in that contentedly round form any cat lover will be familiar with. It couldn't have said why it did not want to contradict Nightshade's words, but it did know the heat from the fire was very pleasant and decided to leave it at that.

"Pitiful, this Sir Platypus fella being so lonesome," Chester commented, casually ambling over to the glass-fronted cabinet that held the rest of the quest party. He clambered upon an enormous footstool and hung his full weight from one of the handles on the cabinet, allowing the door to swing open partway. As Barty and Walnut flew out in relief, the bear helped Mercipolis down onto the floor. "But we all know a thing or two about being one o' a kind. Can't let it get you down, can ye?"

"I couldn't say," Walnut replied as he whirligigged past the bear, "as I've Sunshine, Leaf, and Mold to keep me company. But it has been nice making so many new acquaintances," it added, looking furtively at Barty who flitter-fluttered by just then.

"Yes," Barty agreed, glancing shyly at Walnut. "While most of us are different as can be, that only makes us stronger as a group. We each bring our own talents to help each other out."

"Lovely *sniff*, lovely!" said Sir Preposterous, yanking the handkerchief from Nightshade's paws and sending the mouse tumbling unceremoniously to the ground. The giant wiped his face thoroughly and blew his nose horribly (in exactly that order, fortunately). "I see I have been wrong to keep anyone here to satisfy my every whim like mere playthings. I suppose you are all free to continue on your quest and leave me here alone," he added, waving the revolting handkerchief at them with one hand as he covered his eyes with the other. He reclined his head against the chair in a most pleasingly pathetic pose.

"Or," suggested Nightshade, recovering quickly from their tumble, "you could join us!"

The other members of the quest party gawked at Nightshade in surprise and dismay (except for the Keeylas who was still dozing cattily by the fireplace). It would never have occurred to any of them to invite the giant, who had so lately sought to capture them as specimens, along on their quest.

Sir Preposterous, though touched by the mouse's invitation, felt compelled to decline. "For you see, it is only here that things are sized to fit me. Whenever I try to travel, I fell and flatten, stomp and squash everything and everyone I meet. Not on purpose, of course, but it is one of the hazards of being my size."

Mercipolis had a suggestion. "I transformed Nightshade into a larger form so they would be safer on our quest. I could turn you into a smaller one. Then you could venture out into the world."

"Tempting, but I fear I am too set in my ways. Besides, there is much to do here. This room must be put to rights. Perhaps I will use the occasion to redecorate. What do we think of a gold and blue theme?"

"Gold is my favorite color," answered Grizelda. "I will stay and help you. There is no one as useful as a sorcerer when renovating."

"Says you!" Aloysius cried. "Magicians are much more helpful. Think of all the things I can conjure from my hat. New sofas and curtains. Bric-a-brac, knick-knacks, and tchotchkes aplenty. Even a carpenter to repair the hole in the floor!"

"No need to squabble," said Sir Preposterous. "I would be most grateful for assistance from you both. You have been my faithful companions, though I fear I have not always treated you as such. From today on, we shall no longer be master and servant, but—dare I say?—a family of sorts."

Monkey and goose were so gratified at this proposal, they forgot their quarrel (at least temporarily, as even family members may become cross with each other from time to time).

"Perhaps I will also stay," said the Keeylas, opening one sleepy eye. "It is comfortable here."

The giant leant over and scratched the cat behind its ears. You might think such a dignified and haughty creature would object to this treatment, but a loud thrumming noise was heard that sounded very much like purring.

"You would be a most welcome companion, but don't you want to see the quest through with your friends? You can return after. There will be a place beside the fire for you. For any of you," Sir Preposterous added generously.

"As far as the quest goes," said Celestyna, "it must be up to each member of the party whether they continue on from this point, and no shame to any who remain behind. You must not decide rashly or recklessly. You have gotten us up above the clouds. We should perhaps find our own way from here alone."

"Don't be silly," Chester said, with a wave of his paw as though to dismiss any such notion.

Mercipolis agreed. "We've come too far to abandon you now. Besides, I've a professional interest in finding out if this haven really exists and if there are other wyrms still in existence."

"We'll come too!" said Barty and Walnut (and perhaps the invisible whirligigs also—the world may never know).

The Keeylas rose reluctantly, stretching out each and every one of its six limbs with luxurious grace. "I don't suppose you can manage without me, so I'll come. But keep that fire going," he instructed the giant, "and if you happened to find a soft pillow to lay upon the hearth while you're redecorating, I wouldn't mind."

"I think that could be arranged. And what about you, young mouse?" Sir Preposterous asked. "Have you had enough of adventuring?"

Nightshade shook their head firmly. "Quests will never fail as long as all remain true. My mother told me so and she never lied."

"Excellent," he replied. "Then come with me and I will set you on your way. The place you seek must be beyond my garden walls. Do you know which direction to go?"

"I'm afraid not," said the wizard. "We'd no further plan after reaching the clouds. I was hoping it would become self-evident."

"Hmph," the giant said thoughtfully. "Perhaps we should ask that turtle whatsit. Seems an intelligent sort of animal."

"Turtle?" asked Nightshade. "Are you sure it wasn't a tortoise? We met a very wise one."

"What's the difference?"

"I'm not really sure."

"Perhaps the turtle knows. We'll ask."

Sir Preposterous threw wide a pair of glass-paned doors that opened out into a magnificent garden and ushered the quest party (and the poor ostrich, who was glad to stretch its long legs out of doors) through it. It was obvious the giant collected not only unusual creatures and magical beings, but also uncommon plants. None of the party could have named a single specimen they passed but they were breathtaking in their beauty or weirdness (and sometimes both at once).

Like the giant, they were oversized, as were the butterflies and bees that fluttered everywhere. A blur whizzed by. A hummingbird as big as an eagle. The same thought occurred to all of the questers at once—*Meera!*

CHAPTER 26

A SHOCKING AND TRAGIC EVENT

How could they have forgotten their friend? True, events had been hectic—overwhelming even—but they were much abashed to think none of them had wondered where Meera was until that very moment. They began to ask each other anxiously what might have become of it.

"Meera?" the giant asked, puzzled by the unfamiliar word.

"Our friend," Nightshade explained. "It is a magical being, a being of light, though it is currently in the form of a crystal hummingbird, most lovely to behold."

"I should like to see such a thing. Probably around here somewhere since gardens are natural habitats for birds. Keep your eyes peeled. Ah, here is the turtle," Sir Preposterous said in satisfaction, pointing to what appeared to be a boulder rolling slowly in their direction.

As it neared, Chester and Nightshade recognized the distinctive pince-nez perched on the nose of a tortoise that looked only ordinary-size next to the giant and wyrm but extraordinarily big compared to the rest of the party.

"'Tis Madame Sibyl!" crowed the bear, amazed to see that majestic personage so far from the forest.

"Ah, the bear and mouse," the sibyl said, peering fixedly through her glasses at them. "About time you showed up."

"But what are you doing here of all places?" Nightshade asked.

"I might inquire the same of you, except I foresaw what was to come when first we met. And here you are, more or less on schedule. You met the raven, I believe. Do you remember its prophecy?"

Nightshade had to think very hard, so much had happened since, but the words came back to them:

"THREE TIMES THREE

THE ANSWERS BE

FOUR BY FOUR

KNOCK AT THE DOOR

WHERE STARS ALIGN

YOU'LL SEE A SIGN

A FEATHER DESCENDS

MAKE AMENDS

ALL MUST DIE

DON'T WONDER WHY

BETRAY YOUR FRIENDS

A QUEEN ASCENDS"

The tortoise nodded her head wisely. "Sounds like a raven. They never say anything plainly if they can help it. Let's see. Numbers usually mean math: three times three is nine and four times four is sixteen. You should travel nine leagues in one direction then sixteen in another. You'll find a door where you must knock. Keep an eye on the skies for stars and a falling feather. Make amends? Apologize perhaps for some wrongdoing yet to come. All must die. That is a trifle ominous there is no denying but best not to question it as it suggests—it will only lead to trouble. Betray your friends—that's straightforward enough."

"All must die?" the Keeylas said. "You can count me out of that."

"And we would never betray our friends," protested Nightshade.

"You are being too literal," Sibyl chided them. "Prophecies are slippery and devious things. They rarely say what they mean or mean what they say. Look at how the vine prophecy unfolded. The zingery seeds did bring you above the clouds, just not in the way you expected. Keep faith. Follow the path."

"But what path?" asked Chester. "Which direction?"

"Any will do. I've foreseen you reaching your next destination, so it doesn't matter which direction you pick. By definition, any direction will be the right one since I see that you succeed."

While the bear pondered that conundrum, Mercipolis nervously asked, "And beyond that?"

"I will not say as it is never comfortable to have too much foreknowledge of the future. I will only say one of you here will have to make a great sacrifice, one that can never be taken back lest the good it does vanishes also."

And with that worrying prediction, the sibyl turned and stomped away magnificently—slowly, it must be admitted, but no less impressively for that.

"*A great sacrifice*," whispered Nightshade, and a cold thrill rumbled along every bit of their bones from the tippy-top of their skull down to the tippity-tip-tip of their long tail.

"Best get a move on," Chester suggested, clapping his front paws together enthusiastically. As ever, he was eager for action and impatient with mere talk. "Times a-wasting!"

The Keeylas narrowed its eyes. "What about all this business to do with sacrifices and betrayal and everyone dying? Doesn't that give any of you pause?"

"All quests involve the most absurdly perilous dangers or else they'd just be a nice hike through pleasant country with a congenial company of friends," commented Sir Preposterous. "Or so I have read, never having contemplated such a journey myself. As I've said, any of you who'd rather not are welcome to remain here with me for as long as you like."

The quest members glanced around at each other anxiously, but either they were too abashed to admit they were afraid to continue, or they truly believed in the cause as not one volunteered to be left behind.

The giant nodded his head in satisfaction at this show of solidarity. "Valiant hearts all! I shall open the front gates for you and wave you off on your adventures. I hope you one day return my way so I may hear the end of this tale."

"But what about Meera?" asked Mercipolis. The wizard felt responsible for its hummingbird form and hoped no harm had come to it while its magic was much diminished from normal.

"The five of us will search the garden," Walnut suggested, elbowing Barty, who was roosting next to the whirligig, in the ribs.

The others were confused as to which five Walnut meant, but the flitter-flutter had grown so used to his friend's belief in the three invisible whirligigs that there were times he felt he could almost see them himself.

"Good idea," said Barty, taking off into flight. "Won't take us a minute!"

When a momentous decision has been made, courage has been screwed to the sticking point, and departure appears imminent, any delay becomes both a nuisance and slightly embarrassing. Those remaining stood awkwardly awaiting the return of the search party. If they had thumbs, they twiddled them. Attempts were made at small talk that quickly spluttered and died. Much nervous throat clearing and shuffling of feet was heard.

Finally, the ostrich provided some needed comic relief by chasing an orange and black butterfly as big as itself. The bird's gawky gait and wildly flying feathers raised a smile on every face save the perennially sour Keeylas.

Sir Preposterous guffawed most heartily at the sight. "Capital! Excellent! One might even venture to say first-rate! I should like a whole flock of these things, Aloysius. That is, if you should care to produce them," the giant added, remembering he was no longer in the business of ordering other folk around.

Whether or not the monkey magician was in the mood to oblige, we shall never find out as the search party picked that moment to flutter back into view. Alas, no hummingbird accompanied them.

"We've flown through every nook and cranny, peered around every vine and shrub," Barty reported. "There's no sign of Meera anywhere."

This posed a dilemma. Meera had become an important and much-beloved member of their group. It didn't feel right to continue on without it.

"Perhaps this hummingbird flew over the garden wall and is awaiting you out in the wider cloud world?" Sir Preposterous suggested.

Mercipolis sighed. "Perhaps. In any case, I don't think Meera would want us to abandon our mission."

"That's the spirit!" cried Chester. "I've a good feeling about it. No doubt we'll meet up along the way. Things always work out for the best when I'm around, you know."

(I can feel from here the shudder that ran through you, dear reader, as you hear this reckless boast from a bear who has proven less than skilled at accurate predictions, if we are to put it kindly. If you were to assume some catastrophe is shortly to befall our friends, I would not try to dissuade you from this notion.)

Saying their fond farewells to Sir Preposterous, Grizelda, Aloysius, and the ostrich, who had come to investigate what all the excitement was about, the questing party stepped through the giant wooden gates that marked the entrance to (or in this instance, exit from) the garden.

The world beyond was an outrageous mix of pillowy, puffy clouds and common landscape adornments such as trees, rocks, plants, and even a sparkling stream whose burbling waters were delightful both to behold and hear. Birdsong, the rustling noise of small creatures, and a general buzzy busyness indicated there was life of all kinds out in the larger cloud world.

"Nine leagues in any direction," Nightshade mused. "Does anyone know what a league is?"

Mercipolis pulled a weird gadget replete with a multitude of dials and gears and other whirly bits from his pocket. "I can help there. Follow me!" Staring intently at his mysterious device, the wizard strode forward, trusting in the sibyl's advice that it mattered not which way they went.

It turns out that while a cloud league is not nearly as long as a league as we measure it here on the ground, it was not a short distance either. They were making discouragingly little progress when Celestyna suggested everyone climb upon her by now very broad back.

"Hang on to us tight as tight!" she called to her passengers as she took off.

Slithering speeds for wyrms turning out to be swift indeed, it seemed no time before Mercipolis called an urgent halt and directed her to turn to the right for the next sixteen leagues.

(I can only suppose you are imagining many fascinating things they might have found at their next stop. Possibly they are even more exciting than what was actually there, and if so, I hope you will write your own story one day as I should very much like to read it.)

For the purposes of this tale, what they found was an unfortunately too familiar and monstrous form. Its head was like a vulture with wrinkled pink skin and enormous, piercing red eyes. Its wings were birdlike also, though the sharp, hooked claw at the end of each orange feather was not. Its body was shiny and scaled and as long as a snake but with taloned feet that dug ruthlessly into the cloud upon which it stood.

"Oh, no! It's Pishposh the squish! Poor Meera!" exclaimed Mercipolis with the deepest dismay, for indeed it was the crystal hummingbird returned to its most villainous and hated form. "What has happened?"

"THE WYRM... THE WYRM..." growled Pishposh, stalking toward them menacingly, long tail swishing angrily.

"What wyrm? Which wyrm?" asked Chester, bewildered at this turn of events.

"Perhaps that one," Nightshade suggested, pointing a shaking paw at a figure that suddenly loomed above them, blocking out all light and, one might even suggest, all hope.

It was twenty times the size of Celestyna but, unlike her, was far from elegant or beautiful. Its scales were a putrid puce color and covered with a disgusting pea green slime that oozed and coated every surface the thing crawled over. It grinned maliciously at the group cowering in its shadow with a mouth filled to the brim with crooked and rotting fangs. Those diseased teeth were still effective though, as was too quickly proven to the stunned quest party.

(I will pause at this juncture to advise squeamish or sensitive readers to skip the rest of this most regrettable episode and await the beginning of the next chapter. To those who read on, I do apologize. Stories go where they will, and we authors have surprisingly little control over the unruly things.)

The evil wyrm lunged forward. Everyone tried to climb down from Celestyna's back and scatter, but one was a hair too late. Nightshade squeaked in terror and pain as their wonderful tail was bitten clean off and tossed through a gap in the cloud to the ground below. If anyone had had the presence of mind left to watch where it landed, they would have noted with interest that a pinkish-grey fungi, exactly alike in color to the mouse's tail, sprang from the spot.

It grew and grew until it was a mushroom of towering height, nearly as high as the cloud on which they stood. Or on which they had stood, to be more accurate. For no sooner had the terrible wyrm disfigured Nightshade, and before any of them had a chance to begin to comprehend the enormity of that horrific tragedy, Pishposh, their one-time friend, betrayed them all by knocking them with its tail clean off the cloud to their certain doom below.

And I'm afraid this time it was certain as there was no time to formulate a plan, no magical solution, no *deus ex machina* (which is a fancy way of indicating a miraculous intervention just in the nick of time).

No, I regret very much to report that our friends fell from an immense height and all, without exception, died.

CHAPTER 27

FADING F⬤⬤TPRINTS

H OW QUIET IT IS. How still.

Time passes slowly. The sky darkens. Night falls.

A star begins to twinkle, then another and another. Soon the sky is ablaze. Brilliant jewels, harbingers of tragedy and triumph. How many events have they witnessed in their lives which span such unimaginable eons of time? What stories could they tell?

One star is brighter than the rest and is itself restless. It darts here and there, joining first one constellation then another as though unsure of its rightful place in the heavens.

It spots a rocky patch of ground below where pale dragon bones sprout a remarkable thing. A pinkish-grey mushroom, impossibly long-stemmed and wide-capped. Its delicate gills breathe out soft spores that float down and land gently, oh-so-gently on a ring of prone figures.

The star squints and winks as it takes inventory of the dark forms. One is most definitely bear-shaped while another is sprawled in tangled coils. One wears a pointy hat, and one has six legs. The weirdest shape looks like a bit of everything mashed together and has far too many tails while the unmoving figure next to it has none, else the star might think it a mouse of unusual size.

The last shape of all strikes a chord of memory that resonates deep within the heart of the star. A pale batty thing that heard its secret melody and promised to share it with the world. A flittery, fluttery friend who rescued the star from an obscure and lonely death.

They are all so very, very quiet. So still.

A wailing dirge is heard. An eerie tune of lamentation and mourning. The star croons a tender caress of love and concern that coats our friends like the warmest, coziest blanket you can imagine. Starsong and starshine are two of the most powerful forces in the universe, but alone they would not suffice.

It is the mushroom spores dancing under the sway of this celestial benediction that do the hard work. They sink into flesh and bone. Knit and sew. Smooth and mend every wound. And when all is well, they restore life and breath and hope where there was none.

Satisfied, the star withdraws its influence, its fading light washed away by the coming dawn like footprints in the sand erased by an incoming tide until there is no sign it was ever there. While those it leaves below may never know the generous blessing an old acquaintance bestowed upon them, we know, and we will remember.

CHAPTER 28

THE TOWERING MUSHROOM

AND SO THEY AWOKE to the first sparkling rays of the morning sun.

Chester stretched exuberantly as though emerging from his yearly hibernation, scratching at his shaggy fur with one paw while politely hiding an immense yawn with the other. Not to be outdone, the Keeylas turned on its back, reaching high with its six paws and wiggling its many toes. Walnut and Barty flapped their wings to test their strength, and Mercipolis smoothed out his purple cloak and straightened his pointy hat.

Celestyna luxuriated in her renewed body. She had grown even bigger under the influence of some profound magic she could sense but could not place. It hummed through her shining scales, causing her frills to twirl and swirl in sympathy. She felt more powerful than she ever had before in her life and ready to take on any enemy or challenge.

The wyrm was not the only one to feel refreshed and even changed by their restoration. Boundless joy filled every soul, and great was their rejoicing to see they had somehow survived their fall from an absurd height (though none could quite piece together the details of exactly what had happened after the traitorous squish had swept them from the cloud). They congratulated and even hugged one another in whatever batty, catty, bearish or other fashion best suited them.

Only one stood apart, leaning a paw against a towering mushroom while reaching behind with their other paw again and again for the tail that they knew was gone, though they felt its phantom presence still. How unbalanced, how peculiar, how bereft Nightshade felt, I have not the heart to describe. Their silent grief soon broke through the rejoicing of the others, who formed a semi-circle of sympathy around their friend.

"Your poor tail!" cried Walnut, adding tactlessly, "I lost one too, but unlike you, I have spares."

"Never mind," Chester said. "I'm sure the wizard can fix it, and if not, we'll go visit the giant again. See if the monkey chap or gold duck can't do it, won't we?"

The Keeylas corrected the bear sourly. "It's a goose."

Mercipolis hastened to intervene before another quarrel broke out between those two adversaries of old. "Yes, don't worry, Nightshade. I believe my healing arts are up to the task of regrowing your tail though it may take a few days."

"What a relief!" said Celestyna. "We were so grieved to think you had suffered such a loss on our behalf."

"That's settled then," Chester said with satisfaction, for as we know, he liked nothing better than confirmation that things worked out for the best whenever he was around.

Nightshade spoke softly. "You don't understand. My tail can never be restored. It was the great sacrifice the sibyl warned us of. Any attempt to regrow it will reverse the magic it enabled, the magic which protects us even now."

"How do you mean?" asked Barty. "How can you be sure?"

"The mushroom whispered it to me. Our lives were saved by the magic in its spores and the mushroom grew from my tail, my sacrifice. If my tail regrows and returns me to my former self as though nothing had ever happened, then it was no great sacrifice at all, and the mushroom will disappear along with its magic."

Chester was not pleased a bit at this. "Sounds like so much blither-blather to me. Why shouldn't you have your tail back again? What harm could it do?"

But the mouse was obstinate for they knew more than they had shared. The mushroom had told all. The fall. The bodies, still and broken on the ground. The combined magic of spore and star. All possible because of a sacrifice both permanent and profound, like a promise that must not be broken. Nightshade had no wish to distress their friends with the details, but it was clear if they wished to preserve their restored lives that the mouse's tail was gone for good. They must simply learn to make do without.

The argument went on for some time, even throughout the delicious breakfast Mercipolis produced, but they could not budge Nightshade from their position and as it was the mouse's own tail and sacrifice, what could they do but respect their friend's wishes?

When they had eaten their fill and were basking in a pleasant after-meal daze, their attention was brought back to the quest by a long orange feather that descended lazily from the cloud above them and wafted over the remnants of their feast to land in the wizard's lap.

"Meera!" he cried, stricken that for the second time in as many days, he had forgotten about the magical being. "It hated being the squish and doing harm to others. How must it feel to know it betrayed us and swept us to our certain doom? We must return and see if we can help. Celestyna, you turned the squish away from evil once by biting it. Perhaps that would work again."

The wyrm nodded her heavy head. "Yes, and there is one other there that needs to be turned from evil if it can be done."

"And if not?"

"We are not vindictive or vicious by nature, but such malevolence by one of our kind cannot go unchecked. But first, we must find a way back to the clouds. We believe we can wind our way up this mushroom stem if it is sturdy enough to hold our weight. Perhaps the rest of you should stay here. You have done enough. Some of you more than enough," Celestyna said, looking despondently upon Nightshade's changed self.

You can imagine how that suggestion was received. Not one of the party wished to be left behind, but how to ascend again? More discussion ensued with many arcane plans and wild schemes proposed before Nightshade interrupted.

"The prophecy told us what to do next. Knock at the door," they said.

"What door? Which door?" asked Chester.

"That one."

In the stem of the mushroom, visible now that Nightshade had pointed it out, was a round door large enough for even the Keeylas to enter. There was no need to ask for a volunteer to knock upon it as Walnut in its usual flighty fashion immediately rushed forward and rapped as hard as it is possible to rap with delicate lizardy knuckles.

The door creaked outward to reveal two tiny mushrooms, each no taller than a raspberry and much the same color. They nodded their caps at the crowd and jumped up and down in excitement as Nightshade came forward.

"They bid us welcome," the mouse reported, finding they could understand not only the towering mushroom but these miniature fungi also. "And they offer us use of the stairs."

All peered in to see a winding staircase that spiraled up and out of sight through the core of the mushroom's stem. A multitude of landings and doors of various shapes and sizes indicated there were many chambers within the stem. Other colorful, miniature mushrooms hopped up and down the stairs.

"Looks like a whole village within. A bustling, thriving community," Mercipolis said in wonder. "This is true magic at work. To think it was made possible by your sacrifice, Nightshade."

The mouse's heart lifted at this thought and also at the knowledge they had to all intents and purposes saved the lives of their friends. Though the loss of their tail might be an ache that never completely healed, there was comfort in believing it had not been in vain.

"Not enough room for us in there," the wyrm said. "We will go round the outside and meet you up top."

"Wait for us before going into battle," Mercipolis advised.

"We cannot promise anything as we cannot predict what we may find. The battle may come to us."

"In that case, we'd better hurry," said Chester, entering the mushroom and taking the stairs two or three at a time in cautious bounds while trying to be respectful of the fragile residents.

The Keeylas followed, stepping as delicately and precisely as you'd imagine even a monstrously-sized cat would. As the two largest creatures, they had to be most careful not to step on any of the fungi as there is nothing ruder than squashing your hosts.

Mercipolis trailed behind, taking things a bit more cautiously, while Walnut and Barty decided it was safer and faster for them to flutter their way to the top. Nightshade brought up the rear, shaky on their paws without the familiar counterbalance of their tail to steady them and relying heavily on the railing to pull themself along.

When she had seen her friends safely off, Celestyna began her own climb. She sped round and round the robust stem toward the wide mushroom cap above in secret hope of reaching the cloud and ending any possible hostilities before the others could join in and risk their lives again.

I only wish we were at leisure to dwell upon the many enchanting scenes our friends climbing the interior staircase witnessed as they glanced into charming parlors and libraries, conservatories and dining rooms. This community of magical mushrooms would need its own tale to do it justice, and perhaps one day it will get just that. In the meantime, I will simply leave you with the thought that while the ascent was arduous and time-consuming for our friends, it was not without its compensations.

At the top of the winding stairs was another round door that opened into the cap of the mushroom. There they found a giant room, something like an attic, full of the most unusual and perplexing bits and pieces in every possible nook and cranny.

This space was tended by a tall, gaunt figure who had a permanent hunch in their back from bending low to avoid hitting their head on the sloping ceiling. Their skin was covered with turkey tail fungi which are beautiful things, something like a cross between a paper fan unfurled and a rough dragon's scale. Subtle variations of every shade of green gave the impression of a plant come to life.

"Can I help you?" they asked in a surprisingly high voice, though why this should be surprising now that I think about it, I couldn't really say. "I have many unwanted objects on offer. You may take your pick. Being more or less useless, they are all available at no cost. What are you looking for today?"

"A way up into the cloud above us," answered Mercipolis, still a bit breathless from the steep climb. "We have business there that cannot be delayed."

"Ah, then a ladder would be most useful, so naturally we do not have such a thing," they said with a surprising amount of equanimity for a presumed merchant, who are usually in the business of providing what you do want, not what you don't want.

"I see," said the wizard, somewhat flummoxed. "In that case, I don't suppose you have anything we could use."

"It would be most unlikely. If it were useful, it wouldn't end up here, would it?"

"You mean to say," Chester demanded, "this is nothing but a pile o' rubbish? Why do you keep it?"

"Someone must."

This remarkable assertion brought the conversation to a halt. Rather than stand around awkwardly, everyone poked about here and there, certain that not every item could be entirely worthless.

There was a pitcher made of cranberry-red glass which was crisscrossed with tiny holes, rendering it too leaky for its purpose. A teddy bear whose fur was made from steel wool, not very nice for cuddling. A bow and arrow set, only the bow was strung with a cold spaghetti noodle that snapped as soon as you tried to use it. A bicycle with square wheels and a book with all its pages glued together.

It was a puzzle why such objects were ever produced in the first place, but sometimes mistakes are made. Our friends supposed it was a kindness in a way that these misfits had found a home.

"This is a waste of time," growled the Keeylas. "The wyrm will be up before us if we don't hurry."

"Perhaps, Mercipolis," Nightshade suggested quietly, "you could transform one of these things into something useful."

The wizard was abashed that he had not thought of this himself. Picking up the longest object he could find—a whale harpoon with a barb made of chewed-up bubblegum instead of steel—he angled it up toward the ceiling and tapped it with his wand while saying the magic word (you know the one).

The long pole changed into an oversized wooden ladder sturdy enough for climbing by even the monstrous Keeylas. Mercipolis tactfully sent Nightshade up first in case they were still feeling unsteady and needed a helpful boost from behind. There was some discussion about how to break through the ceiling, but in the end, they settled on the expedient solution of the mouse simply chewing through it with their strong teeth. Nightshade was gratified to find the mushroom was delicious though it seemed a shame to damage it.

The merchant waved away their concerns. "It will grow back. Part of its magical properties. Very handy, unlike my goods," they added with a cheerful grin that showed they were not the least disturbed at the idea of idling away their life among such pointless products. "Good luck to you! Do come again! New stock arriving daily!"

Leaving the jovial shopkeeper behind, our friends crawled one by one out onto the surface of the mushroom cap, Barty and Walnut bringing up the rear in flight. Even as they watched, they could see the mushroom busy healing the damage to its cap, knitting the gap back together until it was as though it had never been.

To bridge the distance between the mushroom and the cloud bottom, Mercipolis retrieved the willow rope from his pocket. Tying a loop and knot at the end, he presented it to Walnut and Barty.

"The two of you fly up and see if you can find something sturdy to fasten this to. Tug on the line three times when it's ready."

"Are you sure it's wise to trust them?" the Keeylas asked cynically as they waited.

"The whirligig, perhaps not," Mercipolis conceded, "but the flitter-flutter has a sensible head on their shoulders. See!" he added in triumph as the rope in his hands jerked three times.

One by one, the rest of the quest party ascended the rope. One by one, they discovered what object Barty and Walnut had decided to attach the willow to. And one by one they agreed it was about the farthest thing from a sensible choice that had ever been made.

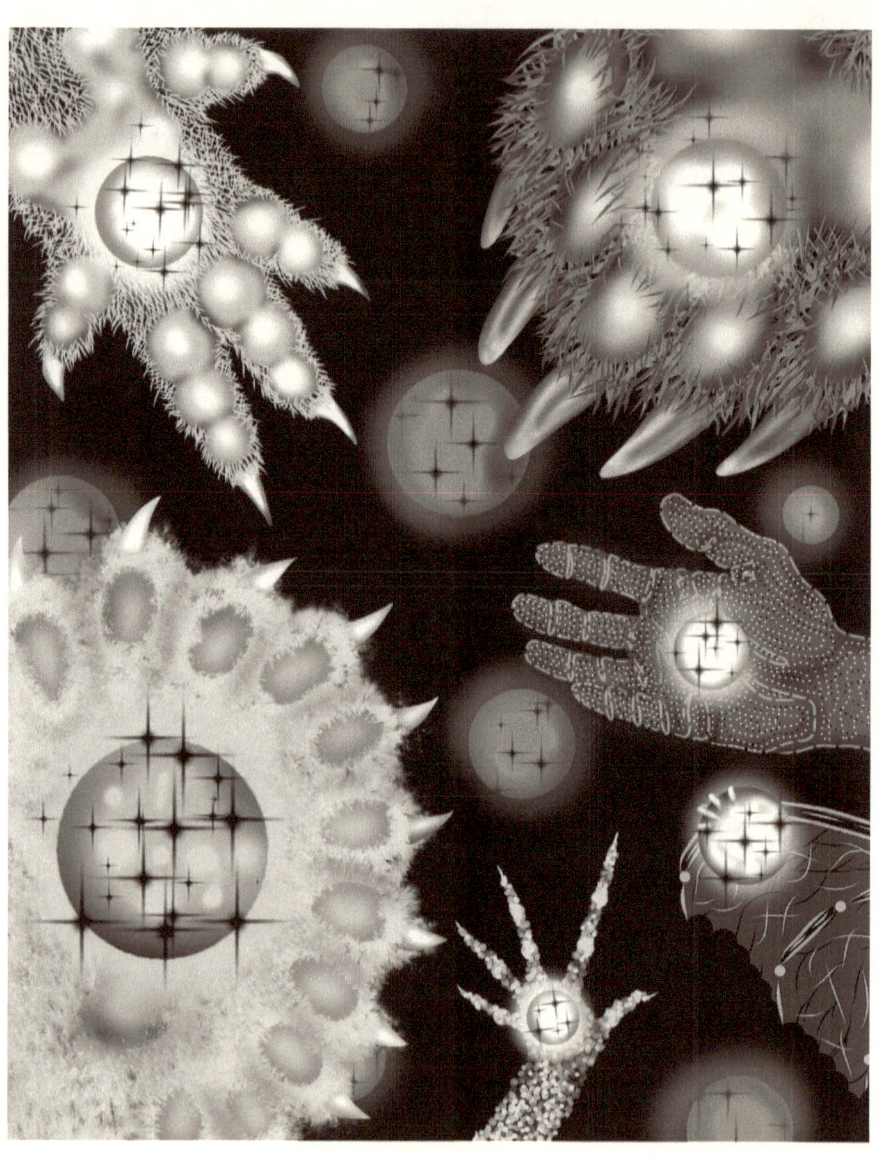

CHAPTER 29

THE THREAD THAT CONNECTS

I F YOU HAD YOUR choice of things to attach a magical willow rope to, which of these would you choose? A sturdy boulder, a stout tree branch, or the sharply-taloned foot of an evil squish. I can only imagine you have chosen one of the two sensible options. Walnut, however, in typical whirligig fashion, had impulsively chosen the least sensible.

It is true that Pishposh was sleeping with its foot temptingly close to where Barty and Walnut had emerged from the cloud base and did not wake even as it was used as a useful (if temporarily) inanimate object by the climbers. Those climbers were less than pleased to find what was on the other end of their rope, and it is extremely unfortunate that in their surprise, more than one let out a groan or shout of dismay.

This had the effect of rousing the squish from its no doubt pleasant slumber (for even evil creatures often take delight in the comforts of a really good nap). Like many of us would be, it was terribly grumpy to have been jolted awake, and a grumpy evil squish is infinitely worse than a non-grumpy evil squish.

It was on its feet in an instant, swishing its powerful, orange-scaled tail in an attempt to sweep the party off the cloud to their doom a second time. However, it was met with a counterattack before it could accomplish its goal. Celestyna arose seemingly from nowhere, coiling her luxuriously long body around the squish. They wrestled thus for a time, with Pishposh doing its best to peck the wyrm's eyes out with its long beak while Celestyna struggled to get the proper angle to bite into the squish's body without killing it.

Growing impatient, the Keeylas intervened, scraping its sharp claws down Pishposh's wings, sending orange feathers flying. This distraction gave the wyrm the opening she needed. She bit down as hard as she could on the squish, then let go and slithered quickly away to observe what effect it had.

As before, the squish reacted violently to Celestyna's bite. Orange scales were shed, feathers flew. Its snaky tail split into two legs and its wings became arms and the elegant orange gown. Meera, that being of light, an Ageless One and their friend, stood before them once again in all its splendor.

Great was Meera's regret and misery, great its weeping and lamentation at the memory of what it had done while possessed by an evil spirit. Overcome with emotion, Meera was unable to speak, but it visited each member of the quest, cupping their face in its hands and bestowing a gentle kiss upon their foreheads. More than a few tears were shed at this bittersweet reunion, and many explanations were owed, but they didn't have the luxury of time.

With a hiss and a spit, the puce-colored wyrm squirmed into view, leaking its pea green ooze and gnashing its horrible fangs. Nightshade started shivering uncontrollably at the sight of the creature that had separated them from their tail so abruptly and completely. Chester, in a rare moment of doing exactly the right thing at exactly the right moment, enveloped the mouse in a fierce embrace, blocking their view of the hideous monster.

"What can we do?" cried Mercipolis. "It is too big and powerful."

It was Meera, willowy and lovely and sacred in some way the watchers could not define, who answered:

"I will make amends."

A blinding light poured out of Meera, a deep and pure magic that only one of the Ageless Ones can call upon. It stroked its hands along Celestyna's shining amethyst and emerald scales, exhaling a sigh that seemed to last a thousand years. When it was done, Meera collapsed upon the cloudy ground and lay still.

Celestyna had sensed many types of magic but none like this. The strength and intensity of it felt like it would burst her free from her own body. Instead, she began to grow at a vastly accelerated pace. Her friends stood back, staring in wonder as her coils shifted and swirled and her scales became as big in circumference as the hot air balloon had been.

At first, the puce-colored wyrm seemed unimpressed, but as Celestyna grew and grew, it lowered its head and backed away, shifting its eyes uneasily from side to side as though searching for a likely escape route. But it left its attempt too late.

Celestyna felt the moment when the magic finished its work. She was now many times the size of her adversary. She considered her options. She thought of Meera and the agony that being had endured as the squish. She thought of Nightshade and the unwilling sacrifice the mouse had suffered with a cruel *snap* of the wyrm's rotting teeth. And she thought of all the other mischief such a creature might have caused or would cause in the future.

When she had thought and considered these things, she opened her mouth wide and swallowed the puce wyrm whole.

It took a dozen gulps or more until the tail of the thing disappeared completely down her throat. It would take as many days to digest, but that simply meant she would have no need of another meal for quite some time, which is actually a very convenient thing when you think about it.

We could pause here to debate whether it was right for Celestyna to eat her opponent without giving it a proper opportunity for negotiations or explanations or a trial by jury for its crimes, and indeed, there is much to discuss around such subjects. But all varieties of dragons share a code of conduct, and one of its most important tenets is never to allow evil to flourish if you can defeat it by any action of your own. As such, Celestyna felt not one moment of regret at her decision but only relief the threat to her and her friends was over.

But alas, that's not all that was over. As they gathered near the fallen form of Meera and waited for some sign, our friends joined hand and paw and claw to form a circle around the light that had been quenched. Celestyna joined them, curling her enormous body round and round, as though building a wall to keep out harm, but the harm had already been done.

It was Barty who began the tune, a melody of mourning, the dying star's song. The others took it up as best they could. Not all could claim musical talent, so it was an eerie, discordant noise, yet splendid in its own way because it was full of tender lamentation for one that they loved and was now lost to them.

The Ageless Ones are forces unto themselves. They were already old when the world was young, eons before you or I were ever thought of. They cannot be killed but may choose to die and by dying transform into something even more magnificent. The dragon that created the Misshapen Mountains was one such, and from its bones grew a multitude of life beyond measure. Now Meera was another, laying down its old self for its friends.

But do not weep, for that was not its end.

As the song continued, the members of the quest watched in wonder as the Ageless One began to glow with a light much softer than before. One by one, gentle sparks wafted over their heads, landing on the cloudy ground around them until nothing was left of Meera's previous form.

From each spark grew a small flame, and as each flame burned low, it left a pile of white ash behind. From each pile of ash, a shining orb, perfectly round and shimmering like a pearl, emerged.

"What are they?" asked Chester, his rumbling voice thick with awe.

Celestyna sniffed at one, then another of the spheres. "Eggs! Dragons and wyverns, wyrms and drakes, all waiting to be born!"

With what joy and infinite care did the members of the quest gather these precious objects, piling them on a hastily built nest of soft leaves and the shining orange feathers that were all that was left behind from Meera's old life. When they were done, Celestyna wrapped herself round to keep the eggs warm until they hatched.

"You shall be their mother," said Nightshade. "Their haven and their queen, just as the raven's prophecy foretold. And when they are born, the magic of the world will increase a hundredfold."

If a wyrm could be said to smile, this one did most lovingly as she replied. "And our children shall be taught the names of Chester and Mercipolis, Barty and Walnut, the Keeylas and Meera, and of a very special mouse named Nightshade. And Sunshine, Leaf, and Mold, naturally," Celestyna hastened to add so as not to hurt the whirligig's feelings. "There is a thread that connects every member of this quest and those we encountered along the way that can never be broken. Blessings on you all."

CHAPTER 30

THE END OF A TALE

THERE IS ALWAYS SOMETHING melancholy about the end of an adventure. While the thread of love and companionship and hard-won experience between the members of the quest would always bind them, they each had their own paths, their own stories, their own threads to pick up and carry on.

They left Celestyna in the clouds crooning lullabies to her children with many promises to come back for a visit when the eggs hatched.

The Keeylas returned to the drawing room of Sir Preposterous, finding to its satisfaction a Keeylas-sized pillow before the fire and a bowl full of warm milk. Thus is a monstrous cat domesticated and turned into a (more or less) tame house pet.

The others descended the mushroom's spiraling staircase before parting.

Mercipolis wished to visit Old Willow and learn the ways of an Elder Tree's magic.

Chester thought to explore the dark part of the forest where the stag had reported seeing a three-legged brown bear with a spot of white upon her back.

Barty and Walnut decided to venture forth together, for they were fonder of each other than either was brave enough to mention—at least, not yet. (We shall assume Sunshine, Leaf, and Mold went with them.)

And Nightshade?

At their urging, Mercipolis returned them to their former size, just right for life within the towering mushroom among its tiny inhabitants. You may find the mouse there many a day, dozing in their own snug little parlor, reaching for a tail that is no more and dreaming of tales yet to come.

ACKNOWLEDGMENTS

Special thanks as always to my usual crew of supporters (you know who you are!) with extra credit to Ian for reading and re-reading several versions of this story and always being its biggest cheerleader. You kept me going many times when I would have given up.

Many thanks also to my loyal readers. Most of my writing has an undercurrent of hope and this one even more so. I hope it brought you some moments of joy.

About the Author

Helen Whistberry (she/they) is the pen name for an indie author and artist who began writing after retiring from a long career working in libraries. They have published three novels in their Jim Malhaven Mysteries series, a collection of forest-themed short stories (The Melody of Trees), as well as contributing horror and fantasy stories to numerous anthologies.

Helen's writing often explores their own experiences with gender, asexuality, alienation, and autism. Their whimsical digital artwork focuses on the natural world. Helen also loves to read and review books by fellow indie and small press authors.

For more information, please visit: www.helenwhistberry.com

ALSO BY THIS AUTHOR

If you enjoyed this book, please check out my other works. Reviews are also always much appreciated!

https://www.amazon.com/stores/ Helen-Whistberry/author/B073 K1P1Z3